AS WE ROT

CAITLYN RISKY

AS WE ROT

ISBN: 979-8-9926263-0-8

Independently published by ART BY CAITLYN.

Cover design by Caitlyn Risky on Canva.

For Tony,
without you this book would've been just another project
in my idea graveyard.

1

Melony

    The scent of onions swirled through the air as the breeze rushed past us. The rising sun beamed down on our heads through the rustling leaves, and I could feel the heat beginning to burn my scalp through my thick brown hair in between each gust of humid summer air. The wind greeted us with the dirt and dust scattered along the road. I shielded my eyes as they began to water. Through my squint, I could see Jonas up ahead. His long strides often led to him leaving me behind, but he always remembered to turn back and check on me.

    As if on cue, he paused and turned to me. The sweat on his forehead glistened in the sun and began to slowly trickle down the arched bridge of his nose. His dark wiry beard sparkled with oil and sweat as though it were filled with fine glitter. His hand crept up and shielded his eyes from the sun as he looked at me from afar. He stopped in his place and swung his bag off his shoulder, giving me enough time to catch up. The veins and muscles in his arms flexed as he forcefully rummaged through the bag.

He sighed in defeat as he glanced up at me from the ground. "We only have another day of rations left, and the sun is getting high. We should find some shelter and rest," he huffed while grasping something inside the depths of the bag.

He then threw his bag back onto his shoulder and held his palm out with whatever he had grabbed aimed at me. I looked down at his hand and chuckled before taking the sunglasses sitting in his palm.

"I found them in a car a few miles back," he spoke with a smile, "they looked your style."

I flicked open the frames and began to rub the dust-covered lenses with the bottom hem of my shirt. The lenses were large and round, lined with thick tortoiseshell-colored plastic. They were an accessory you saw a girl in movies wearing to the beach. I'd always longed for that moment; the sand beneath my feet and to hear the ocean crash against itself for the first time as the salty breeze blows my hair in every direction.

A taste of a different life.

I held the glasses up to the light to check for any missed spots. Once I deemed them clear enough, I placed them on my sun-toasted face.

"How do I look?" I asked as I puckered my lips and posed for him.

Jonas threw his head back with a wide grin, or maybe a smirk. "Beautiful," he chuckled, "like a model."

I gave a wordless reply of a flirtatious smile before I walked forward and bumped into his shoulder on my way around him. I could hear his feet scuffle as he approached my side again.

"I'm pretty sure there's a small subdivision up the road a bit that we could find a place to rest at. Maybe we can find some supplies to reload," he suggested.

I nodded. "Hopefully we can find something worth the time."

Jonas sighed, but this time I could sense a breath of hope. "I know the last few places fell through, but we'll hit our luck soon." He draped his arm over my shoulders and gave me a gentle squeeze. "I know we will," he finished.

I smiled at him before pushing on.

We had been on the road for months, heading south, searching for a place to stay. We'd stay in a house for a night and sometimes get the chance to stay in a place for a week before we were forced to move on. Most of the places we would stay in were already scavenged or completely run down. However, a few months ago, our story was different. We were constantly bouncing from place to place before we finally found something perfect.

It was a motel in the same lot as a small supermarket—the proverbial jackpot of this new world.

The neighborhood it fell in had been lost when the world fell, yet the motel and market remained virtually untouched. They were decaying on the outside, and most of the rooms in the motel had been rotting away as well, but we didn't need all the rooms, we just needed one, and we had found it.

In the check-in office, there was a door in the far back corner behind the counter. The room was locked, but the engraving on the keys that sat behind the counter matched that of the sign on the door. It was ours: the brown peeling wallpaper, the small bathroom with the broken sink, and the supply closet full of clean linens, blankets, and towels. All of it had been ours. We cleaned up the area as much as we could. We rummaged through rooms for supplies and anything that would have made it feel more comfortable for us. We barricaded ourselves in, leaving the only route in and out to be the window in the bedroom that faced the supermarket. It was an easy route to keep our eyes on and the quickest way to get to the front of the store without walking around the building.

The market had been in much better shape than the motel had been. The metal guards over the doors had remained shut since the beginning, and they had kept whoever else was left in the world out. It had been months—almost a year—since the doors had been closed for their final time; dust had layered itself like a blanket over everything inside. The power was a loss, but the food stores and medical supplies inside were gold mines.

I could remember what it felt like when we first walked up to the doors and how it felt when we decided to stay. The energy of the building had radiated over me, and fear pulsed in my veins. We had created a rushed plan, but when we followed it through, I had never felt more excited since before we left home. I remember setting my eyes on everything inside the supermarket and thinking that we had been set for life.

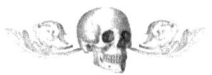

"Are you sure we should go in?" I asked Jonas hesitantly, "What if the doors are closed because people are inside? Or worse, what if it isn't *people* inside?"

I was afraid. Very. I always was. But this time it was different—this fear was fueled by hope. The worst kind of fuel to ignite the emotion inside you. I could feel it twisting and writhing in my gut, trembling in my hands. It was flowing through my body, racing along like a racecar on a NASCAR track, and I couldn't keep up with the thoughts running through my mind; we were most likely going to die where we stood if this went wrong, and we couldn't let something like this go wrong. If this slipped through our fingers, we would die either way.

"Then we join or fight," Jonas stated, "We need the supplies; we need food. I'm not letting you starve."

"Well, I'd rather not die trying to get the supplies or food we need."

He stepped back and began to examine the sides of the building without replying. The moon overhead made his shadow-black hair appear silky and blue. The night sky was full of clouds, and I could smell the rain coming. The wind tickled my arms and sent shivers down my spine. It had been an eerie night, and this was a life-or-death mission.

Jonas took another step backward and placed his hands onto his hips before looking at me and gesturing toward the roof with his head.

"What if we went up top? It's gotta have a roof access. If it does, we can use that to check if anyone is here. We'll be inside and no one would notice," he theorized.

I stepped back past where he stood and craned my neck while my calves strained on my tiptoes. As I gazed up at the roof, I caught a silver glint from a slightly raised section of the roof.

"I think I can see where a door would be," I mumbled to myself before speaking louder toward Jonas. "There's probably a ladder or fire escape around the back of the building. If not, I think I saw a big ice cooler on the side of the building that we could climb on."

"God, you're so hot when you use your brain, *mi amor.*"

I scoffed at his remark. "Are you implying that I'm not usually hot or that I'm not usually smart?"

Without verbally responding, he smirked and began to jog off. I quickly followed behind. As we rounded the front corner of the store, I observed the ivy that climbed the faces of the brick all along the side of the building. The ground was hidden in tall yellowing weeds, and I began to worry about all the possible critters that were hiding amongst it. As we tread through the knee-high weeds, it brought memories of my childhood. I remembered running through the thin stretch of woods near my suburban home pretending I was a spy lurking in the uncut grass and bushes, or I would be a scientist studying the ants that crawled across my hands. I could remember the tiny tickling sensation of their legs as they weightlessly climbed over my skin.

Once we reached the other corner at the back of the building, I spotted the yellow-painted ladder chipping with rust and strands of dying ivy wrapped and twisted along the rungs. I quickened my pace and began to rush over to it before Jonas grabbed my wrist and yanked me backward. When I whipped around, I glanced around in search of him before my eyes trailed down my arm and followed his dark arm to where he crouched down in the weeds. He silently and slowly placed a finger over his lips without sparing a glance in my direction. His line of sight was focused on the trees a couple of dozen yards behind the store.

As I gazed into the tree line, I could sense the darkness of the night creeping along making every shadow lurch and lunge in our direction. It was just our brains deciding we weren't scared enough. A trick of the moonlight. But knowing what was out there, what could have been lurking in those very trees, made me crouch down beside Jonas. The weeds rose and swayed above my head, and the crispy rustling sound echoed around us. I wasn't sure how Jonas had heard anything at all.

After a few extra seconds—which felt like hours—in the tall grass, Jonas decided we were safe enough to move forward, and I believed him. We made our way to the ladder; it creaked and moaned as I climbed ahead of Jonas. It was a deafening sound in the dead of night. My heart raced out of my chest at every step and every eerie screech, but once I made it to the roof, my feet swung over the ledge, and pebbles crunched beneath me. I placed a hand on my chest and closed my eyes to breathe and calm my heart from the rapid thumping that echoed in my ears.

I bathed in the sounds around me. The tall weeds and crickets sounded different from the roof; it seemed more magical. It was soon interrupted by the ladder screaming and crying even louder as Jonas climbed up.

"Let's go," Jonas whispered as he swung his leg over the ledge and walked straight over to the raised mound of metal with the rusty-hinged door.

We had been right about the roof access.

Jonas yanked on the handle and pried the door open. The door swung open and hung wide; the darkness within painted the air black. As I stepped through the doorframe, I felt as if I was walking with my eyes closed. I was blind. The only source of light came from the doorway that was now slowly closing behind us. The door clattered as it softly closed behind us, but the sound echoed as if it had been slammed, and I winced against the darkness waiting for something to pop out and drag us deeper.

Jonas's body pressed against my back, and his hands brushed my upper arms as he slowly and carefully tiptoed around me and shuffled his feet across the floor. After a few inches of shuffling and shifting my weight, I felt the floor drop off near the edge of my toes. I spread my arms out wide like wings on a bird until I was able to graze my fingertips against the walls on either side of me. I felt a thin handrail along the wall and wrapped my fingers around it tightly before carefully stepping down one stair at a time. I could hear Jonas's footfall maybe one or two steps ahead.

"Are your eyes adjusting yet? Because I still can't see," he whispered. His voice was deafening even at a whisper and echoed around me on the staircase. "Oh, wait," he mumbled, "I think I see an emergency exit sign. It's not on, but I can see it."

I began to see it too as I stepped further down the stairs. Jonas came into view; his nose and cheeks were barely visible, but I could see the sweat that outlined them as he stared up at the dead light.

By the time we reached the bottom of the stairs, my heart was racing faster than it had before. I had always been afraid of the dark. An immersive experience was something I had not wished to participate in. However, the longer we were inside the more my vision was adjusting, and I could start to make out the rows of shelves and the few doors that lined the far wall.

When we finally began exploring, we found that the storage rooms and most of the shelves were still fully stocked. No one had been inside the store since the metal door guards had closed. We were beyond happy staying at the motel—it was the best we had come across since we left Brownsburg. We debated on moving into the store for good but wanted to distance ourselves in case someone came along and wanted it for themselves.

Which is what eventually happened.

Months after our move-in, we kept ourselves stocked inside our office bedroom at the motel. We decided that opening the metal doors would make the place seem as if it had previously been looted. We hoped that this would deter any other survivors—not that we had ever crossed any since the first day of the attacks.

Once a week, we would take a daily trip to the market and load up a shopping cart. We'd push it to the lot that sat between the market and motel and carry groceries in through the office window that we always kept open. Going once a week had made our chances of running into something less likely. It gave our new life a routine—a sense of normalcy. We'd cover the window with a sheet when the sun began to rise, and we'd try to sleep. It felt safer to travel at night; we were less likely to be spotted.

During our free time, we'd play card games or tell stories while eating one of our rationed two small meals a day. One evening, while I was dealing cards, I could hear laughing coming from outside. Jonas had heard it too. His head perked up, and he quickly pushed our gaming setup out of the way while I crawled to the window.

Peeking out, I could make out six separate figures standing at the doors to the market. I painfully watched as they cupped their hands over the windows and chatted amongst themselves before they burst through the doors. They had weapons, and it wouldn't have been worth the fight.

Jonas packed everything he could as quickly as he could. Then, we fled.

I could remember the way the glass crunched underneath my feet as I ran through the front lot and straight across the street into the woods. The crunching of broken car windows turned into dried leaves beneath me. My legs burned like fire, and I ran more. I couldn't hear Jonas behind me anymore, but I was too afraid to stop. I wasn't going to risk running into people again. Not like the first time.

I was already so deep into the woods when I hit the ground and collapsed into the dirt. It took five to ten minutes before Jonas found and caught up to me.

That had been our home, and we had to abandon it just like our home before.

Jonas would always say that we'd get lucky again soon, and every morning before we found someplace to lay our heads, I would pray that he was right. I didn't believe that anything was watching over us from above, not anymore at least, but I still tried—still begged. My pleas were never answered.

As Jonas spoke the words to me once more, I didn't feel the same inkling of hope I usually did; I just felt as if he was blatantly lying to my face. I felt numb; the only true feeling I had was the burning sun against my skin. The trees that had been shadowing the roadside were thinning as we neared the next suburb. It would most likely be the last place we would come across for a while.

"You okay?" Jonas asked as he gently nudged me, "You look pretty bummed."

"I'm fine."

"Mel, we will find a place to call home soon. I promise you that," he said as he draped his arm over my shoulder.

The smell of his sweat drifted into my nostrils; it was such a sweet and familiar scent that I'd grown so fond of. I'd already forgotten what he used to smell like; what cologne did he used to wear? I couldn't remember a time when he smelled as natural and as human as he did now.

"How about this—" he paused before offering his bargain, "We play our game and try to lift our spirits. Let's forget about home for now. I know that's what's on your mind."

I cracked a smile, and our hips bumped as we swayed along the road. My mind began to drift to the last time we played this game. Guessing our next treasure. *What would we find next?* Jonas had won the last time we played. His guess had been an overturned shopping cart in a place that wasn't a store or parking lot. We had found it on the side of a freeway propped against the charred remains of a Ford Taurus. It was so specific that I ended up giving him double the points; although, I wasn't sure we were even keeping track anymore.

I often wondered how the cart wound up there. Who parked it there? Who flipped it and why? There were always questions to be asked about everything we happened to see out on the road.

"Are we betting anything?" I asked.

He smirked while his tone was suggestive. "What are you willing to bet?"

I playfully rolled my eyes as blood flushed into my sunburnt cheeks. I felt as red as a ripe garden tomato. I imagined that's what I looked like. A fresh tomato with droplets of water from the mist of the garden hose. What I would give to have a garden ripe with the fruits of my labor.

I couldn't guess any food for the game, even if the chances of us finding something that heavenly were highly unlikely. I would have to come up with something truly specific and weirdly placed to win big, but my mind was stuck on those bright red tomatoes you used to see on canned food labels or grocery store ads.

The color red. Ripe tomatoes. Sunburnt skin. Fresh blood. It reminded me of the bright red bike that Jonas would ride to school every day. We would ride together.

I glanced up at him. His arm was still draped over my shoulders, and he squinted up at the sky blocking his eyes with his other hand. With his face scrunched up, I could see his prominent cheekbones and the definition of his jawline. He was beautiful—a detail that was hard to appreciate while he was covered in sweat and dirt. Through the filth, I could see his eyes with the same hopeful sparkle they always had. It reminded me of our bike rides to and from school. I could almost picture his face when we used to meet up after class and glide past the other kids walking to their buses and homes. I could see how his eyes had that sparkle while I looked over my shoulder after speeding past him.

"Do you remember The Red Devil?" I asked as my eyes drifted along the road, and I squinted at the sky with him.

"Are you kidding me?" he scoffed, "Of course, that bike was my baby. Why? Is that your guess? It's kind of a boring guess."

"Bikes would be very useful," I commented, "and maybe you can find one that's faster than your shitty Red Devil ever was."

He gasped in mock disbelief. "That bike was the best in the entire world. I wouldn't have traded it for anything. It got me where I needed to go and gave me plenty of amazing memories."

"I have a feeling you're about to go on a very emotional tangent."

His smile perked up as he began to lecture. "I was always so worried that The Red Devil would fall apart. Worried that one day I would be riding it and it would crumble to pieces underneath me, but it never did. I would pedal and pedal until I was flying as fast as I could, and nothing would fall off, nothing would wobble, and I wouldn't even budge from the seat. Sure, the handbrakes were on their last life and squealed like a dying hog, but I didn't need them to catch up with you. That bike taught me to hold out hope. You get where I'm going with this?"

I inhaled deeply with wide amused eyes before huffing out and shrugging his arm off my shoulders.

"I get it, Jonas." I chuckled, "You sound just like your mom. Inspirational storytelling and all."

"She taught me well."

We both smiled at this, but I could sense the mood between us beginning to darken.

"My guess for the game is bikes," I declared and rerouted the conversation before it could wander darker, "There will be exactly two of them, both being practically identical in size and color, except the chain on one of them will be popped off and the other will need a handlebar adjustment."

"How big of an adjustment?" Jonas cocked his right bushy brow at me and rubbed his hand over his beard inquisitively.

I seriously furrowed my brows and nodded as I said, "A major one. Those bad boys are completely turned around."

"Super specific guess. Are you willing to take the risk?" he asked and paused awaiting my answer before he leaned in and whispered, "Because it's honestly hot how confident and risky that answer is."

I smirked at him. "Final answer. Locked in."

"Damn, girl."

I giggled and nudged him as he combed his fingers through his sweaty curls, slicking them back from his face. The breeze whistled by, and I closed my eyes to soak in the coolness against my sticky skin. I could feel the air blowing in through my t-shirt, and I felt disgusting. My clothes stuck to me in weird places, and I would have to adjust my necklace often to keep it from becoming stuck to my chest. The breeze dried the drops of sweat against my skin like a layer of glue coated with a glitter of dust and dirt. I felt as if I were caked in mud. A filthy animal.

The heat didn't feel like it would break anytime soon. It was easy to lose track of the days and months. There was no telling how long it had been since it rained or since I had last felt the comfort of a long shower. Running water was nearly impossible to find, and the last thing I had that was close enough to call a bath was over two weeks ago when we made camp near a stream that ran through a ditch along the side of a road. The water was clear and the rocks along the creek bed were large. I had used what was left of my energy rushing down into the ditch and stumbling into the mid-calf deep water. I had scratched my ankle against the rocks along the bank, but I remember being unbothered as I slowly sunk into the water. I didn't even bother stripping free of my clothes until I was completely lying in the cold stream. Jonas had slowly and carefully walked down the hill after me and watched me from the edge of the creek. The setting moon had made him look like he had been carved from stone as he sat on the creek bed watching me strip beneath the clear water.

Eventually, Jonas climbed in, and we scrubbed our skin in the creek water until the sun began to rise and we had to keep walking. We've found a few tiny streams since, enough to pause and fill our water stores along the way, maybe quickly wipe ourselves down, but nothing like that creek.

We both had been the cleanest we had in some time and now we were back to being covered in sweat and stench, our hair greasy, frizzy, and full of filth. We would have looked even worse if I hadn't thought to pack a brush before we began our journey.

Thinking of that creek was beginning to make me thirsty. I pulled my bag off my shoulders and rummaged through it as we continued to sway with each step. When I felt my fingers graze the ceramic coating of my water bottle, I gripped it and pulled it out of the bag like King Arthur with Excalibur. I could hear the water sloshing around against the metal walls of the bottle and couldn't unscrew the lid fast enough. As the lid came off, I looked longingly into the depths of the canister. Less than half. Before I brought it to my lips, I held it out to Jonas.

"You first," he politely declined.

I did as I was told and brought the rim of the canister to my lips taking a few swigs before passing it over. As I reached my hand out, Jonas stopped in his tracks and let out a breathy chuckle. His eyes stared off into the distance. Somewhere beyond us was something amusing enough to take his mind off the water in my hand. I reached my free hand up and lifted the sunglasses from the bridge of my nose to the top of my head. Jonas rushed forward, leaving me behind as he jogged up the road and gracefully stumbled down into a ditch. I trailed behind at my own pace, and as I came upon him, he beamed up at me with a smile I hadn't seen in what felt like ages.

"You were wrong about the specifics," he said emphatically, "but I'll give you the point."

2

Melony

The tires creaked and groaned beneath me, and the force I had to put on the pedals to move was beginning to drain me. We had been riding for a few miles trying to hurry beneath the steadily rising sun for a place to shelter through the day, and my legs were aching. The sweat from my palms combined with the partially melted rubber handles was forming an uncomfortably sticky substance that coated the creases of my palm. The sun-bleached blue paint was splotched with rust and caked in dried mud. The bikes had been in that runoff ditch longer than the world had been barren, but we were lucky to have found them.

I could almost picture the perfect lives these bicycles used to have. They were probably cherished and loved long ago. On the side of Jonas's slightly larger black bike, a name had been etched into the metal framing. Most of the letters were filled with mud or sanded down, like repairing a nail hole left in drywall. From what I could read, the person's name started with a "J" and ended with an "E." After some consideration and a brief discussion, Jonas and I decided it belonged to someone named Jamie. I silently wondered to myself where "Jamie" had ridden their bike. I pictured a young girl riding her bike down the streets with her friend, as Jonas and I had done billions of times before. I could imagine her hair blowing behind her as she kept looking over her shoulder at this friend. Did they ever race? Did they put their bikes down in that ditch? Were they still alive?

I pondered and pedaled until my hips began to cramp. Although the sudden bursts of pain jolted through me, I remained grateful. Time was moving against us as the sun kept climbing in the sky, but we were moving much faster than we had been on foot. However, as my mind continued to drift, I couldn't help but become more uneasy the longer we were exposed in the heat of the outdoors.

"How are you doing?" Jonas called back to me.

For once, he was ahead. On foot, he could take the lead, but on bike, I was usually the one leading the way; that's how it used to be.

"I'm fine," I muttered as my eyes jumped around the tree line, "but I'm feeling paranoid. We need to find a place soon."

He nodded. "We should be coming up on some houses soon."

"I know," I mumbled, "it just feels like—"

"Like we're being watched..." Jonas finished.

I glanced around, and the writhing knot of unease settled deeper into my stomach. As my lips parted to speak, my eyes landed on Jonas, and I watched as he adjusted his position on his bike into a more open stance. With one hand on his hip, his body slightly turned in the direction of the tree line to his left. He glided along the road, riding with one hand and no eyes aimed at the path ahead—not that there was anything on the road ahead to be wary or cautious of.

I could see his shoulders and back rise and fall in a steady motion. He was laser locked and focused on something I couldn't see. My paranoia and nervousness weren't affecting him; he was calm, head on a swivel, body ready to leap off his bike at any given moment. Such small indications in his posture were key details that only someone close to him could pick up on. He appeared calm and at peace, but I could see the tension building along the muscles in his back through the sweat-stained shirt that clung to his skin. Knowing he was on edge only amped up my fear.

There weren't people out here. There hadn't been people out here in ages. We were in the middle of nowhere on some rural backroad that ran through the woods. The next suburb wouldn't be coming up for another five miles based on an outdated city map Jonas had found in a car when we stopped for water. It wasn't *people* who were making us uneasy.

Jonas's pedaling slowed, and I slowly continued past him and took the lead.

"Keep moving," he muttered as I worked my way ahead.

His eyes didn't shift from the trees as he said it. His body was tense, and as I checked over my shoulder for him, he was completely stopped with one leg placed on the ground and the other propped up on one of the pedals. I quickly whipped my head forward and tried to control my breathing because whether I saw something or not, it was out there. We both knew it.

I heard Jonas's bike hit the ground behind me. My body instinctively slammed my feet on the ground to stop myself; I could feel the pavement rubbing through the bottoms of my shoes wearing holes into the rubber soles. When I turned around, Jonas's bike was lying on its side in the road, and he was standing in the tree line with his large folding knife clutched tightly in his hand. He stood there still as stone as if he had been put under a spell.

I began to tune in; my ears perked like a dog. The sound around us seemed to diminish; the birds were no longer chirping, and there was no droning buzz coming from the bugs in the tall grass that ran along the edge of the road. The earth and atmosphere around us were silent. I could hear my heart pounding in my ears and nothing more. Nature had fallen still.

As Jonas stood practically frozen in place, I heard the crunch of a branch somewhere in the distance that echoed like a pen in a silent classroom. That was enough to jumpstart my heart and send me twisting around. I forcefully stomped down on one of the pedals until I began to move. As soon as I pushed off, a loud squealing, reverberating shriek echoed through the trees. The trees and leaves within the woods began to rustle, growing louder and louder into an almost deafening static of noise as my anxiety wedged itself deeper in my chest. The sound felt as if it was following me, and it was much larger than Jonas.

After a few seconds, another shriller shriek filled the air, and everything fell silent except for the squeaking and rattling of the bike chain making its rounds beneath me.

"Melony!" I heard Jonas's shout from behind me.

My pedaling slowed, and before I could come to a complete stop, I was swinging my leg over and letting my bike fall to the ground beside me. I spun on my heels back into the direction I was riding from and spotted Jonas squatting on the roadside wiping his knife in the dirt and grass. His eyes peered up at me from beneath his bushy brows, and I stood still next to my bike as it sat in the middle of the road. He placed his hands onto his knees and slowly pushed upward rising flat on his feet. I could see tiny splatters of black on his sweat-stained shirt and skin. I watched him carefully fold up the knife and tuck it into the pocket of his shorts. He bent down to pick up his backpack and swung it over his shoulder before gripping the handlebars of his bike and standing it back up onto the tires. He very calmly pushed his bike toward me.

"Everything is fine, Mel," he reassured, "I am fine. You are fine. Just breathe."

His head was bent downward, but his eyes remained on mine as if he had been speaking to a wild dog. I stared him up and down with wide eyes before I noticed him glancing down my arms. My gaze followed his down my body to my hands. I was trembling. My hands shook, and I could see my legs quivering as if my entire body was vibrating.

I hadn't even noticed; but once I did, I could feel my knees begin to buckle and feel my weight become too much for my own body to carry. I felt weak and on the verge of collapse. The adrenaline and exhaustion had caught up.

Jonas approached me calmly. The rusty creaking of his bike echoed in my brain, and I began to feel more overwhelmed as the sounds of the bike were the only sounds in the atmosphere around us. The sound of the birds had not yet returned.

When he finally pulled up beside me, he dropped his bike once more, and the clatter made me jump. His hands were hot and sticky against my skin as he grabbed me by the elbows and pulled me into a hug. With one hand on my back and the other on the back of my head, he pressed me against his chest. I could smell the rot on him and could hear his heart racing. Just another sound to bounce around and echo throughout the empty chamber in my mind.

Thump thump thu-thump.

The smell of blackness and death lingered around him. I wanted to gag but couldn't bring myself to pull away.

He didn't seem phased by the smell that lingered in the air around him. It was worse than the stale and sweet scent of the sweat that embedded in the fibers of his clothes. Though he showed no emotion towards it, I could hear and feel his heart beating through his chest.

In another life, he could've been an actor with how composed he remained.

He pulled away and his hands moved to my cheeks and neck as he held me. The sweat and humidity glued us together. Our skin radiated together like a furnace even under the shade of the trees. It felt as if his hands were melting through my cheeks. His eyes were so dark, but the sun peaked through the trees overhead and cast light into his irises. His pupils dilated and as he opened his mouth to speak, a gut-wrenching screech resonated around us. His hands ripped away from my face and pulled along my peach fuzz like ripping away a bandage.

"*Mierda*," he muttered with wide eyes as he spun, eyes darting back toward the woods. In an instant, he picked up my bike and grabbed my wrist. "Ride. Don't turn around. I'll be right behind you, I promise."

With haste, I swung my body over the bike, and while I remained standing, I pushed all my weight down onto the pedals. The bike rocked back and forth beneath me as my legs took turns shifting my full weight onto each pedal. I could feel my knees wobble and tremble with every forceful push, but the exhaustion would have to take the backseat and let the adrenaline drive.

After I gained enough speed, I rested myself back down on the seat. I couldn't hear anything as I sped through the air, just the buzzing sound of the tires against the pavement and the wind whispering in my ears. I felt as if I were flying and wished it were real. I wished I was high in the air, far from the ground, far from this world. I wished to be free and unafraid. I wished to be safe.

My legs began to burn. I felt a fire begin to spread from my thighs into my calves. The ache was screaming through my muscles, but I didn't dare stop pedaling. I kept riding and pedaling through the pain as I came up to an intersection. I didn't stop, not even at the stop sign, because who would've been around to run me over as I pulled out onto the street? I hooked a dangerously rapid right turn, and in the distance, I spotted an old mailbox covered in vines and ivy.

A house.

I unconsciously began to pedal faster. My legs were no longer there. I couldn't feel my body from the waist down. Pins and needles, just pins and needles.

As the mailbox grew closer, I could spot the overgrown driveway to my left and see the small patches of gravel that led through a mini clearing up to a piss-yellow house. I leaned left and felt the gravel catch under the tread of my tires. Bouncing along the crunchy weeds and gravel, I quickly made my way to the shaded porch. Trees covered most of the property, and the house was quite hidden. I wasn't sure how far behind Jonas was, but I knew that this would be where he stopped whether he saw me enter the driveway or not.

I dropped my bike near the front steps, and it clattered softly into the grass. My legs were pulling me up the stairs and in front of the door before I even realized I was standing.

The house was old and filthy. Dirt stained the poorly painted exterior; it formed stains near the roof and dripped down with the remnants of a past storm. Dead bugs and abandoned spiderwebs decorated the exterior paneling, and every window was coated in a layer of crust and dust so thick I couldn't see inside even if I were to wipe it clean.

The wood I stood on creaked and groaned under my feet, and I could feel the planks bow and shift with every step. Leaf litter, brown and green, was scattered across the deck. The welcome mat was folded over next to a pink, cracked, plastic watering can and a pair of foam sandals. On the other end of the porch was a fallen bench swing hanging from a beam by a singular chain, the other side rested against the wood of the deck and quietly dragged and scraped with every sudden blow of the breeze. I listened closely to the surrounding woods before I chose a moment to take a seat on one of the steps. I could hear the bugs and birds like I hadn't been able to before, and that was enough comfort for me to take a second and remind myself to breathe.

Jonas would pull into the driveway at any second and usher me into the house, but for now, I would rest. I could smell a shift in the atmosphere. The air told me it would rain soon, and then we could take our time to refresh ourselves.

3

Jonas: Before

It was the summer after sophomore year, and no matter the weather, we were always riding. Just as we had done since we were kids. Through the summer sun, the heat would beat down on our scalps through our hair, and our skin would burn and darken under the rays.

But the best time, her favorite, was when the rain came down in sheets. The clouds would turn gray, and Melony could always sniff out an upcoming storm the night before it came. She always told me how her grandmother said it was a southern gift; "To smell the water in the air and feel the stormy winds in your veins was a power she couldn't describe," Mel had said.

I took her word for it because whenever or wherever it rained, Mel would be there before the first drop hit the pavement. It was like it called to her. It whispered her name throughout the night and she would wake with a mission. She made it seem like she was some superhero with a special ability, and I loved it.

There were many days when she'd come by unannounced and barge into the house to force me onto my bike and ride. My mother loved her and didn't mind that I spent rainy days outside with a friend, and there wasn't a day in my life where I would've said no to Melony.

As the rain pelted our skin and each droplet stung like an angry bee, she would laugh and pedal faster. She lived for the feeling; she seemed happier in the gloomy spring. Melony had said she was born on a stormy night in her grandmother's house in the middle of nowhere, and I didn't doubt a single word of it. The storm ran through her veins.

I never met her grandmother, but Melony looked up to the woman, and every story of Melony's family I had ever heard was about her. She rarely talked about her mother, whom I knew (and was also hated by), and she rarely talked about her father, but I knew enough not to bring him up in conversation. From the stories I had been told, Melony had gotten a lot of her traits from her mom's mother, and based on that reasoning alone, I think I would have loved the woman.

Melony was as spirited as a summer storm and as refreshing as the spring rain.

So, the minute I heard the pitter-patter of rain against my bedroom window, I immediately slipped my sneakers on—the ones with the caked-up mud and stains—grabbed the slicked windbreaker from the back of my door and headed toward the living room. As I slipped my arms through the sleeves of my jacket and reached for the door, the knob was already turning. A smile pulled at the corners of my lips, and I pulled the door open unsurprised to see Mel, underdressed for the stormy spring chill and rain that had soaked her from head to toe. Her hair was stringy and dripping down in front of her face. Beads of water trickled down her forehead from her scalp and gracefully filled her eyelashes, clumping them together into thick spidery wisps. Her eyes were bright, joyous, and surprised under the shadows of our covered porch. I looked her over and watched the water droplets drip from the ends of her hair as they created a small puddle beneath her at the front door.

"Hi," she greeted softly as the rain echoed above us onto the metal sheeting of the awning.

My smile widened at the sound of her voice.

"You're wearing a jacket?" she asked.

"You know my mom would kill me if I didn't," I said as I stepped out onto the porch and shut the door behind me.

She spun around, quickly jogged down the front steps before me, and picked her bike up from the sidewalk that ran across our yard to our driveway. I stood at the top of the steps, safe from the rain as I watched her maneuver her bike in the direction of the street before she swung her leg onto the other side and looked back over her shoulder at me with a grin. I finally stepped out into the rain and walked around the side of the porch where The Red Devil leaned against the side of the house.

As I pushed it out of the yard and onto the sidewalk, I could hear the storm getting harder through the leaves of the trees. The rain echoed through the woods behind the house and across the street, and the big oak tree that stood strong in the middle of our yard rustled loudly above us as Mel and I passed underneath it. I quickly pulled the hood of my jacket over my head as a gust of wind blew through. I could hear fat drops of water smack against the top of my head.

"What are we doing?" I called out to Melony who was rolling her bike a bit ahead.

She shrugged as she pulled out onto the dead street and stopped to wait for me by the mailbox. The sky seemed so dark yet so bright as she looked up at the clouds free from the canopy of the trees. Her eyes were squeezed shut as the rain pelted her face. She was a strange creature soaking up as much water as possible. A plant thriving in nature. She belonged out here.

I never could understand her obsession with the rain; yes, it was soothing to sit and listen to, but I couldn't stand the feeling of my wet clothes sticking to my skin like a form of paper-mâché. Yet I endured it for her.

When I reached the mailbox, I finally climbed onto my bike and rested my foot on the pedal.

"Are we headed to the clearing?" I asked.

"I didn't really have a plan when I came out," she spoke with her face still tilted toward the sky, "but that seems like a good idea."

"Okay." I pushed off the ground and began to pedal. "Let's go, then."

"Hey, that's not fair!" I could hear her laugh from behind me as I took my "illegal" head start.

As I began to pedal faster to beat Melony to the clearing, my hood flew back exposing my dark curly hair to the rain. I could feel the cold water begin to spread along my scalp as the rain poured harder and harder, stinging like needles against my face. Chills ran along my body under the layers of clothes I had on, and I began to wonder how cold Melony had felt being out here in shorts and an oversized, sopping wet T-shirt. I glanced over my shoulder to check on her only to see her whirling up beside me with her arms outspread like the wings of a bird soaring through the sky. Her bike wobbled back and forth with her hips as she ignored the handlebars. The smile on her face morphed into a smirk as she spotted me staring and quickly surpassed me.

As I trailed behind her, we pedaled out from the suburbs and turned left onto the side of the calm county road, swerving to avoid small debris or twigs in our path. We were cautious to watch for incoming traffic before we took another left onto her neighborhood street.

The clearing was near Melony's house down an old hiking trail that was uncovered years ago. On the right, along the property line of the Parkers' residence, the entrance to the trail was in the woods. Melony had told me about it a few years back.

Her grandmother was friends with Mrs. Parker, a round and wrinkly woman who would plant hundreds of flowers during the spring and summer months. Her yard was covered in a wild assortment of colors and floral scents. Melony and Mrs. Parker had found the trail together one spring while Mrs. Parker was babysitting her.

Melony had told me she was just a little girl when they found the hiking trail. I remember she said they were planting zinnias—Melony's favorite flower—when Melony had tried to remove a fallen branch out of the way of Mrs. Parker's flowerbed and she discovered an old sign for a hiking trail. She said the trail was so overgrown it was difficult to find the exact entrance, but after a while, they uncovered it together.

Years later, when Mel met me, the hiking trail was one of the first places she took me to explore. It was one of her favorite places to go, especially when it rained. There were plenty of springs after where we would join Mrs. Parker in her flowerbed and help her plant Melony's zinnias. Mr. Parker—who started a woodworking hobby after he retired—would go out and clear the path for us to ride; one summer, he installed a sign he had handcrafted that read "The Zinnia Path" as a gift for Melony.

I think they thought of her as one of their grandchildren, especially after Melony's grandmother passed away.

We pulled into the driveway of the Parkers' home, pedaled up the pavement, and through the wooden gate. Small puddles ran across the backyard, and a small section was boxed off and full of old soil and mulch. It was too early in spring to plant the flowers, but within the next few weeks, on a day when the sun would be shining, Melony would be knocking on my door again ready to help Mrs. Parker plant her zinnias.

The Zinnia Path was dark under the overcast clouds and shade of the canopy above. The trail was narrow and covered in a thin layer of mulch. The heavy rain became a trickle dripping from the leaves above as we pushed our bikes onto the path. I could feel the water and mud slowly soak through the fabric of my old worn-out sneakers, and I could hear the birds quietly chirping as they hid in their homes from the rain high above us.

It was quite magical, like a fairytale adventure from some old movie.

I looked over my shoulder back toward the trail entrance as it slowly grew smaller and smaller the further we walked through the mud. The rain poured out there, gray and deafening, but not on the trail. It was sparkling and vibrant green; the trees whispered, and the birds chattered. I could hear Melony's feet squishing into the mulchy mud. I would never get over the feeling days like this gave me.

"It's like another world, isn't it?" Melony spoke softly. Her voice was quiet and drew my eyes away from the woods around us onto her.

"It is," I murmured as her hazel eyes gazed into mine.

"I'm glad I get to share things like this with you."

We were moving at the same pace now, pulling our bikes alongside each other between us. Our bikes both creaked, and our shoes squished like sponges beneath us. Her hair dripped onto her arms and shoulders, and I could see goosebumps rising over her skin.

"Are you cold?" I asked, ready to rip my jacket off and hand it to her if she needed it.

"No," she replied, "it's refreshing."

"Liar," I quietly scoffed, and she smiled in return. "You need to start wearing more layers when you go out into this," I nagged, "My mom worries about you getting sick more than she worries about me."

She laughed, and the leaves rustled as the birds scattered around us.

"I'm serious, Mel," I chuckled nervously, "She's always asking about you, especially after rainy days like today."

"She doesn't need to worry."

"You say that like I can just tell her to stop," I chuckled, and she did the same.

She sounded like heaven. She looked like an angel.

Her skin was glowing and glistening under the bright gray light that peaked through the canopy. All the freckles that were scattered across her cheeks mapped out so many new and unknown constellations. No one could compare to her in my eyes. She wore the rain as if she was the one who brought the storms—as if she was made from the very water that fell from the sky.

"You're in your head," she whispered playfully as the clearing began to come into view ahead of us. "What are you thinking?"

I think I'm in love with you.

4

Melony

Jonas rounded the edge of the drive at a dangerous speed, and I leaped to my feet at the sight of him. More of the thick black substance painted his shirt and splattered over his hands and forearms. As his bike hit the ground in a loud clatter and he jogged up to the porch, I could smell what had happened.

"Are you okay?" I asked, not trying to hide the worry and fear on my face; he could sense it anyway.

"I'm fine," he said in between breaths, "I think we should be okay for the night."

"No scratches? Cuts?"

"Melony," he soothed. His voice steadied, and his eyebrows lifted as a small smile tugged on the corners of his lips. "I'm fine."

After a few more seconds of eyeing him, he finally broke eye contact and headed up the steps toward the front door.

"Have you checked it out?" he asked as he looked over his shoulder at me while his hand was wrapped around the doorknob.

I shook my head as I approached him.

He *reeked*.

Not the same musky scent of onions and garlic—sweet sweat and body odor—but the horrid stench of death and decay. It swirled around him in the air and hung onto the hairs inside my nostrils; the stench began to nestle into my lungs.

Jonas was unbothered, or if he was, he did a particularly good job hiding it.

He began to push on the door as he turned the knob. His arms flexed, and his shirt began to cling and stretch along his back. I could see the outline of his spine and the bulky protrusion of his shoulder blades as the amount of force he used grew stronger. The wood frame began to crackle, and the door started to slowly budge free from its grip. I could hear the bottom of the door scrape and drag along the old and crusty carpet behind it as I watched the door slowly and steadily open from over Jonas's shoulders.

The room beyond was dark; it would've been pitch black if not for the blinding light we were letting in. As we entered, the floor creaked beneath us, and the air was filled with dust. It felt stale in my lungs, and the dust floated around as if there was no gravity.

The door had opened into the living room. The windows on either side of the door were covered by ratty quilts with dirt and stains, and the carpet was stiff with time and layers of crusty debris from a home forever locked in the years before. The couch was along the left wall of the room; the upholstery was a floral fabric torn and eaten away by bugs and rodents exposing the underlying cushion. Apart from the damage, it reminded me of the couch that my grandmother and I would sit on as we watched TV or looked at old photo albums.

In the center of the room was a squat rectangular coffee table. Coasters with mugs of evaporated liquid and mold still sat in their places on the surface. A small vase of crunchy stems and dried petals sat in the middle next to a framed photo.

I cautiously stepped toward the table, trying with everything in me to avoid the creaky floor and remain quiet. I bent down and picked the photo up. The dust was caked onto the glass of the frame, and I attempted to wipe the layers off with the bottom of my shirt.

The photo was taken on the beach. An older woman and man stood on the shore holding each other. Her hair was short and gray, and her sunglasses hid her eyes, but the smile on her face was pure bliss. She was shorter than the man by about a foot. He was smiling the biggest grin I had seen in quite some time. His hair was white, and his face was clean-shaven. The man's eyes were barely visible as his cheeks bunched up with his grin, but you could tell he was having the time of his life. The legs of his pants were rolled up to mid-calf length, yet they were still darkened with seawater. I could almost hear them laughing as the waves crashed behind them.

I had only ever seen the ocean in videos and movies, but I imagined that the experience would feel magical. I had always hoped it would be something I could visit and experience before the end of my days. It would be like visiting another world; different from the magical feeling of the woods in the rain, different than the strange feeling the city gave me. The ocean would be peaceful and cinematic. That's how I imagined it. I would get sand in between my toes and drench myself to the point my clothes would be dragging me down. I don't know if I would ever stop smiling.

I'm not sure I would ever really know that feeling. Not like this couple had known it.

I flipped the photo frame over and began to pull the prongs up from the backing. I pinched the corner of the photo and removed it from the frame to examine it deeper before swinging my bag off my shoulder and setting it on the table. With the photo in one hand, I used my other to open my bag and dig deep into it, blindly feeling for the leather texture of my photo album. As I pulled it out of the bag, the light from the doorway made the leather look new. It was a deep forest green, and photos poked out of every available side.

The album was a gift from Jonas that I received years ago and have been using for a long time. When he gave it to me, he had already filled the first few pages with pictures of the two of us. All kinds of moments and memories lined the pages. Since the world flipped upside down, I had been filling it with other people's photos and memories to keep them alive just as I was keeping the best parts of Jonas and I alive within the pages. There was so much darkness and rot in the world, these people needed to be saved from that like Jonas and I had saved each other.

This couple belonged to my album. They deserved a spot and a chance to live on even if I had no clue who they were.

"You find anything?" Jonas whispered as he peeked his head around a wall leading into another area of the house.

His voice startled me even as his deep whisper matched the volume of the buzzing and chirping coming from outside. I shook my head in reply and tucked the photo into the book before shoving the book back into my bag. I swung my bag over and tugged the straps onto my shoulders, gripping them as I pivoted and stepped deeper into the house.

The shape and layout of the house mimicked that of my own childhood home. The entry led to the living room and further back the kitchen; there was a hall to the right—where Jonas had disappeared to—and a door on the left wall next to the couch marking the end of the living room and beginning of the kitchen that I assumed was the master bedroom.

I maneuvered myself around the furniture and headed for the door. I passed a small wooden furnace in the corner and backtracked toward it to grab a fire poker from the rack before I made my way back to the mysterious door and placed my hand on the handle. I took a deep breath to mentally prepare myself to fight something off.

The door was cold against my hands and shoulder. It was a refreshing touch in the summer humidity. The house was virtually silent other than the noises echoing inside from the open front door. I could hear my heart pounding in my head and chest. My fingers throbbed with a pulse against the dusty metal doorknob, and the wood and sweat prickled at my palms and fingertips.

I began to twist the handle. The latch clicked, and the door slowly began to creak open. A draft in the room rushed through the opening I had created, and the musty smell of wet, rotting wood and dirty linens smacked me in the face like a sack of bricks. I had the urge and instinct to just slam the door back shut and be done with it, but Jonas and I needed supplies more than anything. I resisted my urge and pushed the door open completely. The door creaked and groaned as I poked my head in after my makeshift weapon, leading the way with my extended arm and fire poker. Once I determined the room was free of imminent danger, I stepped inside and examined the scene.

The obvious thing that drew my attention was the jagged hole in the ceiling. Water had damaged the roof and soaked into the wooden beams. Brownish stains circled the hole, staining like ripples on the surface of a lake. Broken pieces of wood and crumbled drywall dangled from the gaping mouth above. It was like staring into a portal. The trees and leaves overhead swayed as the wind began to pick up, and the scent of rain was growing stronger. I could almost smell it already painting the pavement and gravel. The trees had shed into the home. Leaves and branches dangled from the rotting wood above and were scattered along the mushy and moldy carpet. I suppose a fallen branch had been what made the roof collapse in the first place.

The blanket that had been tacked over the window was falling, allowing an extra source of light from a different angle. The light from the window aimed directly at an area next to the bed in the middle of the room—a folded quilt resting perfectly on a storage ottoman at the foot of the rotting mattress. My eyes continued to glaze over the entire room.

The dressers and nightstands were from a wooden antique set like the one I remember seeing in Mrs. Parker's home except I believe her husband had made those by hand. These were not handmade. The wood was chipped, and the medium-toned stain was a patchy variant of dark and light wood grain across the entire surface. The bed in the middle of the room was framed in a similarly stained wooden frame and headboard. Scratches and termite holes ate away at the probably once beautiful finish. After observing and absorbing the extent of the damage to the room, I began to walk around it. I carefully swiped and dragged my fingers along the surfaces of the dresser. The wood grain and dust particles etched into my fingertips, filling my prints with grime that turned my skin gray.

I opened jewelry boxes and drawers; I scanned through the clothing and found pairs of socks and changes of bottoms for both Jonas and me. After looking through the bottom half of the dresser, I turned my attention toward the top.

I found myself staring at a dull mirror.

The top half of the dresser was a vanity. The mirror was cloudy and covered in grime, but I could make out my silhouette in it. I reached into one of the drawers, pulled out a shirt I had decided wouldn't fit either of us, and began to wipe the mirror off in circular motions. When I pulled the cloth away, it revealed a semi-clean smeared circle.

It had been so long since I had seen myself.

My hair was frizzy and pulled back into a loose ponytail. Wispy strands of caramel brown were glued to my face with sweat. My neck and cheeks were streaked with shine and dirt, and my eyes were set deeper than I had remembered. The tan on my skin was nothing compared to the darkness of my undereye bags. My freckles were more abundant, my eyebrows were bushy, and my lips were cracked and dry. The loose clothing I wore was covered in filth and stains. My silver chain and locket pendant hung out from underneath my shirt, and I brought a hand up to clutch it.

It wasn't me. I was looking at someone completely different. It was as if I was seeing someone else wearing my skin, and I didn't know if I could stomach looking at her any longer.

I could hear Jonas walking around in the other room, and my eyes started to drift away from the person I was staring at in the mirror to what was behind me.

The dresser and the bed were facing each other. I could see the debris from the open ceiling—drywall, wood, branches, leaves—piled up onto the mattress.

But there was something else that appeared… off.

Under the debris, a quilt—not unlike the one folded at the end of the bed—was draped across the mattress over two lumps that elongated from the pillows to the end of the bed. I turned and faced them head-on. I stared at the lumpy mattress from the foot of the bed frame. Slowly and cautiously, I took small steps toward the bed. I could almost feel the carpet's texture through the soles of my shoes; with each step, the smell of mildew wafted up around me, and the crunchy fibers of the carpet mixed with the rotted squishiness of the sponge padding beneath was making my stomach churn. The queasiness began to spread through my abdomen the closer to the bed I became.

My eyes shifted and focused through the debris until I could make out the shapes of two people in the bed. They lay side by side covered in the quilt; it stopped at their neck and shoulders, and a pale blue flat sheet was pulled over their faces.

I didn't need to see their faces to know they had been there for a long time. A black rot mold had spread over the lumps remaining under the sheet. It appeared in such a balanced yet chaotic pattern like splattered droplets of watercolor paint.

The queasiness in my gut became a roaring churn of twisting knots. I could feel the acidity of my empty stomach burning as it slowly climbed, and with no time to move, I dropped the fire poker, hunched over, and began to retch over the carpet next to the bed. Little to nothing came up, but the feeling lingered in the back of my throat. As I placed a hand over my stomach, I heard a hurried footfall rush into the room from behind.

"Are you okay? What happened?" Jonas asked rapidly, his voice was no longer a whisper.

I nodded as I remained hunched over with my hands now on my knees. My eyes watered, and I could feel a few hot tears begin to trickle down my sticky face. I brought the back of my hand up to my mouth and wiped away at my lips. I could feel the skin scratching at the back of my hand and all I could taste was salt and acid.

"I'm okay," I grumbled.

Carefully, I straightened my back and turned to face him. I could see his gaze shifting between the roof and the bed.

"The house is clear," he informed as he ignored the obvious scene in front of him. "I went ahead and locked up the entrance—barricaded it too."

I nodded and inhaled deeply; I could still feel the burning sensation in the back of my throat and nostrils.

"Why don't we get out of this room?" he suggested.

"Yeah, um…" I glanced back toward the mirror, unable to see the messier I had become, but I could feel it. "I think we should block it off. Anything could get in through that hole."

He nodded in agreement before stepping out of the doorway and motioning for me to exit.

"I found a few changes of clothes, socks, underwear. I didn't get to look for any new shoes," I informed as I stepped out and brushed past him.

With the door closed, the house was back to being dark, but I noticed that Jonas had rolled and tied off the bottoms of the blankets covering the windows to allow some light back in.

"That's okay," he replied as the bedroom door clicked behind me, "I found some old shoes in a room down the hall and some boots by the back door. Both sets are a little big for either of us, but they should work for a while."

He stepped away from the door and headed for the couch. His strides were long and even, and he reached his destination in no time. He reached down and plucked a pair of black and purple sneakers tied together by the laces from the couch and tossed them to me. I clumsily caught them and checked the sizing; only one size too big.

"You did good," I chuckled.

"Oh!" he exclaimed excitedly, "I also found you this."

He reached over the edge of the couch and picked up an aluminum bat streaked with neon green branding. He outstretched his arm and held the bat by the barrel with the handle pointed toward me. I reached out and gripped it, pulling it out of his hands I could feel the weight and the cold metal in my clammy palm. There was a thin layer of grip tape around the handle which scratched at my skin, but it felt nice. It reminded me of home.

5

Jonas: Before

Melony reached into the bag that she had set in the grass next to her and pulled out an old and dirty baseball.

"You down to play a little?" she asked as she reached her other hand to the side pocket of the bag and gripped the handle of a bat.

The sun was out today; it beamed through the trees and onto the grass of the clearing adding to the heat of the already hot and humid summer air. You could hear the bugs droning and screaming in the trees and grass.

Melony often brought some form of entertainment for us on days like this. The rainy days were to sit and enjoy, and the scorching ones were for us to sweat our asses off. I suppose she kept me in shape.

We would come out to the clearing and play games of kickball, fútbol, baseball, and any other sporty idea Melony could think of. On days like this, she would always wear a tank top and a pair of shorts, even when her mother gave her a skeptical eye and questioned what she was *actually* doing out here with me. I'd only seen this kind of interaction once before and remained as respectful as I could—it was how my parents had taught me—but I couldn't stand the way they treated each other. I couldn't stand the way her mother treated *me*.

But no matter what Mrs. Harper said to Melony, if the sun was up, she'd be outside wearing whatever she felt, and spending as much time as she could playing games with me.

I respected her rebellion as much as I would respect her compliance.

Sometimes her arguing with her mother would get worse over the summer months because she wanted to spend more time outdoors. I would come home frustrated with Melony's situation. It wasn't any of my business, but family is something important to me, and a lot of the time I couldn't wrap my head around how she and her mother treated each other so differently than I always treated mine. My mother would try to explain that not all families are functional. She would tell me that people express emotions differently and that everyone grows up differently and is raised differently. Generation after generation, certain behavior sometimes follows. She would tell me that my father grew up so close to his family in Mexico; he worked a job from a young age to help my grandparents pay bills, and he would spend every night helping his mother in the kitchen, and every morning he would help his father repair what needed fixing. She would then explain to me how she grew up distant from her parents and only remained close with her brother as time went on. She empathized with Melony, and I think her tenderness and love for Mel reflected that.

We all grow up differently. Different cultures, different worlds.

"C'mon," Melony grunted as she pushed herself off the ground and headed for the center of the clearing.

My eyes were at her thigh level as she reached out a hand to assist me off the ground and I zoned in on the bat she held at her side. Her knuckles were white as she adjusted her grip from the knob to the handle of the bat. I could see her fingernails picking and digging into the foam grip.

Today must have been a difficult day.

I placed my hand in hers and felt her gently squeeze as she pulled me up to my feet. When I came face-to-face with her and the sun was no longer glaring into my eyes, I noticed a glossy redness in her eyes.

"Are you okay?" I asked softly.

Melony wasn't a sensitive girl. I had always known her to be fierce and energetic even on days that weren't exactly good. She would talk me through the details in such a calm manner; her voice rarely ever wavered, and I rarely ever witnessed her cry. She was strong and tended to brush off any minor nuisances. Although she never really showed her emotions, I could usually sniff out when something was truly bothering her. I could tell when she was too in her head or hiding some sort of pain.

She tried to hide it today.

As I stared down at her face, I could see her cheeks grow more flushed underneath the rosy redness of a sunburn. Her earthy eyes began to water, and her lips parted as if she were about to speak before she quickly closed her mouth. Her lips began to tremble, and the façade began to fade.

"I—no," she stuttered and stopped herself before quickly shutting her mouth again.

"I can hear the strain in your voice, Melony," I murmured, "You don't have to hold it back with me…"

Her eyes flickered across my face and tears began to roll down her cheeks. I realized I was still holding her hand and gave it a gentle squeeze. Our palms were sweaty, and I could feel a more intense heat radiating from her than the summer day.

"I just want a normal day," her voice was weak and scratchy, but she had said enough to allow the gates to spill open. "I want a normal life."

"Let's sit back down…" I suggested as I slowly began to pull her back into the shade of the tree line surrounding the clearing.

She followed without hesitation, and after we sat back in the itchy grass, she began to spill.

"I see all these families: Mrs. Parker and how she is with her kids and grandkids, you and your parents, literally random fucking people in the grocery stores or on the street. Everyone seems so happy, so normal." The words tumbled out. "They're all so whole."

I sat back and listened. I didn't speak. I didn't interrupt her to give my feedback. I just listened to her emotions. I listened to her trembling voice turn into a calm and flowing river of thought-out feelings. She talked about how her mother treats her and how that makes her feel. How her grandmother was the opposite and how she misses her. She told me about her father's death and how it's been affecting her lately even though he passed so long ago. Her tears soon faded, and she just began to... talk.

The heat of the day began to cool down as the sun disappeared from above the clearing and began to peak through the trees in the woods. The birds were no longer chirping, and the sounds of the bugs had begun switching to the night shift. The evening air felt damp and dewy as the sky was painted with oranges and purples.

"I think I should be getting home," Melony sighed.

"You don't have to," I finally said.

Her look was confused and inquisitive.

"You can," I corrected myself, "but I think you should come to my house for a bit. Talk to my mom."

"I don't know if I wanna tell your mom all of this."

I shook my head. "You won't have to. She'll do the talking for you."

Melony was hesitant but ultimately agreed. We rode our bikes down the county road, back into my neighborhood, and up my driveway. The ride was silent as the sky darkened to a navy speckled with stars. The porch light illuminated the yard as we approached the porch, and I could sense the tension in Melony's breath the closer we got to the front door. We rested our bikes at the steps, and she swung her bag off her shoulders, leaning it on the ground beside her bike. The metal of the bat in the side pocket clattered against the metal frame.

"Just come inside and calm down a bit," I soothed as she slowly made her way up the steps and in front of the door.

She glanced back down toward her bag and bike as if she were planning to bolt. A small smile grew on her cheeks.

"We didn't even get to play today."

"Another time," I replied.

6

Melony

I could feel my eyes grow heavier as the sun became golden through the small crack in the makeshift curtains. The room grew hotter from the rays beaming in, but it still felt better than being directly in them.

Jonas had pushed the coffee table off to the side of the room and spread a sheet he had found in the linen closet down the hall across the carpet. We sat facing the barricaded front door, our backs pressed against the ratty sofa, sharing the insides of a can of fruit cocktail found deep in a cupboard. Earlier, Jonas found several canned goods in perfect condition, only briefly past the expiration date, tucked away in the cabinets. We decided to make the rest of this day feel like an achievement and treat ourselves to something on the sweeter side.

Ergo, fruit cocktail.

The sweet syrupy mess of soggy fruits touched a sentimental string in my heart. It felt as if I were enjoying some dessert—the toppings of a sundae. It pulled me back to what the world was like before. Being free to grab anything you craved or wanted to eat from the cabinet and cook up something nice for yourself.

Now, we ate anything we could. No questions asked.

Some things were better than others, and I had enough knowledge about edible plants to get us the nutrition we needed when we didn't have it. I'm lucky I spent so much time planting gardens with Mrs. Parker as a child. We would read through the benefits of certain flowers and plants before we decided to plant—which ones had vitamins, and which ones worked like medicines. Pansies and nasturtium flowers are full of antioxidants and anti-inflammatories; they can help with headaches and swelling. During the spring, I would bake cookies with Mrs. Parker and decorate them with pansies, she would also show me how to make oils and salves. She avoided removing weeds like dandelions from her flowerbeds.

"You could eat this whole damned plant!" she would say.

She made me help her plant zinnias in the flowerbed for the first time, and when I asked her what kinds of things they helped with, she didn't know. I went to the library the next day and began to do my own research. Zinnias are antifungal and antibacterial; they help with stomach aches and help treat wounds. I rushed to Mrs. Parker's house the next day and told her what I had learned, and she officially added them to her garden every year after. The zinnias bloomed that summer, and

I had never seen a more beautiful flower. It was strange to see how something so natural and lovely could help in so many ways. Flowers and gardening became one of my hobbies.

When I became a teacher, I would often use our free time and science lessons to share my knowledge with the elementary kids. As a project, we made dandelion salves in class. It took six long weeks, but the kids were so excited when their creations were finished. It was a messy experience at first, but they got to create the labels for their tins, and some even decided to give them to their mothers as a Mother's Day gift before the school year had ended.

I felt as if my knowledge and hard work as a teen paid off; it became especially useful when the world fell to pieces. Except, I didn't have a place to plant a garden now. I didn't have the seed, the flowerbed, anything. Instead, I had a can of fruit cocktail, and no medicine for if it made us sick.

Our spoons began to scrape the bottom and sides of the can with a brain-itching racket as the metals scratched against each other. When the can was empty, Jonas took it and set it on the coffee table. He closed his eyes and leaned his head back onto the cushions of the couch. I could hear him release a deep breath before he turned to me and gazed at me with his dark chocolate eyes.

"What's one thing—one food—that you miss?"

"Ice cream," I said bluntly with no hesitation.

He chuckled at my speed. "That *would* be nice right now, especially with this heat wave that we've been moving through."

"It'll rain tonight."

"I trust that you're right about that," he smirked.

I scooted my body down and turned more to my side to face him. His eyes were soft and tired as his gaze bounced around my face. His greasy curls fell back onto the couch behind his head like midnight ocean waves, and a few strands clung to his forehead appearing like curving rivers on a map.

"Do you remember the first time I told you I loved you?" he whispered sincerely.

I furrowed my brows in confusion at the sudden seriousness in the air, but answered, nevertheless. "I'm not sure. Maybe the first night we had a sleepover. 'Goodnight, love you.' You let me sleep in your bed while you slept on the futon you had in your room."

He shook his head and pushed his entire body to face me head-on. "No, no. The time I said I was *in love* with you," he added.

"Prom. Junior prom."

He nodded and a nostalgic smile rose upon his face. "You look just as beautiful now as you did that night."

I laughed.

"I'm serious. The end of the world may take everything from us, but it will never take that from you, *mi flor*."

"I've always loved when you call me that," I smiled.

"I guess it also won't take my spectacular charm," he playfully smirked at me causing me to giggle.

"I'd be blushing if my face wasn't already red."

"Good," he stated.

The sun beyond the windows was falling lower and lower. The coolness of the night began to seep into the poorly insulated house and through the gaping hole in the other room. Jonas sat up and stretched as the living room grew darker.

"There's a bed in another room down the hall. We should go ahead and make ourselves comfortable. It's as clean as we'll get for a while," he said before he grunted while he pushed himself off the floor and extended his hand out to me.

His fingers gripped around my wrist, clammy and hot, and he tugged me to my feet. After picking me up, he reached down and grabbed our bags from the floor. He handed me the bat that was resting against the arm of the couch and began to lead me down the hall to the bedroom.

The vinyl wood flooring down the hall matched that of the kitchen. The thinness caused the creaking of the floor to be much louder than that of the carpeted living room. The hall was significantly darker than the rest of the house, but I could make out the outlines of frames on the walls and tears in the wallpaper. Jonas opened the last door on the left and waved me in. It appeared to have been sectioned or sealed off and unused by the last people who lived here. The window wasn't covered how the others were, and the room was clean. The bed was made and just collecting dust in a layer as if it was just another sheet to add to the bedding. In the other corner of the room, across from the bed and under the window, a desk sat coated in a blanket of gray fuzz still messily organized from the last person who used it. Jonas brushed past me as he squeezed in through the door and closed it behind us. He headed toward the partition doors in the corner of the room next to the dresser that sat along the same wall as the main entry and pushed them open. He rummaged for a moment before he turned around holding a dark-colored wadded sheet and a folded blanket. Jonas set the sheet down on the tabletop and passed me the blanket. He instructed me to remove the first few layers of bedding from the bed and remake it with the blanket while he searched for something to pin the sheet over the window.

I turned toward the bed and pulled up the quilt that lay on top as well as the white flat sheet that was sprawled out underneath. The mattress was soft to the touch, and as I pressed on it with my hands, I could feel myself begin to weaken and melt into the fibers. I felt heavy and exhausted, but I carried on. I pulled back the blankets until they hit the carpet with a soft thud, and I unfolded the blanket Jonas had handed me and spread it flat over the fitted sheet. I grabbed each pillow that rested at the head of the bed and smacked them. Under the moonlight that had begun to pour in from the window, I watched as clouds of dust exploded into the air and swirled around like a swarm of tiny bugs. The dull glitter floated around the room in the sparkly white light, more and more with each smack of the pillows.

When I had finished fluffing and "cleaning" the pillows, I arranged them back on the bed with the previous dust-covered side facing down and the clean side up. When I turned around to check how Jonas was doing with the sheet, he was reaching up with one corner gripped in his hand trying to push a thumbtack into the wall above the window.

I took this moment as an opportunity to claim my spot on the bed and flailed myself back onto the mattress. Jonas's head snapped at me with concern on his face before he realized I was finally relaxing. He chuckled to himself and moved to the other corner of the window with the other side of the sheet.

"Is it nice?" he asked.

I released a sigh of contentment, and I took it that that was the only answer he needed as he shook his head while playfully rolling his eyes. I outstretched my arms and turned my face upward to the ceiling as I sprawled myself out across the mattress. My legs dangled off the bed at my knees, and my feet hovered above the carpet. My body ached, and I could feel my muscles release the longer I remained still. I was melting. As I stared at the ceiling, my eyes began to grow heavier and burn the more I tried to keep them open. My breathing was steady and deep, and I felt as if the mattress was engulfing me.

It opened and swallowed me whole.

The room was dark. Were my eyes closed? I could hear my breathing echoing in my head as if I were deep in a cave. Water dripped somewhere in the distance. The sound was much deeper—a faint dripping; *plink, plink, plink* resounded throughout the cavern. I began to see a blueish light form around me and shine off the rock walls that surrounded me. I was encased in a tomb. Blue, black, and gray filled my vision. The light sparkled off the damp cave walls, and I could see the reflection of water up ahead. *Plinkplinkplink.* It was growing louder and faster. Was I moving?

A screech erupted and my eyes shot open. I had drifted to sleep.

Jonas had repositioned me fully onto the bed and scooted his way in next to me. My shoes were no longer on my feet, and I was wearing different clothes. I quickly sat up and looked around the room, my breath heavy and trembling, and my body shaking under the covers as I let my eyes adjust to the darkness.

The dresser that was once in between the closet and entry was now pushed in front of the bedroom door barricading us in. Our bags sat in the corner next to the window, and my bat was leaning against the wall next to Jonas's head. Outside, the rain poured down onto the roof of the house; I could hear the drops hitting the window, and I could smell the water in the air. I breathed deeply and began to ground myself.

In through the nose, out through the mouth.

I turned to check on Jonas. He lay on his side facing me, one arm was across his chest with his hand tucked under his head, and the other arm was tucked up underneath my pillow. His breathing was steady, and a small rumble would call out into the night with every other breath. He looked peaceful.

I smiled to myself and slowly laid back on my pillow trying not to disturb him. I rolled onto my side and stared at him through the blue darkness around me. His eyelids fluttered as he dreamed, and I began to feel my own eyes grow tired once again.

The rain pattered against the window, and I started to drift away. I could feel my mind slowly lifting out of my body. Floating in and out of sleep as the window rattled against the breezes of the steadily growing rain. I wasn't dreaming. I felt awake and asleep at the same time, sailing between worlds like the rocking of a ship at sea. A few seconds later, a thunderous crack rumbled across the house and jolted me back into my body. My awareness came to me in the blink of an eye. The storm had picked up. I could hear the quiet whistling of the wind and the consistent slaps of water against the window. The shadows of the water and leaves smacking against the window created illustrations against the sheet in the moonlight. Lightning illuminated the room in a dull flash of light, and I saw a shadow standing next to the bed for a brief second.

I froze in fear and slowly reached out to Jonas next to me; nothing.

I stared at the shadow as it inched away from the bed and toward the door. It was humanlike aside from the extra-long limb that extended to the floor, dragging along the carpet. I could feel tears swell in my eyes and my lungs rapidly filling with air. My lips trembled and a whimper tickled the back of my throat. I remained perfectly still as the shadow turned to me while tears streamed down my face.

Another flash of light bounced off the walls illuminating the figure standing feet away from me. The light reflected on dark black curls and shadowed the arched bridge of Jonas's nose.

I squeezed my eyes shut as relief ran through my body in a wave. Tears streamed back into my hair as my head pushed deep into my pillow, and I released a trembling breath. My eyes began to adjust to the darkness, and as I opened my mouth to scold him for scaring me, he placed a gentle finger over his lips and nodded toward the bedroom door. I furrowed my brows and eyed him up and down.

The extended limb I had seen was the bat clenched tightly in his hand.

My eyes widened, and I froze in fear once more. Jonas tiptoed slowly, avoiding the creaks and groans the floor had emitted earlier. I watched as he pulled the bat up into a swinging position, and I held my breath. I listened to the air around us. The pattering of the rain practically filled every inch of the house; then there was the sound of Jonas's breathing—his inhale and exhale was so faint beneath every drop of rain against the window. I waited for a second, and then another, my lungs burned and begged to gasp for air.

But within the waiting, there was a sound.

The all-too-familiar faint clicking almost mimicked the rain pelting the window. Almost. It was too rhythmic, too vocal.

I stealthily began to slide myself out from under the covers with enough caution and care to remain silent. I swung my feet off the bed and gently placed them against the carpet. The fibers itched at the bottom of my feet through my socks, but I continued to move at a snail's pace. The floor did not make a sound underneath me as I tiptoed around Jonas. He held out the bat to me with one hand as his other dug into his pocket for his knife. Only when he pulled out his new weapon did I take the bat from him. I slowly moved back, toe to heel, bat raised in front of me with both hands gripped tightly around the handle.

Jonas nodded his head toward the closet.

"Hide..." he mouthed.

I furrowed my brows and shook my head furiously.

I wasn't going to leave him. I wasn't going to hide. Before, out on the road, we both had the chance and option to run. We had the distance and the bikes. Now? The hall was blocked, and the window would have caused more trouble now than it would have provided us with an escape. We were trapped.

We needed to remain silent. If they didn't find us, if we didn't make a sound, they would leave. They would leave eventually. They wouldn't stay here. There have been several instances in the past where we could escape past these creatures going unnoticed, and only a couple of cases in which we were forced to fight for our lives. Neither of those occurrences totaled up to enough run-ins to grow used to this kind of thing. There was no *getting used to it.* Being alive meant being in danger and being at risk of coming across these... monsters.

But there was a chance—a small, miniscule chance—Jonas and I would survive this. Not just this night, but this new world. We had already come so far. Would this really be our last night together?

I took another step back, and in an instant, the idea of surviving this night all came crashing down. My hip bumped into the edge of the desk and a cup of pens toppled over. It rolled across the desk with a clatter that echoed throughout the house. My eyes widened as my body went into shock, and I immediately began to cry. My breath caught in my throat, and Jonas turned and ran to me with a speed unknown to man.

There was no more hiding. They knew we were here.

An inhuman screech broke through the air, clawing and ripping at my eardrums.

Jonas grabbed me by the shoulders; his fingers dug into my muscles, and I could hardly see him through the tears in my eyes. Everything began to blur together. Colors. Shapes. Everything blended into a single shade of dark blue as Jonas brought his face inches from mine.

There was a banging on the door.

Bang after bang reverberated through the walls, and I could feel the vibrations through my spine as my back pressed against the wall. The dresser in front of the door wobbled, and the drawers began to slide out inch by inch with each ram against the door, but Jonas still stood inches in front of me.

He was mouthing words I couldn't hear. Was he yelling? Why couldn't I hear him?

Thump. Thump. Thump. Crack!

The door was breaking. The wood of the doorframe was splintering like snapping a branch in half.

The more the door cracked, the more I could smell death.

I could smell the rotting stench of spoiled raw meat left in the sun. It was as if I was standing in an abandoned butcher shop or had come across a bloated animal lying on the side of the road. A metallic scent was carried in with the rot, so strong I could almost taste copper and old pennies at the back of my throat. The scent wafted under the doors and filled the room.

Jonas began to pull me toward the closet, but I couldn't move. He tugged and tugged on my arms, but I felt like a brick wall. Frozen. Glued in place. Brick and mortar drying in the sun. I felt like a tree taking root deep in the carpet interweaving within the beams and posts in the foundation. Immovable. But as the leaves of a tree produce oxygen, I felt as if mine was being taken. The stench was growing so strong as it continued to blow in from the hall and I could feel the queasiness churning in my gut as I held back my gagging as long as I could.

Yet the scent was nothing compared to the sounds coming from outside the room. With each bang, the hinges on the door rattled, and the dresser barricading us jumped forward inch after inch. I could hear a sickening squelch with each ram, and the cracking of not only the wood of the door but the bones of the creature that wanted in.

It was going to get in.

Another bang erupted followed by the crashing sound of the dresser as it wobbled one last time and tipped over. After it fell, I could see the familiar thick black substance oozing in from underneath the door and staining the carpet like a spilled bucket of tar.

Finally, my body and brain synced. All the blood in me rushed through my body as if I had just been revived.

"Melony!" Jonas shouted.

I turned to him with panic running through my veins faster than lightning in the sky. Thunder rumbled outside, a shriek filled the air after it, and then the banging grew harder. The door cracked once more. Louder. Sharper.

Oh. My. God!

Jonas yanked hard on my arm, and I practically flung myself into the closet. The bat, which I had forgotten I was holding, dragged alongside me and bounced off the doorframe.

"You're gonna be okay," Jonas said planting a firm kiss on my forehead before he slammed the closet door, shutting me inside.

My fingernails dug into the grip tape on the bat, and I brought a hand up and covered my mouth. I could feel vomit rising in my throat as the smell grew stronger, and my breathing was so unsteady I began to feel faint. Tears continued to pour down my face and neck. I was sobbing and could barely hold back the whimpering as the door crashed in.

The slats in the closet door provided enough of a visual into the room. Jonas stood with his feet planted, hips turned, facing the door. His left arm was stuck out as if he were holding an invisible shield and the knife in his right hand glistened as he held it up. I couldn't see the creature that had been banging on the door, but I didn't need to.

I leaned forward and held my breath as a gray blur leaped from the hall, over the dresser, and straight for Jonas. In the blink of an eye, Jonas was pinned against the wall. A blur of gray and black flailed around in front of him attempting to maul him.

I could see it now.

Its skin was gray, covered in holes and tears. The black goo oozed from the wounds like blood from a cut. Its limbs were spidery in length and bones protruded from the flesh into newly formed joints as it sprinted like an animal; though jagged and broken, the arms and legs extended like a human.

But this was no human... *not anymore.*

Its spine stuck out from the skin on its back as if the flesh were merely thin sheets of paper draped over the bone. Scaly and leathery like patches of dried animal hide, it clung to the creature with small bubbles like blisters of blood pooling across the skin. It was a living rotting corpse. With cloudy eyes, it blindly clawed at Jonas as its mouth hung agape; its jaw barely remained attached to its skull. The entire right side of this creature was torn and smashed to pieces. Its arm hung limp at its side; shattered bones ripped through its shoulder and neck from ramming against the door. The pitch-black tar glistened over its entire face and wounds. It screeched and swung wildly as Jonas used his arm to push it back. Black blood splattered onto him, and I began to pray internally.

I wasn't a believer. Never really had been religious growing up, and especially wasn't after the world began to rot. But in a moment like this, what harm could it do? These beasts carried a disease. A disease with no cure—the disease that ended the world. We didn't have much information about it, but we knew that the moment you got a cut, a scratch, or even a tiny drop of its blood in your system, you were dead. I had seen the change happen once… and I'd pray to any god that I'd never have to see it again.

I muttered some hopeful words under my breath as Jonas struggled and pushed against the creature. I saw his hand come up in the darkness, and within seconds, the creature released a deafening shriek before it fell limp at Jonas's feet.

Jonas leaned his head back against the wall and stared at the ceiling. His breath was heavy, and I could see his chest rapidly rising and falling as he tried to maintain his breathing. The look on his face showed his exhaustion. His energy was depleted. Through the crack, I watched him push himself off the wall and gaze down at the creature in disgust before he stepped around it and headed toward me. But deep within the house, underneath the sound of the rain, I could hear another.

A faint clicking traveled from somewhere inside. *No, no, no.*

"No," I whimpered aloud as Jonas reached for the door.

Confusion darted across his face as he opened the closet door and saw me. His eyes widened in concern before the clicking bellowed from inside the room. The sound was deep and guttural, and I could see the source from where I stood in the corner of the closet.

The corpse stood on all spidery fours on top of the fallen dresser with its mouth hanging wide open. Its blood dripped from its mouth and puddled onto the wood with a thick squelchy splatter. With solid white eyes and a nose structure that resembled something so human, it pointed its face toward the ceiling. Jonas slowly pivoted on his heel and faced the gray being. We both watched in terror as its throat swelled and a knot bulged from underneath the skin before it bellowed another set of clicks like the slowed rhythmic drumming of a woodpecker.

We didn't have a chance to move; it had already heard us and leaped forward with a ferocious speed immediately tackling Jonas to the floor.

Lightning flashed throughout the room, and without thinking, I stepped out.

The creature screamed and screeched as if it had crawled from the pits of hell. Wildly flailing, it missed Jonas by millimeters with every swing.

As it raised its grotesque arms, I used every fiber of my being to raise the bat. Adrenaline raged through me. It was a fire I had never felt before. Both hands were wrapped so tightly around the bat that I could feel my fingernails digging deep into my palms, and I could feel the warm sensation of blood on my fingertips. My arms tingled with pins and needles, and I brought the bat down onto the beast's head.

Clunk.
And again.
Clunk.
And again.

7

Jonas: Day One

The bell above the door jingled as it flung open and someone walked in. I looked up from my magazine spread on the counter with a half-assed smile preparing to greet one of my first customers of the day.

My father would scold me if he were here to see such unenthusiastic work.

"*Hola!*" Melony greeted me as she entered the store, and the bell jingled again behind her.

My half-assed smile quickly morphed into a real grin as she approached the counter and placed her tote bag over my magazine. She lifted her round-framed sunglasses and rested them on the top of her head. The temples of her glasses tucked into her hair that she wore pulled back into a styled loose ponytail. The end of her ponytail was full of curls, and the thin pieces that framed her face stuck to her sparkly lip gloss from the breeze outside.

"*Hola, mi flor,*" I murmured against her lips as she leaned in over the counter and kissed me.

Her lips were soft but sticky, and I could smell a hint of vanilla and coffee in her breath. When she pulled away, her flirtatious hazel eyes remained focused on my lips.

"I love it when you call me that."

She leaned forward again and pecked me softly before she came around the counter, draped her arms over my shoulders, and interlocked her fingers behind my neck. I gently wrapped my arms around her waist and looked down at her sweet smile and bright doe eyes. She looked as beautiful as always. Her mid-calf length skirt was breezy and thin with silky pleats and a gorgeous navy-blue floral pattern; she paired it with a white polo and dull red cardigan to match some colors from the flowers on her skirt.

When we were kids, you wouldn't have caught her dead in a skirt or dress, but damn did she rock the hell out of one now.

Her locket was untucked from her shirt and resting against her chest with the engraved side facing me. It was a pendant the size of a quarter shaped into the intricate design of a zinnia; a tiny latch and hinge could be found on opposite sides of each other, and on the back, engraved into the metal, were the Spanish words for "my flower".

The locket had been a gift I had gotten her for our first anniversary. I had first told Melony I was in love with her at junior prom. It was the first time I had seen her in a dress since we met when we were ten, and I couldn't take my eyes off her. We had decided to go together as friends, but I wasn't sure exactly what to label the relationship we came out with.

My father had let me borrow the car to drive us there even though we lived less than ten minutes away from the school. I picked Melony up, helped her buckle in, and drove back to my house so my mother could get pictures. My mother's smile was like none I had seen before. I think she knew something would happen that night, or maybe she was just happy she got to see us like that before she passed.

Melony wanted to leave the dance early that night so she could come back to my place and tell my mother every detail before she went to chemotherapy the next morning, and I agreed to leave. When we got to the car, I put the key in the ignition and confessed my feelings before I even pulled out of the parking space. Melony didn't speak a word, so I pulled away from the school, down the road, and into my driveway. She unbuckled herself in silence and exited the car. I sat outside alone in the car for thirty minutes while she was inside my house talking to my parents. I can still remember the feeling in my chest as my mind raced, and I questioned everything. I was too afraid to lose her.

But then the porch light flicked on, the front door opened, and Melony stepped out. She stood at the top step of the porch with a smile on her face still in her pistachio-colored satin gown basking in the warm glow of the bulb above the door, and everything I was worrying about was washed away.

A year later, at graduation, we celebrated our first anniversary, and I spent a week's check working at my father's store to buy her that necklace. I had a hell of a tough time getting one of our prom photos down to size to fit in it.

I think Melony would have loved to show it to my mother, and I like to think my mother would've been proud of me for doing something so sweet.

"What's on your mind?" Melony cocked her head to the side and asked.

Her ponytail whipped and flicked around as she moved.

"You're beautiful," I replied before I gently pulled my arms back, dragging them along her waist and hips as I did.

She blushed and turned away as I let go. She leaned against the counter and pulled her tote—and my trapped magazine—toward her. She reached into the bag and began pulling out her sticker-covered laptop. A few of the stickers I recognized as duplicates of ones we had on our bikes so long ago, but it seemed like every day there were new stickers pasted on from students who brought them for her.

"How was your day?" she asked with a bright smile while opening the screen and bringing up a bunch of minimized tabs.

I shrugged and gestured around us. The store was dead. It was always empty during the week until around six p.m. when we'd get a few regulars who stopped in for a candy or drink on their way home. In the early mornings, an older gentleman named Easton would stop by, buy a coffee from the automated machines, and sit in the two-seater booth watching the news from the television hanging in the corner. He made intellectual conversation about topics I did not know of and was quite an out-of-date comedian, but he was the only company I had in the early morning and a customer who stuck around after my father passed. If he was here when Melony stopped in on her way to the school, she'd playfully flirt with him, and I swear it got him off every time.

Easton didn't show up this morning, and it was nearing six with no jingle of the doorbell other than Melony.

"Has it been like this all day?" she asked as her eyes flicked down into the corner of her screen to the digital clock.

"I don't know what's going on," I said nonchalantly.

I should have cared about getting customers because this was my father's business. When he passed a few years after my mother, I was in year three of my business bachelors. His death was sudden, and he had been showing me for a long time how to run the store, so naturally, I came home at the end of the semester and started taking my classes online. Melony stopped by a couple of times a month while she was still on campus, and the customers were the only people I got to interact with. It was a hard change to adjust to, but I worked with what and who I had.

But it'd been several years, and I'm not sure I cared to be confined here anymore.

Melony pulled up a browser tab and her fingers flew across the keyboard.

"*Qué haces?*" I asked and leaned onto the counter.

"Searching if maybe anything is going on in town or Indianapolis. I had a few kids out today as well with no notification from parents or anything. I know there's that new flu bug going around, but it's still weird."

"Hm," I mumbled to myself in thought before I said something, "I've had local news playing all morning. No events are going on—not in town at least."

Melony clacked away on her keyboard and moved her fingers down to the trackpad. Her white nails, spotted with blue polka-dots, scratched along the smooth surface.

"Oh, wow…" she muttered to herself, "an ambulance flipped over on the way to a hospital in Indianapolis. They've got the entire highway shut down."

She pushed the screen back a smidge and scooted the laptop in my direction so I could read the article. I thought back to what Melony had just said, and my eyes flicked up to the television above the corner booths with growing curiosity about why I hadn't been hearing anything today about the new sickness spreading. Every other morning, there are a few short videos and shots warning people to distance themselves and wash their hands. The news anchor, Allison Taylor-Brown, used her emphatic news voice as she explained the steady climb in hospital visits and new cases of this "outbreak." They were the normal announcements they made when the flu came back around each year, but it was still strange they hadn't aired today.

On the screen ahead, an aerial view of a crash on I-465 played. Lights and sirens swarmed the vehicle as it lay on its side smoking. The news chopper circled the wreckage, panning their cameras from the billowing smoke to the drivers standing outside of their vehicles on the highway,

"It's on the news," I informed as I nudged Melony and gestured toward the TV. "Great, now we don't have to read."

Melony chuckled lightly at the joke as she diverted her eyes toward the screen. We both watched in silence as the video footage continued. The volume was low and garbled; every other sound in the shop overpowered it. The fluorescent bulbs buzzed overhead, and the whirring of the air conditioning was deafening as I tried to tune into the TV. The more sounds I was beginning to hear, the more frustrated I was growing. I grumbled to myself and stomped my way around the counter and toward the corner. The remote to the television was placed on top of the ledge that came out from underneath the screen. I snatched the remote in my hand and began to crank up the volume. I could feel Melony's eyes boring through the back of my head, and I could feel her silently giggling at my frustration.

The helicopter camera zoomed into the wreckage, zoomed back out, and as it began to pan toward the hundreds of people standing in traffic, the camera blurred due to a sudden whip in motion. An anchor off-screen, and not on the scene, unfolded the known details that led up to the traffic jam while the video was unclear and out of focus. The camera wobbled and moved as if it were chasing down an image; tiny pixelated dots and shapes floated around the screen before everything slowly came back into focus and the people below were now running. They pushed past each other and bounced off cars like pinballs—almost climbing over each other like ants. The camera panned back to the overturned ambulance now up in flames. The flames weren't large, just the beginning of a fire, but smoke billowed into the sky and a gray and black blur almost like a shadow darted across the screen onto the highway. Allison Taylor-Brown interrupted the live feed as the footage morphed into a blurry pixelated mess.

"What the hell just happened?" Melony mumbled as her footsteps approached.

"I have no idea," I replied in utter confusion, "The camera was obviously having difficulties, but that felt insane."

"Why were all those people running? Was it just the fire? I mean people stand around and video stuff like that all the time. They wouldn't just run frantically... right?"

"Yeah..." I mumbled hesitantly.

My mind began to wander to the moments when I scrolled across videos on my phone of people in dangerous situations and not having a single care in the world. Melony was right. It made no sense for people to run from something like a fire on a highway. Most of the time, people would just pull out their phones and record without hardly a care for another person's life. This felt different. Strange. Something in my bones was making me nervous. Call it instinct or intuition, something did not feel right about the whole situation.

And what was that black blur?

"Well," Melony said as she spun on her heels and headed back toward the counter, "I hope everyone is okay."

Suddenly, almost before she could get out her last word, the television began to beep the most ridiculous and annoying ringing tone. The ringing burst through the speakers and seemed to break the sound barrier in the shop. Blocks of color and static rolled across the screen like an emergency broadcast, but nothing came on after. No words appeared on the screen. No newscaster. No warnings. Nothing but colors and static and noise.

God, the noise!

"Jesus, fuck!" I shouted as I fumbled the remote in my hands and slammed my thumb against the power button.

The screen went dark, and the store fell silent. I couldn't hear the droning of the lights or the whirring of the air conditioning due to the deafening tone from the television still ringing in my ears. Silence. I stared at the black screen in complete disbelief and utter confusion as to what had just happened. Never in my twenty-seven years had I experienced something so strange. Not even severe weather alerts here in Indiana were as loud and outrageous as that had been. Did the news station have a malfunction? Was my television broken?

"I think we should lock up," Melony spoke softly from behind me.

When I turned around to face her, she was behind the counter sticking her laptop back into her tote. The evening sun beamed in through the glass doors and illuminated her. I could see her hands shaking from across the room.

Melony was an overthinker; she hadn't always been, and I didn't know when exactly it started. It seemed like one day she came to visit, and a switch had been flipped. At first, I was simply confused by her sudden shift and her sudden anxieties, but I quickly grew used to it and learned how to help her in the most effective ways. She was more fearful as an adult than she had been when we were younger.

"Hey, hey," I comforted as I rushed over to the counter.

When I made my way around, I gently grabbed her face in my hands and aimed her gaze at my face. Staring into her eyes, I could see them watering. They glossed over like mossy ponds while she exhaled wavering breaths.

"Mel," I said softly, "it's okay to worry, but let me worry with you. Talk me through it."

She slowly blinked away tears and took a few deep breaths before she tried to speak.

"It's just so close to home, and if this sickness thing is a big deal," she breathed, and I could hear the tension in her voice as tears started to come back. "I just don't want anything to happen. I-I want things to stay normal. My brain is… just questioning a lot of stuff."

I nodded and remained silent.

"Like how did that ambulance crash in the first place?" she continued, "Is this tied to the sickness going around? What if you get sick? What if *I* get sick?"

I smiled and pulled her head into my chest.

"It's okay," I whispered. "We will be okay. I know how vigilant you are about getting sick. We've both got killer immune systems, plus it's likely just another flu."

I brushed my fingers through her ponytail and rubbed my hand in circles on her back. I could feel her chest rising and falling as her body pushed against me, and after a few seconds, she pulled away from the hug.

"But what about the news, Jonas?"

I shook my head and kissed her forehead.

"We can look up more articles about it later, okay? Usually, they always explain what happened a few hours after the fact. But for right now, we—" I went over to the register and popped it open to snatch the keys from the extra compartment in the drawer. "We are going to lock up, and I'm going to drive us home."

Melony quickly agreed to the plan, so we packed up our things and began to close the store. Before we left, Melony grabbed a few snacks from the shelves and tucked twenty dollars in cash underneath the locked register. She shoved the few packs of ramen, two eight-pack boxes of granola bars, and a candy bar into her bag. It bulged and lumped into a more rounded shape than the original rectangular tote she carried earlier. I waited by the door for her to catch up. She swung her bag over her shoulder and walked toward me with urgency.

I held open the door for her, and she pulled her sunglasses back over her eyes as we exited the store. The sky was painted with beautiful shades of oranges, pinks, and purples and lit Melony with an angelic golden hue as she walked through the parking lot. She waited at the door of my old Honda Accord while I locked the front door.

I fumbled around my keychain for the key fob to the car and pressed the unlock button. When the car hiccupped its horn, Melony pulled the passenger door open, plopped herself down in the seat, and began to make herself comfortable. I made my way around the front of the car, planting my ritualistic tap on the hood before I climbed into the driver's seat and turned the key in the ignition. The car rumbled to life with a whining cry and creaked as I put it in reverse.

The noises were routine. After a few minutes, they died down and the car drove like normal. I had the money to get it fixed, hell, I had the money saved up to buy a *new* car, but there are just some things I can't let go of. I always had Melony's car if anything happened.

Melony had a strange routine when it came to her vehicle. She started living with me after my father passed and she had returned home from college, so most of the time her vehicle sat in my driveway. She hated driving; she claimed it felt unsafe and made her feel trapped. So, she rarely drove unless she needed to be somewhere important and didn't want to inconvenience me—not that it would.

On weekday mornings, we'd wake up together, go to the store, and she'd help me get ready to open.

Around seven a.m., before the store officially opened, I would drive five minutes to take her to the elementary school; it gave me a break from setting up the store and cleaning, and I got to wish her a good day at work. After school, Melony would indulge the thirty-minute walk back to the store. She said it gave her time to think and absorb nature. It seemed like her own personal therapy to have that time alone. She needed it and deserved it. Every day she entered the store with a bright smile on her face, even on days that weren't her best. I think the walks refreshed her, especially when it was pouring rain. At the end of the day, she would help me close the store, and I would drive us back home.

It was around seven-thirty when we pulled onto the county road. On any normal day, the store wouldn't get closed until around eight p.m. and we wouldn't leave until nine or ten depending on the day we had. The roads were usually dark by then, so it was strange driving us home underneath the setting sun. It was also strange the amount of traffic and cars that backed up the roads.

The county road was usually somewhere between slow or no traffic—at least during the time of day I drove it. But today, the traffic was out of control.

Cars were parked on the sides of the roads, crammed into gas station lots waiting for pumps, and people were leaving the small stores with shopping carts piled high.

"What the hell is going on?" Melony's attitude and fear were rising as cars were forcing their way back onto the main road and people were hanging out the windows yelling at each other.

That odd feeling began to sink into the pit of my stomach like I was being pulled toward the bottom of a lake with a cinderblock.

The car in front of us shifted their car into park and began to get out to yell at the car cutting them off. Their voices were muffled, but Melony's panic was growing more visible by the second. I didn't want to sit here and wait anymore.

"Okay," I sighed deeply as I patted Melony's thigh before gripping the wheel and checking my blind spots.

"Jo?" Concern dripped from Melony's voice as I began to pull out from behind the car and into the lane of oncoming traffic.

No cars were on this side of the road, and I knew there was a shortcut through a subdivision up ahead. I wasn't sure where all these other people were headed, but I was just trying to get us home. I drove further up the wrong side of the road using caution and staying well below the speed limit. The cars alongside us were still. Some vehicles were missing their drivers, others were sitting with the doors wide open and people inside; there were a few more vehicles just pulled into the grass off the road shoulder. Up ahead, I could see the flashing of red, white, and blue lights and police vehicles blocking both lanes of traffic.

I glanced in the rearview and grew more uneasy with the amount of people stopped on the road. I wasn't even sure if this many people had lived in this area.

A few cars had pulled out of the line and begun tailing me as I made it to the side road and drove through the neighborhood. After a few short minutes of turns in silence, we pulled into my driveway. The train of cars that were behind me continued to trail on down the back roads until they too came to a complete stop, and soon the neighborhood was filled with cars struggling to turn around.

I quickly unbuckled and jogged around the car to the passenger side and opened the door for Melony. I helped her climb out and steady herself on her trembling legs. Her pulse raced against my palm wrapped around her wrist as I walked her to the door. When I unlocked the door and pushed it open, I ushered her in and sat her down on the couch. I hurried back to the front door and deadbolted it while peeking out of the window along the top.

The scene was chaotic. People were honking and aggressively slamming against their steering wheels. Most cars were jam-packed; people sat in every available seat, and their trunks were bungee strapped down; SUVs and truck beds were stacked high with luggage. It was as if all these people were on the run. Escaping.

I calmly made my way back to Melony and squatted down in front of her. I placed my hands on her knees and gazed at her dewy face. She stared off into space with wide eyes, and her teeth dug into her bottom lip. Her cheeks were flushed and shining under the ceiling light. She mindlessly picked at her nail polish as her hands lay balled up in her lap.

"Mel, *mi amor*," I tried to get her attention and gently squeezed her knees. When her eyes flicked to me, I simply smiled softly and continued to speak to her,

"I'm going to step outside real quick and see if the people out there know anything, okay? I will be right back, I promise."

She replied with a numb nod, and I trekked toward the door. I made sure I still had the keys before I unlocked the door and exited; I also made sure to safely lock Melony inside the house in my absence.

Once I double-checked the door, I placidly tucked my hands into the front pockets of my jeans and walked down the driveway toward an SUV blocking the end of my drive. I gave a kind smile to the family inside as I knocked on the passenger window and waited for them to roll it down. The driver skeptically looked at me as he reached for the button on the panel. The window cracked about two inches.

"How can I help you?" the man asked rudely.

"Hi, I was just wondering if you knew what's going on. I was just driving on the main road back there, and it was a mess." I patiently waited for a response.

The woman in the passenger seat turned to the driver and whispered a few words before she turned back to me with a smile and rolled her window down further.

"Did ya see the local news earlier?" she asked and without a response from me she continued, "Well, we listened in to the radio after thinking maybe the station went down or somethin', and they're on there talkin' about people going crazy in Indy and attacking people. Conspiracy guy on another channel said he thinks it's zombies like in those movies."

"Zombies?" I chuckled.

She laughed along before the man nudged her and she stopped.

"Maybe," her chuckle died out, "but with this new sickness thing and every other thing happenin' in the world, we just wanted to head up north to some family just in case."

"Okay, that's enough," her husband blurted and began rolling the window up.

"Well, thank you!" I shouted before the window fully closed, and I threw them a wave before I trotted back up the drive and unlocked the door.

Melony snapped her head in my direction.

"Did you find out anything?" she asked frantically before the front door even closed behind me.

"Yeah," I chuckled, "and it's going to sound ridiculous."

"What?"

"Zombies."

8

Melony

The blood on the carpet smeared in streaky lines and faded as Jonas crossed the bedroom threshold onto the vinyl flooring of the hall. The sheet covering the now open window moved like an ocean wave as the stormy breeze blew in. The chilly air following the rain nipped at my toes through my socks. I scooted further back and deeper into the bed pulling my knees up to my chest and wrapping my arms tightly around them. From the waist down, my body began to tingle and grow numb. I rested my head against my knees; the skin felt rough and gritty on my chin. I could feel the tackiness of blood speckled across my face like a new set of freckles. I didn't know how bad I looked, but the way Jonas continued to glance at me gave me some insight.

As the breeze rushed in, I could feel thin and frizzy wisps of hair tickle the back of my neck. The sensation as well as the chilly wind rushing through the threads of my shirt made me shiver. The air around me smelled of tangy sweat and pure rot. It would have been sickening if I had not grown so used to it over the last hour.

The rain still fell in a chaotic pattern of taps; with each breeze, the sound would soften and grow faint or pour in a much faster rhythm. The white noise that began to fill the home drowned out any thought in my brain as I stared at the stains on the carpet.

I listened as Jonas opened a door somewhere in the house, and after some faint shuffling, the door closed again. His boots tapped against the false wood flooring on his way back into the room.

"Damn," he muttered, "it still smells horrible."

I couldn't notice the smell anymore, but the streaks on the carpet were seeping deeper into the fibers. The stench would probably linger for weeks.

The curtain moved like a wave, and a splattering of raindrops darkened the thin fabric. The thunder outside had calmed down, and the pouring rain had turned into a trickle. I could hear the wind rustling through the leaves above, and the birds were beginning to chirp.

The sun would come up soon to prove we had survived the night.

"The front door is no longer standing, but for now I think I've got it mostly blocked up," Jonas paced the room in front of me.

His clothes were covered and soaked in a spattering of black. Behind him, leaning in the corner between the wall and desk, the bat dripped black into the carpet. It looked like it had been dipped in paint; the black oozed down the barrel of the bat and soaked into a puddle on the floor. Eventually, the carpet wouldn't be able to absorb any more, like water rolling off a full sponge.

Jonas continued talking, "After you fell asleep, I went ahead and set our bottles out in the backyard to catch the rainwater. We can filter and boil it later. I think now we should focus on cleaning ourselves while we have the chance," Jonas suggested as he finally stopped moving and turned to me. His voice grew softer. "C'mon, Melony, let's get you up."

His clammy, black-stained hands glued to the skin on my arms as he gently pulled me from the bed and onto my feet. Mindlessly, I followed him out of the bedroom and into the living room.

The black streaks from the room continued across the floor toward the door marking the end of the living room and beginning of the kitchen. The rain was louder here. The front door hung from its hinges with cracks and blood sprayed across it; the couches and other furniture in the room were now stacked in a neat and stable pile in front of the door. But with the door still wide open behind the barricade, you could hear the rain smacking against the tin roof of the covered porch and the swing grinding back and forth against the wood in the breeze.

"The back door is still fine, so we can safely go out there without being out in the direct open," Jonas informed, and I followed.

The back door was directly across from the front door in the open dining room. The doors were sliding glass covered in old, pasted newspapers and trash bags. The squatters before us sure tried everything to keep themselves hidden.

Setting on the dining table next to the back door was a pile of towels and rags along with a new set of clothes for each of us. Before opening the door, Jonas walked around the kitchen counter and grabbed a soap bottle he must have pulled from a bathroom or closet somewhere in the house. He walked back around while shaking the bottle in his hand and opened the door. The sliding mechanism creaked and groaned an awful metal-on-metal screech before stopping halfway. The crack remaining was just enough to squeeze us through.

I turned to the side and shimmied my way out; the metal framing scratched against my back in between my shoulder blades. I could feel my skin starting to burn as I stepped out onto the back porch and gazed out into the tree-lined property.

The dawning air was breezy and sent goosebumps all over my skin, chilling me down to the bone. This porch was as simple as the one in the front of the house—a wooden base with a metal roof that echoed and sang as the rain splashed against it. The patio furniture consisted of a few plastic chairs with moldy and mildewing seat cushions and a small glass side table with an ashtray. The yard itself was fairly open with a steppingstone path that sank into the dirt and mud. The shade of the trees darkened the yard from the moody blue sky and rising sun, but I could see the colors around me brightening in front of my eyes.

The grass was overgrown with a sprinkling of small white, yellow, and purple flowers. From where I stood, I could see dandelions and henbits around the framing of the porch. Small patches of clovers were scattered all over, and the morning birds began to chirp in the trees. Along the perimeter of the yard, a chain link fence was crawling with ivy and bushes, a few small trees seemed to be growing and interweaving themselves through the metal.

Nature prevails, especially when the people rot.

I walked toward the edge of the porch, slipped my socks off my feet, and stepped down onto the first step. The rain sprinkled and splashed my skin with a refreshing chill, and I began to crawl out of the mental static and numbness I was starting to feel trapped in.

I turned my face toward the sky and saw how the trees seemed to open above the yard. The leaves overhead fluttered against the gray and blue sky as raindrops fell in and out of focus. The air smelled of wet gravel and mud. I inhaled deeply and began to erase the smell of death that lingered in my nostrils. I could hear how the wind brushed against every leaf and tree before it touched my skin. It whistled and sang and wrapped around me with tender arms. It was beyond refreshing; I felt alive.

It felt like the clearing back home. It felt like walking down The Zinnia Path. I stared up at the brightening sky and watched the gray clouds feather and drift as raindrops filled the corners of my eyes like miniature ponds. With every drop, the muscles in my face twitched and my eyelids flinched.

Home...

I squeezed my eyes shut as the feeling of tears began to push against my eyes. My bottom lip quivered and trembled as the tension in the back of my throat warped into a burning pain. I coughed up a breath as the dam began to break, and I collapsed to my knees in the grass and mud.

We were so far from home...

The rain began to collect on my skin and drenched my clothes in a way I hadn't felt in quite some time. The front of my shirt began to drape over my thin body and stick to my skin. The weight pressed against my chest and back like a hug. It felt as if the world was holding me, as if maybe it was apologizing for everything it put me through. As I blinked through the tears, I could imagine myself lying in the grass in the middle of the field down The Zinnia Path. I could hear myself calling out to Jonas who stood warily in the tree line watching me as if I were insane. He had always watched me carefully as if a bolt of lightning would strike me down for standing in the middle of the field in the rain.

It had been so long since I thought of the clearing or thought of the happiness I was forced to leave behind. Why hadn't I remembered how the sky opened up, or how magical the rain felt underneath the trees and shaking leaves? The cold mud between my toes? The wet clothes clinging to my skin?

The world had taken so much from me. I would never be who I was.

I brought my hand up and clutched my necklace. My grip was so tight that the metal engraved petals dug into my palm; I was afraid if I moved my hand there might be blood.

As I sobbed sitting in the grass covered in dirt and drenched from head to toe, a warm hand pressed against my hunched-over spine. I glanced over and saw Jonas kneeling in the mud beside me staring up at the clouds.

"It feels like home, doesn't it?" he asked.

"It's more than that."

"I know." His voice flowed like a calm creek underneath the sound of the rain. "Ya know, after mom died, I felt like I was forgetting her. I couldn't see her face in my memories anymore; she was starting to get fuzzy. She wasn't there to talk to after school, wasn't there for dinner. It was like something was taken from me." I could hear him swallow back his sadness as he spoke. "I was so mad at the world for taking someone so lovely, someone so kind and caring. But every day, you would come over and check on me. You would go out of your way to be there for me even when I knew deep down her death was hurting you just as much.

"Then, when my dad died, you supported me even more. You moved in with me and took care of me. You loved me when I was struggling, and you tried to rebuild the home I had lost. Every day after that, waking up next to you, I would remind myself that even though

I lost a part of my home, a piece of it would always be alive as long as I had you.

"Every time I look at you, I will always remember the place we came from. I will always be reminded of all the happiness we were rooted in because *you* are my home. Not someplace we lived in, but all the memories I share with you, and that's what will be my home forever."

9

Jonas: Day One

The radio static fluttered and squealed as I turned the dial and filtered through the frequencies. I had found the old emergency radio in my parents' bedroom closet stashed inside a box of other things they had once brought from Mexico. Dust had coated the device and filled the tiny holes in the speakers, but with a new set of batteries and a wipe from a damp cloth, it appeared almost new.

After coming in from my chat with the people in the SUV, Melony and I spent some time trying to find any information on what was going on beyond the limits of Brownsburg. I had pressed the power button on the remote only to be surprised by the color blocks and TV static that had plagued the store TV earlier. Melony tried searching for articles, browsing social media, and calling her mother which all resulted in the same screen and automated voice messages. No internet. No service. Try again later.

By that time, I had remembered the old radio my father used to listen to broadcasts during bad storms, and I rummaged through every closet in the house to find it. Melony and I had gathered at the dining table and hunkered down next to the speakers as they garbled nonsensical squeals and static.

The sun had set hours ago, and we still sat filtering and listening for a clear station. We had no more information than what we started with, and the night was only growing darker. People were still parked outside along the streets; some had decided to set up camp in the neighborhood. Flashlights and porchlights illuminated people walking up and down the street chatting with the others they were stranded with. I could see the silhouettes and light through the closed curtains in my living room.

"I don't think we're going to find a clear one," Melony spoke with exhaustion and despair.

"There can't just be nothing," I grumbled before I yawned. "Radio stations and emergency broadcasts still play during natural disasters. I don't understand what's going on."

"I think we should just close the curtains, lock the doors, and go to bed. I don't like how many people are just waiting outside. If they get desperate, they might try to scavenge houses," Melony turned away from the radio and stared at the front window.

The lights in the neighborhood still illuminated the vehicles and tents set up outside. How long had they been out there, and how long were they planning to wait? Even this many hours later, were the roads still backed up? Too many questions began to scramble in my head, and I could feel the piercing throb of a headache coming on. I sighed and switched the radio off before getting up from the dining table and resting a loving hand on Melony's back.

"You're right—" I yawned again. "Let's get some rest and hope this thing is over with when we wake up."

She leaned into me as she remained seated at the table; her head fell at my waist as I rubbed small circles between her shoulder blades. Just this simple touch made my heart flutter, and a smile began to grow on my face. After a few seconds of standing by her side, she shifted in her seat and brought herself up next to me. She tucked her arms underneath mine and wrapped them around my back before laying her head against my chest. Her body was warm as she pressed against me, and I could smell her tea tree and lavender shampoo. I leaned further into her and bent down to kiss the top of her head. She smelled like a garden. I wrapped my arms around her tightly and pulled her in closer; I would pull her into my skin just to feel closer if I could. My hands began to drift along her back. I traced along the ridges and bumps of her spine and shoulder blades, the curves of her waist, and the small indentations of the dimples on her lower back. I could feel her details through her clothes; I knew them like a map tattooed behind my eyelids. I studied her as if she were the muse of my art, the model for my canvas. I felt her and traced her like the water that rolled off her body in the rain. My hands began to separate as one began to travel up to the back of her neck and the other began to lightly tug at the white polo tucked into her skirt. I wanted to feel her skin.

With my hand at the back of her neck, I traced soft fingers along the side of her neck and pushed them into her hair. She tilted her head back into my hand with a soft yet sly smile as she gazed up at me with seductive eyes that transported me through woods that I could forever get lost in. Her eyes flicked from my eyes to my lips, and I didn't feel tired anymore.

I could feel my blood rushing through me. All over me. Waves of heat and a pulsing beat throbbed through every part of me. My other hand pulled her shirt free from her skirt, and I slid my hand underneath it. Her skin felt like velvet under my fingertips, and as my hand glided over her waist and to the small of her back, I could feel goosebumps perk up over her body. I was so lost in her. A ship in the middle of the sea. Wave after wave pounding against the sides of the ship. I felt as if I couldn't breathe properly without her. She was the oxygen I needed.

God, I needed her.

I gripped her waist as she brought her arms out from around me and up to my shoulders, draping them around my neck. She began to push me back, forcing me away from the bigger windows and into the kitchen. She softly dragged her fingers and nails down my neck and to my chest. She felt like a gentle breeze with a tickling touch. So delicate and sweet.

The throbbing began to grow.

I brought my face down and traced her lips with mine. Blindly, I paced backward, my hands rummaged under her shirt, and I began to fumble with the clasp on her bra as I roughly bumped into the kitchen counter. Our lips continued to collide, and our breathing grew heavier. I couldn't take it anymore. In a sudden movement, I wrapped an arm around her lower waist and scooped the other under her bottom as I lifted her off the floor and sat her on the counter. I could feel her breath hot on my face as she giggled and bit my lower lip.

The sound of her sweet voice made me erratic, and I began to strip her of her layers. One after the other, her cardigan and polo hit the kitchen tile. She looked so perfect. Carved in marble. Her skin was creamy and soft in my hands, and I couldn't get myself off her. Her bra was unclasped and loosely draped over her still covering what I wanted to get to when she began to pull my shirt over my head and undo the button on my jeans. I quickly found the bottom of her skirt and ran my hands up her legs. I dug my fingers into her thighs, and she let out a tiny moan at my touch. I groaned and smirked at the sound of her tiniest pleasure before I gripped her thighs and yanked her toward the edge of the counter.

A small yelp and giggle escaped her as her lips fell back onto mine. Her kisses were wet but neat and her lips smooth like honey in the mouth. I could feel her nimble fingers trailing along the skin at the top of my jeans before she tucked her fingers in and began to pull them down—my boxers slowly went with them. After they were off my thighs, gravity did the rest of the work, and she brought her hands to her shoulders and slowly began to slip her bra away from her chest.

I pulled her even closer and felt everything press against me. Her breasts were silk pillows as they pressed against my chest, and I could feel her wetness soaking me down below through her underwear.

My lips gently left hers as I moved to her jawline and began to plant tiny, fragile kisses along it. I traced a delicate trail down her neck and over her collarbones as my hands searched higher upon her legs. She released quiet moans and pants with each touch of my lips. I could feel her legs rise, and she wrapped them around my hips trying to pull me in before I could even get her panties off.

"Not yet," I whispered in her ear, and she released a soft gasp.

"Jonas..." she quietly begged and moaned.

I looped my fingers into the top of her underwear and began to pull them down past her thighs and over her knees until they hit the floor. I wrapped my arms under her thighs and began to pull her toward me. Within a second, she tightened her legs around me and forced me in.

I groaned and moaned as I felt her warmth surround me. My fingers gripped and squeezed her, moving between her thighs and waist. My hands found their place at her hips, and I began to hold her in place as I pushed myself deeper.

Melony tilted her head back and braced herself against the counter. I was delighted to hear the sounds coming from her. Her pleasure fueled me, and as I grew more lost to the heavenly angel in front of me, I began to forget about the worries that had plagued us only minutes before.

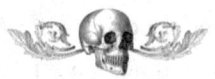

I leaned down and picked up our articles of clothing from the floor. In the other room, I could hear the water sprinkling from the showerhead and the sound of Melony humming through the walls. I loosely folded our clothes over my arm and adjusted the waistline of the pair of clean boxers I had put on. My curls dripped icy water onto my shoulders and trickled down my back. A shiver ran up my spine as I carried the clothes down the hall, pushed open the laundry room door, and tossed the clothes into the hamper. As I passed the bathroom on the way back into the kitchen, I heard the metal squeak of the knobs, and the water cut off. I spun on my heels and jogged back down the hall toward our bedroom.

The hinges quietly creaked as the door opened. I reached over to the dresser by the door and pulled the cord on the lamp that sat atop it. The warm light revealed the same charcoal gray walls and terracotta color scheme I'd had since high school as well as all of Melony's small houseplants that I've become the adoptive father of. I stepped inside and felt the warmth of the plush carpet on the arches of my feet. The room had a slight chill but was ultimately toastier than the tiled portions of the house.

I pulled open the top dresser drawer and sorted through the neatly folded clothes until I found a cute pajama set for Melony—her favorite lavender shorts, and a striped light cotton t-shirt. I set the clothes on the bed and headed for the small laundry basket filled with a clean mix of our underwear that was placed on the futon across the room. I dug through it until I found a pair she would be comfortable in and tossed them onto the bed next to her pajamas.

The bathroom door opened down the hall, and I could hear Melony's damp footsteps coming toward the room. I turned and glanced over my shoulder as I grabbed the crocheted blanket folded on the futon and wrapped myself in it.

She entered the room wrapped in a towel. Her dark hair was slicked back and full of stringy drenched waves. She smiled at me when she noticed me staring.

"I set some clothes out for you," I informed as I gestured to the bed.

"Thank you," she spoke; her voice was soft and sincere.

She looked like an angel straight from the sky as the towel she was clutching at her chest dropped to the carpet will a dull thud. My eyes followed along the curves of her waist and hips, trailing the path laid out up and down her spine. She leaned over and pulled the underwear up her legs and wiggled herself into them. She was so candidly beautiful; out of anything in the world, I'd wish for her to see herself through my eyes, to see herself the way I did. Her outer body matched her inner perfectly; she was just simply who she was.

"Stop staring at me, you perv," she playfully giggled as she rounded her side of the bed now fully clothed in her loose-fitting tee and short shorts.

"I'm not a perv," I chuckled along as I rounded the other side of the bed and began to tuck myself in beside her.

Her skin was cold under the sheets. Her legs brushed against mine as she rolled onto her side and faced me. The hairs on her legs were a few days old and prickly as they gently scratched against my lower thighs and knees. The feeling didn't bother me, although she often complained about the feeling of my leg hair against her bare skin when she rubbed her legs against mine as if we were a single cricket in the night.

But tonight was a colder night in the house; there would be fewer complaints and more cuddling for warmth.

She scooted closer toward the middle of the bed and draped an icy hand over my stomach and side. I winced at the sudden shock, and she mindlessly murmured an apology before closing her eyes. She took a few deep breaths and wriggled in the sheets every few minutes before she could find a comfortable enough spot to doze off.

I always envied her for her ability to fall asleep like throwing a rock into a river—she just sunk into it. Of course, there were always days when she would stay up later with me and entertain my mind as it kept me awake. She was always the first to break, though. She'd fall asleep on my chest or with her head in my lap halfway through a sentence. I would always be there to watch her eyes flutter as she drifted and how still she was after she succumbed to her exhaustion. Her chest would rise and fall as her deep breaths echoed in the silent room. Her breaths would often be the reason I finally fell asleep. It was almost a meditative rhythm like waves crashing on the shore. I had grown slightly dependent on Melony being with me. She touched every aspect of my life for as long as I cared to remember. I felt as if my life was bland and meaningless before I met her.

I'm not sure how I'd ever live without her.

I stared at her side profile and how her wet hair draped over her pillow. The light from the lamp cast her features in a comforting, angelic glow. Her nose and cheeks shimmered from their recent cleanse, and I couldn't help but feel hypnotized by it. The bridge of her nose was long and only slightly bumped over her bone. Her eyelashes were light while her eyelids fluttered smudged with faded black stains from her previous make-up. Her mouth was barely cracked open and drool clung to the corners of her parted lips.

I adjusted my pillow and shifted my body into a more comfortable position to better suit my need to stare at her. I draped my arm over my body and tucked my hand under my pillow while I extended my other arm and wedged it under her pillow. As her pillow moved and shifted with me, she was as still as stone. She didn't budge. You could've mistaken her for being in a coma.

I rolled my head around on my shoulders to stretch my neck before I relaxed back onto my pillow. I took a deep breath and could feel my eyelids grow heavy. As I drifted, the sounds of the crickets outside grew louder; their screams echoed along with the frogs calling from the pond down the road. I could hear them through the walls as if I were sleeping in a tent outside. I dozed away and my light, sensitive sleeping emersed me into the woods.

I was standing in the clearing, a place Melony and I hadn't been in quite some time since we had gotten older. The grass was much taller now. Wildflowers bloomed around me, constantly growing and rising toward the sky. They swayed and continued to blossom petal after petal. I could hear Melony calling for me. Her voice reverberated around the clearing as if we were in a steel drum.

"Jonas!" I could hear her call through a smile.

Her voice was joyful.

"Ven conmigo, mi amor," her whisper whistled through the evergrowing grass like the wispy wind.

I looked around, my head swiveling on my neck as I briskly searched for her. But the further I pushed through the weeds and the grass now standing high above my head, her voice became more distant. I felt my heart racing in my chest as I frantically searched. The weeds and grass climbed up my legs and tightened around my limbs, holding me in place. The sky thundered and I could still hear Melony calling for me— this time her voice sharp and afraid. My breathing quickened and my lungs began to burn, but then I felt a hand on my shoulder.

The grass fell away, and the flowers shed their petals. The clearing was normal again. Just as I remembered it. I could feel the hand on my back growing warmer as the thumb gently rubbed back and forth in comforting support. As I turned around to face whomever the hand belonged to, I was shaken awake.

"Jonas," Melony hovered above me, her face inches from mine as she whispered breathily in my face.

I grunted in acknowledgment as I rubbed my eyes. Through a squint, I began to examine my surroundings. The room was dark, the lamp was no longer lit, and the night sky was barely lightened by the soon-to-be-rising sun.

"What time is it?" I grumbled.

"Not important," her voice was frantic, "something is going on outside."

The alarm in her voice perked me up. I quickly became alert and sat up in bed beside her.

"What do you mean?"

She quickly jumped from the bed and scurried toward the bedroom door waiting for me to follow. As my eyes better adjusted to the dark blue light of the upcoming morning, I noticed she had already changed for the day. She wore plain black leggings with a baggy graphic tee. She wasn't dressed for work.

My brain began to bounce around ideas and worries about what was going on that would have her so frantic and not going to work on a schoolday.

As I entered the hall in just my boxers, I watched Melony in complete confusion as she stealthily hunched and crouched along the wall as if hiding from something. She paused at the end of the hall and peaked her head out toward the front door before she hurried along the room in the dark.

"*Estas siendo rara*," I muttered as I rubbed my eyes and stepped into the living room.

"*Agachate!*" she hushedly shouted at me from behind the couch. Her spanish was usually soft and simple, but this was much more aggressive.

I skeptically lowered myself into a squat and began to crawl across the floor to her. She continuously peeked around the corner of the couch at the front window as I scooted into hiding beside her.

"What the hell is wrong with you?" I whispered harshly.

"Keep your voice down," she mumbled as she turned toward me and finally planted her paranoid self onto the floor. "I got up earlier to go to the bathroom and heard some noise outside. When I went to check, before I even got to the door I heard someone scream. I don't know what's going on, but I'm not risking it happening to us."

Her voice was tired and wavered as she fell in and out of breath. Her eyes blinked slowly, and I could tell exhaustion was getting the best of her. Her damp hair was loosely thrown up into a thick, unbrushed ponytail. Little wisps and frizz poked out around her face and back of her neck. Her anxieties from the night before must have crept into this morning and prevented her from getting enough sleep.

"I'll check it out," I whispered, "just let me run—well, I guess *crawl*—back to the room and put some clothes on."

She mumbled an approving hum before I rolled onto all fours and began my journey back to the safe coverage of the hall. The tile froze my palms and knees into popsicles, and I'd probably feel the upcoming bruises and soreness on my bones for the next week. When I made it to the bedroom, the sky was beginning to shift into a lighter shade of blue peeking through the cracks of the gray curtains. I pounced upward to my feet and immediately began to search the dresser by the door for a pair of pajama pants and an old t-shirt.

I slipped into my clothes and began to crouch down as I exited the room. Melony's eyes were half-open while I nearly crab-walked down the hall at what I guessed was five or six in the morning.

I crouched around the back of the couch toward the front door and window. My toes were beginning to numb from the cool tile floor beneath me, and the poor blood circulation flowing below my knees was starting to send pins and needles of pain through my legs. Luckily, I reached the door soon after and was able to bring my squatted crouch to a semi-stand and allow blood to flow back into my legs more comfortably. I slowly brought my face up to the small window near the top of the door and tried to peek out. The condensation and fogginess of my warm breath against the cool window blocked my view, and I quietly growled to myself as frustration began to overcome me.

I took a deep breath and stepped toward the main window. The morning was growing brighter, and the sheer curtains were allowing the light outside to enter and fill the house. I could hear the birds chirping outside and the sound of Melony's deep sleepy breathing from across the room.

With my back pressed against the wall, I leaned into the window and carefully pulled back the edge of the curtain to provide myself with a sliver of a view outside. Upon first glance, I noticed that a lot of the vehicles that had been parked outside were empty with the doors wide open. Packaged food, blankets, pillows, and empty plastic water bottles spilled out into the street. A few tents had been set up throughout the night, but from where I stood at the window, several tents were left unzipped with no one inside.

"These people just left all of their stuff..." I whispered mostly to myself.

"What do you mean 'left all of their stuff'?" I heard Melony's gentle sleepy voice whisper from the other side of the couch.

"I don't know. There's no one out there, but they left everything behind."

"Are you sure there's no one?" she sounded just as confused as I was.

I left her question unanswered as I closed the curtain, crouched back down, and waddled to the other side of the window for a different angle going up the street. When I pulled back the curtain, I saw more cars and tents left abandoned. A few tents were ripped along the sides as if something had cut or clawed into them. Down the street, a few houses away, I could see a person lying limp halfway hanging out of the passenger side of a truck. Blood trickled down their arm and into a puddle on the pavement.

"What the fuck..." I muttered as I rushed away from the window and toward the shoe rack.

I quickly slipped on a pair of slides and unlocked the door. Before I could hear Melony protest, I was already outside and quietly shutting the door behind me. The brisk morning air sent a rush of chills across my body, and I crossed my arms over my chest in a failed attempt to hold in some warmth.

It was eerily quiet; I couldn't hear the birds singing anymore, and the usual distant sound of cars rolling down the county road was missing. The SUV that I had approached last night still sat in front of the driveway, but now there was no driver or woman in the passenger seat. The front doors were left open, and the lights on the dash blinked red as they continuously dinged. The keys were still in the ignition.

The trunk of the car was still packed with luggage and bags of groceries. A phone lay with its shattered screen face-up on the pavement outside the passenger door, and a purse sat on the floorboard.

I backed away from the vehicle and gazed up and down the street at all of the other abandoned cars in the same conditions. Keys in ignitions. Belongings left behind. Some cars were still running idle. I tiptoed around vehicles and briefly scanned inside each one before moving to the next.

My stomach grumbled and gurgled, and I began to feel nauseous. I was uneasy. That hair-raising feeling from the drive home last night was returning stronger than I had ever felt before. The next vehicle I passed was a black Silverado with a toolbox resting in the bed. I leaned over the side of the truck bed and peered down on the mud-caked plastic lining. The first thing I saw was a crowbar, so naturally I reached in and armed myself with it. The uneasiness and hunger inside my gut spun circles inside my stomach.

The sky had brightened into a baby blue streaked with orange, and I was beginning to feel restless. My knuckles whitened as I clenched onto the crowbar with each tent that I passed. I was gaining distance on the car with the body, and my nerves were rattled.

The only time I'd ever seen a dead body was in movies (totally fake) and at funerals (quite real) but movies and funerals are staged. They're dressed up, wearing makeup and clothes that make them feel as if they're sleeping even when you know they aren't. I had watched cancer slowly take my mother. She was sickly and pale, fragile and thin; when she eventually passed, it wasn't gory or gruesome, she was at peace. She took her last breath holding mine and my father's hands. When my father died, there was no blood, no terror or horror on his face. He had a heart attack while lifting a crate at the store, I called the ambulance and sat with him to the hospital. He recovered that night but died in his sleep two nights later due to a second heart attack. The doctors said it was most likely quick, and he probably didn't even realize the pain.

I didn't often see blood. Sure, Melony gave me the scares of lifetimes when we were younger when she'd flip down a hill on her bike or any other dangerous thing she enjoyed doing, but not to the extent she bled out.

Whatever I was walking to was a true-horror dead body. This was a real stranger dripping blood on my street. It would be shock-inducing, and I had to mentally prepare myself for what I might see.

I came up to the back of the truck with my eyes locked on the arm dangling out of the open door. I watched the blood slowly trickle down and drip into the puddle before I took a deep breath and stepped forward with the crowbar cocked back into a swinging position. As I stepped out next to the passenger door, I observed the massacre in front of me.

The arm dangling out of the passenger door was connected to a man slumped against the dash—dead and *covered* in blood.

"*Oh, Dios...*" I mumbled as I accidentally stepped into the puddle of biohazard on the road.

My hands began to tremble as I stared at the man. His lifeless eyes stared at the floorboard and his mouth hung agape as if he had been mid-scream. There was an indescribable horror written across his face; it soaked into his wrinkles and dripped right into the puddle. Most of the blood that trickled down his arms and splattered across his face was dried, but the initial wound on his neck still bled. It oozed thick black liquid like nothing I had seen before. It was as if his blood was rotting.

I quickly spun on my heels and began to jog back toward the house. As I ran, I glanced down at each tent I passed. Masses of blankets and lumps of pillows and clothes lay on the ground. A lot more of the tents were torn and scratched to shreds than I had initially thought. I shook the thought of what had caused this out of my head and directed my focus toward the houses. Every door was wide open. My neighbors, friends, and people I grew up with were just... gone.

I stopped dead in my tracks and began to pace in circles as I looked around the neighborhood. Everyone was gone. Front doors and garages were left open and porch lights were still on. It was as if everyone just got up and left in the middle of the night. Almost as if they had gotten some warning we hadn't.

What is going on?

As the sun finally began to beam on the horizon, the singing birds returned and the eerie silence was once again filled. I brought my hand up to my head and pulled my hair back out of my face. I took a few deep breaths to calm myself before I hunched over and hurled onto the sidewalk. I stood there with my hands on my knees for a few minutes just trying to shake myself out of shock. I stared down at the ground and breathed deeply before I noticed the red outline of my slides that trailed along behind me.

I had stepped in someone's blood, and it was seeping through my sock.

10

Melony

The rain had grown heavier again and poured down on us out in the open backyard. Jonas had set out a bucket next to us to catch water as we "showered." Our clothes were getting soaked and washed of their filth as they draped over the railing of the porch, and we were using washcloths to help each other scrub away dirt and stains from our bodies.

It was strange being so vulnerable out in the open. So naked in nature. Back then, this would have been a crazy idea that I would have quickly laughed off. Now, there was no one left to see. It had felt as if we were the last people on Earth for quite some time, so the idea of getting naked in a random person's backyard didn't bother me. It was quite freeing. I could feel the small breezes caressing my back and chilling my breasts. The falling rain on my bare skin was unlike anything I had felt before. It didn't feel like taking a shower. Or maybe it did? I hadn't had a normal shower in so long. Maybe I had taken for granted how heavenly they had felt.

The cold morning rain trickled in streams down my face and off my chin into a waterfall that dropped off onto my chest. The water tasted salty as it washed away dirt and sweat and ran along the creases in my lips. Water droplets seeped into my hairline while I tilted my head back and faced the rain; a tickling sensation rolled along my scalp, flowed toward the back of my head, and down my neck.

"Do you need help reaching anything?" Jonas spoke from behind me.

I spun around and caught him in the middle of scrubbing his inner thighs. He scratched and rubbed at a grayish-brown dirt stain near his knee. As I stared, I realized I almost couldn't recognize him. He didn't look like the same man he used to be. Maybe it was the fact he was mostly clean now, or maybe it had just been so long since I had seen him and stared at him so vulnerable and exposed.

He was slightly thinner; I could see his muscle tone and the outline of his ribs beneath his *Virgen de Guadalupe* tattoo. His beard was thick and messy, not the same neatly trimmed stubble he kept years ago. There was a scar that dragged across his chest and left shoulder; it was a raised welt that had marked his body since we saw the first of the creatures, but it was still so strange to see.

He was so different. Still *my* Jonas. Still the man I loved, but it had been so long since I had seen him so bare in this light. It's easy to forget what details lay underneath the filth when you're constantly worried about surviving.

"You're staring," he murmured as he stepped closer, rag in hand.

He held the cloth toward me and motioned toward his back. I took the rag and held it out under the pouring rain to wring it free of dirty water before I started scrubbing circles on his back. My eyes trailed along his skin slowly to observe and absorb every little detail I could.

His back was spotted with the occasional freckle and thin hairline scars. On the back of his right shoulder was a small half-dollar-sized tattoo of a flower—a zinnia.

I had forgotten about it.

"You okay back there?" he asked as he glanced over his shoulder at me. "You stopped rubbing. You finished?"

"Yeah…" I replied. "No cuts, no scratches, no dirt. All good."

I passed his rag back to him, and he draped it over his shoulder before sticking his hand out and plucking my rag from my other hand. He silently twirled his finger in a circle motioning for me to spin. I reached up and pulled my drenched hair to the side over my shoulder while I turned. He began to gently and slowly rub scratchy circles around on my bare back. I didn't realize how much I itched until now. I could feel my body relax and accidentally let a quiet moan slip from my lips as the washcloth scratched my spine between my shoulder blades.

Jonas chuckled at my pleasure and continued rubbing. His hands traveled outside the limited range of my back. He scrubbed up on my shoulders, around my hips, down my ribs until he eventually stopped moving. His bare finger slid down a sensitive spot running along the right side of my ribs.

"I still think about that day," he murmured.

I raised my arm and glanced down at the spot he touched and remembered the long gashed scar that ran diagonally toward my back.

"You should've stayed inside," he said.

I furrowed my brows and turned to face him as I placed my hands on his chest, reaching up and dragging my thumb over the scar running across his collarbone and shoulder. His eyes gazed into mine as rain streamed over the topography of his face. The rustling of the rain and leaves around us droned away, and all I could hear was his breathing. His finger still brushed against the scar on my ribcage, and I could feel his heartbeat underneath my palm pressed against his chest.

His eyes were so dark and deep chocolate brown as they flicked around the features of my face. The drenched waves of his hair fell forward and dripped in front of his eyes. His hand left my scar to tug and smooth his hair back.

I couldn't take my eyes off him. I had been so afraid and worried about staying alive that I had forgotten how it felt to just see him and feel him like this. I pushed my hand up his chest and caressed the side of his neck. I craned my neck and tiptoed upward while pulling him into me. His lips were as soft as I remembered.

His hand came back down and found its place on my waist as I kissed him. He gently squeezed before he wrapped his arm around me and pulled me in tighter. The rain pooled between us as we pressed our bodies into each other.

Both his hands ran down my body as he lowered himself and gripped behind my thighs. In a simple motion, he lifted me, and I wrapped my legs around him as our lips stayed connected with sloppy wet kisses. It had been so long since I felt this way—since I felt *him* this way—and, *God*, had I missed it.

I could feel every inch of him pressing against my bare skin and body. *Every inch.*

I pushed my fingers toward the base of his skull and up into his wet tangled hair. I clenched my hands and gently tugged as I gasped for air at every touch of his hands under the cool rain. I could feel him rubbing against me. So bare and warm. I was sensitive to his touch.

One of his arms remained wrapped around my waist while the other hand groped freely around my hip, waist, and thigh. He pulled away from my lips and began to kiss my jawline and neck. I panted over his shoulder trying to catch my breath as he slowly and carefully paced through the grass back onto the covered porch. He made his way up the steps still holding me before he patted my thigh signaling for me to hop down.

I did as told before he hurriedly made his way to the sliding door and attempted to tug it open further. I could see the frustration building in him as the door wouldn't budge. His muscles flexed, and I could feel myself tingling and pulsing intensely.

I *needed* him.

After a short few seconds of messing with the door, he turned back to me, quickly swooped back over, and scooped me up. His grip was tight, and I could feel the frustration and blood pumping through his body.

"Fuck it," he growled as he squeezed my waist, smashed his lips against mine, and aggressively forced me back between him and the exterior wall of the house.

11

Jonas: Day One

I continued jogging down the street until I got to the house. I stopped at the SUV parked outside, walked around the front of the vehicle, and climbed into the driver's seat. With the doors still hanging open, I turned the key in the ignition and found myself surprised as the vehicle rumbled to life. The battery wasn't dead yet.

I pulled on the shifter and reversed the SUV giving me enough space to shove it in drive and pull the fully stocked vehicle into my driveway next to my car. As I turned the wheel and began to pull forward, my eyes landed on Melony standing in the driveway bundled in a cardigan.

"What are you doing?" she shouted.

I motioned for her to move aside, and she did. I quickly pulled the car up next to mine and shifted the car into park before I hopped out and rushed toward her.

"You need to get back inside." I looked back over my shoulders in paranoia. "Something isn't right."

"What do you me—"

"Just get back inside!" I ushered, "Please, just go inside and try to call 911 or listen to the radio stations again."

Her eyes widened in shock that I had raised my voice at her, but she ultimately listened and quickly made her way back into the house. I rushed back to the vehicle, flung open the back door, and began to rummage through the belongings. I pulled out suitcase after suitcase, grocery bag after grocery bag, and set them on the paved drive. Once the SUV was empty, I hunkered down and began to unzip the suitcases. Mostly clothes filled each one, but small luggage bags were full of medications, first aid supplies, batteries, and feminine hygiene products. I grabbed everything I could carry, aside from the clothing, and began to haul it all into the house. Melony frantically helped me set the bags on the couch and quickly began to bombard me with questions about what was happening. Questions I didn't know how to answer.

Emergency dispatch didn't pick up, what do we do? What happened? Is everyone gone? What had these people heard? What were they planning to flee from in the first place?

No answers.

I began to filter through the bags and hand Melony things to take to the kitchen while I laid first aid out on the coffee table. We did our work in silence; both of our minds shuffled through scenarios and solutions.

Nothing I could come up with seemed to make sense. There was no news, no radio, and no one to tell us if everything was okay. We were surrounded by abandoned cars and houses. There was a dead body down the street, and I had no cell service to contact authorities.

"We still have power," Melony finally blurted, "so we should still have water."

"How do you know that?" I furrowed my brows at her.

"A student told me," she spoke plainly, "The kids teach me as much as I teach them. Water will last a while even after the power goes out."

"Okay." I began to dissolve into my thoughts. "Well, maybe we should go ahead and fill some bottles. Store them just in case this is a national emergency thing."

She nodded and rushed back into the kitchen. I could hear her rummaging through the cabinets. The sound of clanking metal and clinking glasses filled the house as she pulled cups and metal tumblers out of the cabinets. I was feeling rather lucky that we had been such active children and had a collection of styled tumblers and bottles to keep us hydrated in the summer months. I remembered how my mom would get Melony a new one every Christmas to match her ever-changing styles. When Melony moved in, those were some of the first things she packed.

I heard the creaky faucet turn and water gushing into cups as I continued to organize the supplies I had brought in from the SUV. Blood pressure medication, topical steroids, antinausea tablets, nasal sprays, and all kinds of random stuff pulled from a random family's medicine cabinet. It was as if one person held the bag open and the other swiped the contents of every shelf into the bag.

After a few minutes of stacking bottles and laying out tubes of creams, I slouched back on the couch as Melony appeared in the entryway to the living room and crossed her arms over her chest. She leaned against the wall and zoned in on the items piled on the table and couch. I could see her biting the insides of her cheeks while she sunk deep in thought.

"I still haven't heard from Mom," she informed quietly.

I could hear the sadness and worry creeping through her words as she reached up to her neck, wrapped her finger around the chain of her necklace, and fished out her pendant. She clutched it in her hands and rubbed her thumb over the textured petals.

"She was in Indianapolis for work staying at some hotel," she continued.

"There's no need to worry," I replied as I patted the spot on the couch next to me.

She pushed herself off the wall and slowly made her way over before plopping herself down onto the available space on the cushion next to me. I could see her fingers tremble as they squeezed her pendant and gripped a handful of her cardigan.

"You don't know if she's okay," she mumbled, "you can't know. We don't even know if *we're* okay, Jonas. What did you see out there?"

I looked down at my feet and the blood stain that covered the big toe portion of my sock.

"It's just empty," I said while wiggling my toes against the brown stain. "Everyone is gone. We must've slept through it, but it seems like everyone just walked away in the middle of the night."

"Well, we could door-to-door and ask aro—"

"*Everyone* is gone, Mel," I restated, "not just the people parked outside, but the neighbors, too. At least from what I could tell, most—if not everyone—who were outside last night have left."

"I don't—" she hesitated and stammered, "I don't understand. I-It doesn't make sense. There haven't been any warnings or alerts, and all these people just run away? Disappear?"

"I don't get it either, Mel."

"What if those people come back for their stuff?"

I thought back to the other cars outside, and all of the personal belongings left behind. The cars were low on gas, and batteries were dead. It had been hours since they were abandoned, and a voice deep within me was saying these people wouldn't be returning.

"We'll worry about that if it comes to it," I mumbled, "I think I'm gonna go back out and find some more supplies just to be safe."

"Are you sure?"

I nodded in return.

"Okay, well I guess I'll start putting these supplies away." She sat up slowly. "Maybe I'll go ahead and start packing us some emergency bags in case we need to leave."

"Good idea," I encouraged.

I watched her push herself up from the couch and walk down the hall before I stood up and headed back toward the front door. While I twisted the deadbolt to unlock, I picked up the crowbar Melony had taken and set against the wall earlier. I stood in front of the door for a few moments contemplating.

My entire body felt numb as my heart raced with anxiety. A trembling feeling began erupting from deep within my bones. My legs felt weak, and for the first time in over a decade, I felt deeply afraid. The fear crawled and slithered all over my skin like a snake tightening its grip. My breath felt trapped in my lungs, and my heart was pounding out of my chest like the rhythmic echo of a war drum. Waves of heat washed over me in surges, and sweat prickled at my forehead.

I couldn't let Melony see me like this. My fear would only terrify her.

I inhaled deeply and held it in as I twisted the doorknob and pulled the door open ready to bear witness to blood-sucking monsters and brain-dead corpses wandering the street beyond the safety of my home. I anticipated something to lunge toward me and rip me apart and go for my throat as it had done to the man in the truck.

But nothing happened.

The door creaked open, and the spring morning breeze blew in through the entryway. The sun cast shadows around the cars and houses as it did every morning before. The birds chirped, the bugs began to buzz, and the leaves and trees around the houses rustled and whispered with each gust of wind as if today was no different than yesterday morning. It was a bright and beautiful spring day.

I exhaled and took a step beyond the threshold. The morning sun was growing brighter against the vibrant blue and fluffy white clouds in the sky that peered through the leaves of the big oak in the front yard. I trotted down the front steps and into the grass as I walked toward the driveway. The further I stepped into the outdoors without any incident, the more my nerves began to settle. The eeriness that had lingered around me was fading as the world seemed to fall back into order. Everything felt so clear and calm. If not for the unusual cars and shredded tents, I would've thought this was an ordinary day. I would be stocking shelves and dropping Melony off at the school.

I clenched my hand tighter around the crowbar as I walked down the drive. The blood on my sock scratched at my toes with each step and began to irritate my skin. I didn't think to change them before I left. Maybe I should have. I couldn't take my mind off the way it dried to my skin like a scab.

"It'll come out in the wash," I muttered to myself as my slides thwacked against the pavement beneath me.

Deep down, I knew that the stain would linger. I would permanently have a reminder of that man slumped in the passenger seat. His horror and terror will forever be engraved in my mind. Soaked into the stitching and seams of my brain like the sock.

At the end of the drive, I hesitated on which way to turn. There were so many vehicles, and so many bags to sort through. I was starting to feel overwhelmed by the possible routes and ways to start maneuvering around the chaos, but as I looked up the road and took another glimpse at the lifeless arm that dangled from the truck, I quickly made my decision and began walking in the opposite direction. I was afraid if I caught another glimpse of that man that I would create another vomit stain on the concrete.

The car that had been parked behind the SUV was a small sedan filled to the brim with someone's life. I was fairly certain that this person had left their home empty aside from furniture. Their entire existence had to have been packed into this car. I reached the back passenger door and tugged on the handle. With a small pop, the door opened and items immediately began to tumble into the road. Pairs of shoes, balled-up clothes, Clorox wipes, and various snacks tumbled out on the street in front of me. The mess was nothing like the organized suitcases and luggage I had combed through earlier. I wondered if this person had been living in their car before this or if this was just a panicked frenzy of packing.

"Jesus," I mumbled as I watched the pile shift.

I stared into the mess in search of some form of bag to carry everything I could and spotted a backpack tucked underneath everything.

"Great…" I grumbled to myself as I reached in and grabbed one of the straps.

I tugged on the bag slowly and gently until it slipped free with minimal spillage. I began to carefully stuff the bag with the packaged food that had been roughly piled into already-full boxes. As I sorted through the junk, I found a gallon ziplock bag filled with a bottle of hand sanitizer, a pack of disposable masks, and a small box of nitrile gloves tucked away in the pocket behind the driver's seat. I held the bag in my hands and stared at its contents. The gears in my brain began to spin and grind in overtime as I quickly shoved the ziplock into the backpack and rushed to the driver's seat. I hastily plopped myself down and leaned forward to pop open the glove box. I tore through everything; I pulled papers, packs of gum, and any other item from the compartment. When nothing turned up, I directed my attention toward the center console.

I wasn't sure what I was searching for, but I was sure that this person might have had answers. If this person was so afraid of getting sick that they kept masks and gloves, it would have been for a reason. No one ever seemed this scared to contract a normal flu, unless they knew deep down that this wasn't a flu at all.

I yanked handfuls of trash and random junk from the center console. Chapstick, trash bags, old car air fresheners. I rummaged and dirtied the passenger floorboard until I reached the bottom of the console and spotted a packet of folded papers. I reached down and grabbed the stack of papers with more care than the other contents of the car. On the front page of the stack was a printed newsletter from the Center for Disease Control containing information on the new flu. Except, the words "NOT A FLU" were scrawled in bright red ink at the bottom of the page.

I quickly ruffled through the sheets of paper. Notes in red ink were scribbled on every page; circles and scratches covered most of the text, annotated and edited by hand. The stack contained printed social media threads filled with conspiracies, survival tactics, and articles about rabies in wild animals. None of the information correlated or made any sense—at least not to a normal person. At the back of the stack of papers was a shrunken U.S. map printed on plain paper. The map had small red circles scattered throughout the United States with no written notes.

I sat in the driver's seat and stared at the pages in my hands until my eyes began to burn from strain. I brought my hand up to rub my face and leaned my head back against the headrest. My eyes met with the tinted sunroof of the car, and I blankly stared up at the morning sky as I filtered through the new questions rising in my brain. There was only one thing my mind could settle on that was quite obvious: the new sickness had something to do with this.

As I raced through my thoughts, a distant whirring filled the air above me. I furrowed my brows and leaned out of the door to stare up at the cloudless sky. The mechanical whirring increased in speed and intensity. I folded the papers back up and shoved them into the backpack before I stepped out of the car and searched for the source of the noise. The whirring was directly above the neighborhood before my eyes finally spotted where it was coming from. A helicopter buzzed overhead, heading in the direction of Indianapolis. It appeared so small in the sky but seemed a lot lower than what it should have been. It must've been landing soon. My eyes followed it as the whirring of the blades became deafening and then quickly distant once again as the helicopter passed. I watched as it disappeared past the treetops.

My mind flicked back to the pages and the conspiracies entailed within them before I heard faint footsteps and looked up toward the house. Melony stood in the driveway clutching her thin jacket closed as the sun began to beam down on the back of her head. She squinted at me in the brightness of the growing day.

"Was that a helicopter?" she called out.

I nodded.

"Was it military?"

"I'm not sure," I replied, "Go back inside."

She nodded and began to speed walk toward the front door. She disappeared behind the tree in the front yard, so I listened for the sound of the closing door to ensure she was safely inside. I stuffed the backpack full and rested it in the driver's seat. Before grabbing the bag and rounding the front of the car, I froze.

I hadn't heard the front door shut.

"Melony?" I called out to her.

No answer.

I jogged up the driveway, and by the time I was halfway up, I spotted Melony standing on the porch with her back toward the door. Her eyes were wide, and I could see her lip trembling from where I stood in the driveway.

"Melony?" I called again. This time, concern dripped off her name as she stared at me in fear.

She didn't move or speak, but I quickly saw why. A shadow of a man stood behind her against the shade of the covered porch. His gloved hand crept up on her shoulder, and his other held something against her ribs. His face was covered with a mask and a hood as he stood a few inches above her. He nudged Melony forward, and she stepped closer to the edge of the porch. I watched him without a word. His fingers twitched, and his eyes flicked back and forth to the houses around us. I shifted my weight onto my back foot, and his eyes darted at me like daggers.

"Don't come any closer!" he commanded. His voice was deep, but not menacing; if anything, he sounded afraid.

"There's no need to hold her, man," I called back as I slowly reached my hands out, palms up in surrender. "You can have anything you want."

"We want that car you pulled into the driveway. Saw it runnin', so we need it."

"You can take it," I offered. "Keys are still inside. All these cars out here have supplies too. Take anything you want, just let her go."

The man pushed Melony closer to the edge of the porch, and I caught a glimpse of silver shimmer against her ribs. He had a knife. My heart pumped faster, and I couldn't take my eyes off his hand pressed into her ribs. I inched forward while he glanced down at the stairs.

"Just stand back!" he shouted as he carefully made his way down the front steps.

I paced backward a few inches with my hands still in the air. He carefully took each step, dragging Melony down each one with him. As they grew closer and stepped further into the light, I could see the tears in her eyes, and she winced at every step. The blade was noticeably poking into her ribs.

I stopped stepping backward and was about to inch forward once more before I felt the cold sharp tip of a knife press against my throat. The blade edge laid against my collarbone while the point pierced my skin, and a tiny prick began to burn against my neck.

"I don't think so, buddy," another man whispered from behind me. "Keep fuckin' still."

This man was more harsh and more intimidating, and I could tell he would be willing to kill me to save himself just from the firmness of his knife to my throat. As he held the knife, his hand was steady. He reached his other hand up to grip my arm and hold me still.

"Drop the crowbar," he grumbled.

And like a dog doing a trick, my hand released, and the crowbar hit the pavement with a metallic clang. The sound seemed to echo against the newfound silence surrounding us as the sounds of the morning birds seemed to drop away.

The man holding Melony flinched, and she whimpered at his sudden jerk. They inched closer and closer to the driveway before a horrible stench filled the air around us.

"Oh, God," the man holding Melony mumbled.

"Get in the fucking car, Paul!" the guy behind me shouted.

In a quick second, Melony was pushed forward and yelped in pain as the man ran around the side of the car to the driver's door. She clutched her ribs as red began to soak through her shirt. I gritted my teeth and pushed forward against the knife. A burning sensation ran across my chest, and the man behind me began to shout and curse in panicked breaths as I pulled away from him. I scooped up the crowbar and cocked back to swing when a piercing shriek filled the air, and a blur of black and gray leaped from the hood of the car over my head and tackled the man to the ground. My eyes went wide as the creature flailed and clawed wildly at the man's abdomen and face. The man screamed in such horrendous pain and agony that I wanted to rip my ears off to avoid the sounds that escaped him.

I spun on my heels and ran to Melony, who stood frozen in shock at the bottom of the stairs. Her hands shook and rattled as they clutched her side. I swept my arm underneath her in a rush of adrenaline and beelined it for the front door. I didn't turn back as the man's screams morphed into loud pained gurgles of blood. I could hear the creature shriek again as the SUV rumbled to life, and the tires squealed out of the driveway.

With Melony in my arms, I climbed the front steps, pushed open the front door, and kicked it closed behind us. I laid her down on the couch and lifted her shirt to check the wound. I had no idea if he stabbed or sliced her, but it would be detrimental to being able to save her.

The red-soaked fabric clung to her like a wet bandage, and blood stained across her abdomen and ribs as I exposed her bare skin to the air. When I finally reached her wound, I released a breath of relief I didn't realize I was holding when the gash along her ribs didn't appear to be too deep. He had sliced her while running away.

"Jonas," Melony panted through fearful tears, "you're bleeding."

She reached up to my shoulder, and I glanced down at where she was headed. A hole ripped across my shirt and blood soaked my chest. I pushed her hand back down and pressed it against her ribs.

"I'll be fine. Hold pressure there for me, okay?" I waited for her to nod before I jogged to the bathroom and pulled the first aid kit from under the cabinet.

Our first aid kit was a tackle box full of bandages, gauze, suturing supplies, ointments, shower caps, and rubbing alcohol. There were even folded and pre-packaged plastic sheets that looked like puppy pads. A lot of the contents had never been needed, but my mother was cautious when I was a child and bought almost everything you would need to start an at-home clinic.

I flipped the clips holding the box closed and sorted through the different supplies inside before deciding to slam the box shut and carry the entire crate into the kitchen. I set the kit down on the dining table before heading toward the kitchen counter and laying out one of the plastic sheets. I rummaged through the tackle box for all the pre-packaged and sterile utensils I would need and set them out on the sheet before I grabbed a few pairs of gloves from a Ziplock bag in the kit.

After setting up the area, I went and grabbed Melony off the couch. She protested as I picked her up, but I refused to let her walk into the kitchen on her own and carried her in any way. I sat her up on the counter, and she angled herself in a position that stretched out her torso while remaining comfortable.

Melony took steady and deep breaths while I handed her a warm wet cloth to clean the surrounding blood away. She winced with each wipe, and the skin around her wound was already beginning to bruise. I slipped my hands into a pair of gloves and doused them in rubbing alcohol as I held my hands over the sink. They were tight to my skin and pulled on the hairs that covered my hands.

"Don't you think you're going overboard?" she asked.

I shrugged. "I've never exactly given stitches before, but I don't want you to get an infection so I will do anything to make this as clean as possible."

"Good call," she mumbled as she glanced back down at the now pinkish-red stained towel.

I reached over and opened the suturing supplies to prep them before I took a deep breath and peered at Melony. Her eyes searched mine as we stared into each other. She was afraid, I could sense it, and so was I. I had watched so many doctors do their jobs as a child when going to appointments with my parents, but *I* wasn't a doctor. I observed from the sidelines as if I were watching reality TV, *not* as if I were going to ever use the skills.

"Are you ready?" I asked, completely unsure if I was asking her or myself.

She forced a playful smile on her face and winced as she pulled the towel away from the gash on her ribs. The fabric stuck to her red-stained skin, and I could see white and purple coloration forming around the wound. She attempted to mask the pain with a chuckle before she spoke.

"As long as I get to stitch you up next."

12

Melony

The storm pushed on, and with each day it pushed, I began to feel more at home. Every night, I fell asleep to the sound of the rain tapping against the window with every wind gust. The wind would blow, and the rain would whisper back as it fell through the trees into the grass. The walls that surrounded us began to feel like home. It was beginning to feel as if the world was turning back to normal. We had shelter, water, and comfort; I felt the calmest and more at peace than I had in almost two years.

After the second night, Jonas and I wandered down the road after the storm let up for some hours and scavenged a few houses. We managed to find enough food and clothes to keep us sheltered for another week, but the houses were in more disrepair and not worth moving into. Instead, Jonas found a piece of siding and a toolbox from one of the houses, and we brought it back to our temporary home to fix the front door. When the rain started to pour again and could mask any sound, Jonas took his chance to hammer the siding over the empty doorway in the living room. It was safe enough.

Jonas and I would spend our time at the house reading books we found on the shelves, playing card games, and telling stories that were imprinted in our minds—stories that we had already told each other so many times before. Other things occupied our time; an intimacy that we hadn't experienced in a long while.

When the world changed, we had to adapt to it. We changed the way we moved, the tone at which we spoke, our eating habits, our sleep schedules, everything about our normal day-to-day routines had to change. I don't think we took the time to realize that the world had changed the way we loved each other too. Our passion and affection had turned mild and cautious, but now that we felt security and comfort, it was like no other.

Every time he touched me felt like the first time all over again. He gave me butterflies just as he used to. It had been so long since we had felt each other this way; it was ravenous. We had been starving even when we were so close, and now we were satiating our hunger, devouring each other every chance we could get.

Six days had passed like the second hand on a clock, and eventually the storm began to fade. Once the rain had stopped, it was only a matter of time before we had to move on. We would run out of books to read, games to play, and stories to tell. We would run out of food and water. The home we had made here would no longer be safe. It always came full circle, and the hope we held out for would always fade just like the storm.

Jonas's hand brushed my hair out of my face as his arm draped over my bare waist, and the wind gushed in from the cracked window behind him. The bed was warm with his touch, and the room dark like his eyes.

"You know since the rain has passed, we'll need to be moving soon," he whispered as his thumb gently traced my jawline.

"You think we could ever come back?"

"It's not stable here for the long run." He smiled softly. "The house is practically falling apart, and we can't find food here."

"We could hunt and fix the place up."

"With what weapons? I don't have a gun or know how to set traps. You damn sure can't kill a squirrel with a bat, and fixing this place up wouldn't be worth the time and effort."

His tone was unserious, but his words were the exact opposite. We wouldn't survive here. We had proven ourselves to be scavengers, not hunters. I knew a few herbal remedies and minor first aid from teaching, but where would that get us? We couldn't survive on herbs and flowers. I was beginning to ask myself how we had survived this long.

"Okay," I finally mumbled, "but you must promise me that when we get to the next city, we find a library, and we learn. We can't survive much longer out here without learning anything."

"I promise," he replied with no hesitation as he stared into my eyes.

The sun came just as it had gone the night before. Jonas was up before the orange skies began to peek through the curtains, and he had already packed most of our belongings by the time I woke up. Our bags were leaned up against the wall near the closet. The carpet underneath them was still stained as black as tar. The fibers appeared shiny as if the stain was still wet, but it wasn't. The bedroom door leaned splintered and cracked with broken hinges against the wall where the dresser should be. I could hear Jonas moving around in another room of the house.

I swung my legs over the side of the bed and shuffled my sock-covered feet over the carpet to feel the grain scratch against the arches of my feet one last time. I pushed myself up and lightly bounced down onto the mattress to feel the soft cushion of the bed; I'd probably ache for weeks before I had another chance to sleep in a bed again. I closed my eyes and bathed in the silence of the house. It wasn't truly silent as Jonas shuffled around in the living room; pots and pans gently clanked against one another, his boots tapped against the floor, and I could hear the floorboards creaking with each step he took. There was never true silence, but I bathed in the quiet atmosphere of the house because it would be much different once we were out on the road. There wouldn't be a peaceful night's sleep. One of us would have to stay up to keep watch while the other prayed for enough shut eye to stay awake through their shift. The crickets and frogs and nocturnal critters that surrounded us would chatter and cry all throughout the night. I would feel the bugs and the grass and the twigs poke at me whichever way I turned. We'd have to sleep with one eye open.

There would never be peace like there was in the house. The world outside would shift around us as it always did, and we would have to run and hide in the shadows. With every turn, we would have to look over our shoulders no matter where we were as we had always done. I was a fool for letting myself grow used to this feeling of normalcy and for thinking everything would be okay.

We would leave here and walk for days. The hot sun would torch us, and our water would run out eventually like time and time before. The sounds of the outdoors would make me forget about the peace I felt here, and the smell of the fresh air would make me forget the comfort.

The house had a lingering smell of life that was different than the smell of the outdoors. The air was trapped and not flowing, and the musty scent of dust and old linens drifted in every room. It wasn't clean—it was lived in. The house didn't smell fresh, but it didn't smell of death. The smell of rot from the black blood on the floor had aired out quicker than I thought it would, and the regular air of the house replaced the stench. It was a scent that bounced off the corners of your mind, and you remembered parts of your life you had forgotten. It reminded me of my grandmother's house, a part of my life so long ago that I wouldn't have remembered it if it wasn't for that recognizable scent. The only things missing were cigarette smoke and ashtrays.

I pushed myself off the bed and outstretched my limbs as I stood; a yawn immediately pried at my jaw and my lungs began to rapidly fill like water pouring into a cup. The floorboards under the carpet released a muffled groan underneath me, and Jonas's footsteps began to approach from out in the hall.

"Mostly everything is packed and ready to go," he said before he appeared in the doorway. He leaned against the doorframe and tucked his hands into the front pockets of his shorts. "Go ahead and check around. Make sure we aren't forgetting anything."

I replied with a nod, and Jonas pushed himself off the doorframe to disappear back down the hall. I wandered around the room and began to rummage through the nightstand. The drawer was full of nail polishes, lotions, candy wrappers, and a bible. I reached in and picked up the leatherbound book; small sticky notes and book tabs poked from each page, colors ranging across the entire rainbow. A thin gold ribbon was tucked into the middle of the book holding the place of a reader long gone.

I stared at the embroidered cover. The brown leather was worn and scratched from a lifetime of use, and pink and gold thread embroidered a cross with roses on the center of the cover. My fingers traced over the rough threads and knicks in the leather.

Jonas's mother had a beautiful, embroidered bible that sat on a bookshelf in their living room. I never saw her read it, or ever touch it, but it rested on a shelf

142

next to a small porcelain figurine of an angel. When the conversations drifted off-topic as we sat in the living room, I'd find myself staring at it questioning why she had it. I had never known her to be a religious woman, and she never mentioned it before.

There were instances in my life where I wondered if God truly existed. I questioned if there was anyone out there watching over me. After my father died, I overheard someone telling my mother that we would be in their thoughts and prayers. I was young and didn't know much, so I tried to pray for him, and I prayed that my mother would be okay again. In my roughest times, I tried to pray in the hopes that maybe someone would come swooping in to save me. Eventually, I gave up trying. I felt I was contacting someone who wouldn't contact me back—I was calling a disconnected phone line or getting my call declined and sent straight to voicemail.

I hesitated before I pulled back the cover. I never read the bible, never really cared to, and maybe that was the reason God never helped when I needed him. The spine quietly cracked under the new pressure, and the sheer pages clung together and fluttered as I flipped through to the ribbon-marked page. The page was marked in pen and annotated in beautiful cursive penmanship. Transparent colored sticky tabs were placed over certain passages, but there was only one pink tab on the page.

*31 But they that wait upon
the Lord shall renew their*

strength; they shall mount up with wings as eagles; they shall run, and not be weary; and they shall walk, and not faint.

I looked at the top of the page. Book of Isaiah. I flipped through the rest of the pages, scanning the notes and assorted colors. Squiggles and small doodles filled the margins where no notes were taken. I gently closed the book and walked over to my bag; I squatted down and unzipped the large pocket. The book felt heavy in my hands as I stared down at the embroidered cover in contemplation before I pushed my thoughts aside and shoved the bible into my bag.

The personalization alone fueled my urge to keep it. Something in my gut told me I would need it someday. I had a hopeful dream that maybe life would return to how it used to be, and someone out there would want to have one.

Life before was strange to remember. Driving to work, going to church, watching television at home. We had to worry about bills and putting food on the table, or for others, making it on time to Sunday mass. Now everything was about surviving. We had to constantly keep death at bay or else it would come for us and consume us. My mother used to tell me that I would regret not believing. She used it as a scare tactic to get me to listen. She wasn't truly devoted, but she would go to church on Sundays and holidays, forced to leave me alone at home. If I knew it were to happen this way—If

I knew that life as I had once known it would end as it had, I would've gone back and shared another Sunday morning with her. I would suffer the conversation and ignore the snide remarks. I would give her one last chance to scold me before God plucked her from this plane.

After stuffing the bible in my bag, I moved on to the desk drawer. As suspected, it was mostly full of office supplies and stationery. A few textbooks were stacked in a deep-set drawer, and a zippered fabric pouch was placed next to them. I reached into the drawer and removed the pouch from its resting place. The pouch was stuffed with sanitary pads and tampons, a small tube of mascara, and a mini pack of Kleenex. I plucked out the tube of mascara and left it on the desk before rezipping the pouch and packing it into my backpack with the bible.

I struggled to slip my new sneakers on but quickly got them tied after they were snugly in place. I swung my bag over my shoulder and picked up my bat with one hand and Jonas's bag with the other before marching out of the bedroom door and placing the bags on the living room floor next to the couch.

"You find anything?" Jonas asked as he poured water from a pot into his tumbler.

The water glugged as it filled. He screwed the lid on and set it on the counter next to the two one-gallon jugs and plastic bottles filled with water.

"Nothing too important," I replied as I made my way to the counter and began carrying the bottles and jugs toward our bags.

I set the two one-gallon jugs on the coffee table as well as the plastic bottles before splitting the stores amongst the two backpacks. Each of us was to carry a gallon jug and three water bottles as well as our metal tumblers. The bags would be heavy, but necessary.

"Okay, well, after I fill this bottle, we should be good to go. I've checked the rooms, packed up anything I could find already, just waiting for you to be ready, mostly," he huffed.

I knew that Jonas wanted to stay just as much as I did, and I assumed he knew that I understood that we needed to leave. Everything he had said before was true. We would run out of food, we didn't know how to hunt, and our water stores would run out. It was better for us to get going now than to grow too attached to the house later and have to abandon our home.

I sighed and pulled my bag—now double in weight—onto my shoulders before picking up my bat.

"I'm as ready as I'll ever be," I replied with slight irritation, "best get moving now before I change my mind."

Jonas chuckled before he screwed the top onto the last bottle and tossed it to me. I clumsily caught it as he strolled toward his bag, picked it up by the strap, and threw it over his shoulder as if it weighed nothing. He marched over toward the backdoor with a shimmy to balance out the weight of his pack. We both squeezed through the opening one after the other and made our way down the porch steps toward the side of the house where the fence gate was covered with ivy and locked into place by the tall weeds. Jonas easily raised his leg and pushed himself up over the fence while I jammed the toe of my boot into one of the holes and lifted myself off the ground and onto the top of the fence. Jonas politely held out a hand and helped me down onto the other side.

We walked down the small overgrown footpath around toward the front of the house, retrieved our bikes, and began pushing them down the drive. Once we reached the end, I glanced over my shoulder back at the piss-yellow walls.

The last few days had been comforting. They had brought me a small sense of hope for the future, but now I was just worried about what was to come. Hope lingered in me no more. Fear began to slither in through my veins and attack whatever hope I had left. Poison in my bloodstream. We were moving on, and I had no idea what the future would hold.

13

Melony

"Do you think a library will be deep into the city?"
I asked as I looked at the faint city skyline poking above
the treetops ahead.

"I'm not sure," Jonas said as he squinted in the
same direction. "It might take us another day or two to
get there. We're heading south toward the Ohio River,
but I'm not even sure the bridge is still intact."

"What will we do if it isn't?" I asked, full of
concern.

"There's plenty of bridges going from Indiana to
Kentucky," Jonas informed, "we'll just find another and
take it."

"Do you think it'll be worse there?"

He fell silent. No nod, no shake of the head, no
shrug. I couldn't tell if it was hesitation to answer in fear
of embracing the truth or hesitation in his lack of
knowledge. The more I stared at him I didn't think it was

hesitation at all; his silence and expressionless face appeared more like contemplation. He was making some kind of mental decision and pulling apart every possible outcome. He seemed to be trying to find a way to piece the words together. Either way, hesitation or contemplation, he didn't respond.

"Why did we ever decide to move south?" I asked, "We could've gone any direction. Maybe we could go east toward the coast; I could finally see the ocean. I wouldn't have minded going north toward Canada either. Maybe they have it more contained there, maybe it didn't happen at all. We could always change our mind while we aren't too far from home."

Jonas still didn't answer. His eyes were focused on the road ahead, unmoving. He didn't even spare a glance in my direction. It felt as if he was keeping a secret. There must've been a voice in his head that didn't want to let me in on the plan. The silence between us was easily snuffed out by the bike chain groaning with each grinding cycle of the pedals.

"You could at least say something," I muttered. "It doesn't even have to answer my questions. Just talk about something."

The words that finally escaped him were more of a realization than a question, "You've never been to the ocean…"

"I thought you knew that?" I chuckled at the thought of him being so clueless about something so obvious to me.

"I did," he replied, "just forgot that was an option."

"Like I said," I tried to persuade in singsong, "we could always change course."

He returned a satisfied nod before he fell back into his thoughts. The silence returned and awkwardly hugged me. I needed to spark an actual conversation.

"So..." I playfully nagged knowing he would say no, "is that a yes?"

He chuckled dismissively. "Maybe someday I'll take you to the coast, and you can see the ocean. Maybe we'll even go to *Mexico*."

Out of the country? I didn't have a passport—not that it mattered anymore. I was sure in another life Jonas would have taken me sooner when I would've actually needed one, or maybe in that other life the world never ended, and we'd retire on the coasts of Mexico. In another life, I would've seen the bustle of the streets and the vendors with food I couldn't ever imagine trying in our small town. I would hold Jonas's hand as we toured museums and soaked up the knowledge I had dreamed of and was meant to know. I would get to see the trees that grew through the sands of the beaches and the Mayan temples that rose high from the ground. Another life.

"Do you remember Mexico?" I asked as I drifted into thought.

Jonas clicked his tongue against the roof of his mouth as he assembled an answer in his mind. "My parents met there. Mom was in college—taking a semester off, or something like that—when she met Dad. He had dual citizenship and was on vacation to visit his parents when they crossed paths. Dad used to tell me it was love at first sight for him. He'd tell how he spotted some beautiful white woman smiling and greeting people in a foreign country. He said he was so surprised she spoke such good Spanish. I could still hear the emotion in his voice when he told the stories. He sounded so raw and in love.

"Mom would tell it that she saw him standing there just gawking at her, so she began to ask for directions. He just dropped everything he was doing and walked her to her destination. I always thought that was destiny for them, or at least that's what destiny looked like.

"Mom always told me that they moved back and forth, and she'd stayed in *Mexico* for as long as she could before she always had to come back. She and Dad always traveled with each other, and I guess that's how I came along. She ended up getting pregnant, and they married within a few months. I was born in *Mexico*, but they decided after I was born that they'd move back to the States for good. I remember a few vacations where we would go down and visit *mi abuelitos*—my dad's parents."

He paused, and I took a moment to ask another question.

"What was it like?" I softly asked so as not to disrupt his thoughts too much.

He seemed to be cherishing a sweet moment in his head, one I don't think I knew of.

"I was little, so I don't remember much. I only remember the people and the colors. It was so vibrant. Mom was the one to make the details come to life. She'd tell me stories of how beautiful it was there and teach me about the culture that she learned. She wanted me to know and be proud of where I came from." He turned to me with watery eyes and finished, "I think you would have loved it."

Jonas's smile was wide, and his eyes brimmed with tears as he browsed memories of his parents. The look on his face was bittersweet as he talked of them and the moments lost to the years. I felt it with him. I grew up with his parents more than I had mine, and with all honesty, I probably missed them more than my own. I felt deep shame and regret that I hadn't taken the time to hear these stories straight from them.

"I would have loved it…"

Our conversation faded back into the humming sounds of nature around us. The cooling shade of the trees that lined the sides of the road turned from little dots of light speckled on the pavement to massive chunks of sun beaming directly onto us. The woods around us thinned the further we rode out, and small neighborhoods turned into city blocks. Stop lights marked every intersection, but there was no electricity and no traffic to be guided. Cars still sat with doors open at gas stations and corner stores. Jonas and I had to maneuver our bikes through the lanes of vehicles that never made it to their destination. It reminded me of how backed up the roads had gotten at home after Day One.

A feeling bubbled inside my gut as we passed vehicle after vehicle. Windows and doors were left open to expose the interiors to the elements. Luggage and personal belongings were left behind. It was all a scene I had been too familiar to. Everything someone once cared for was left out in abandoned cars. Picked over and rummaged through by passing-by scavengers.

Of course, Jonas and I did the same. We went through any cars that seemed to still be worth checking. It was difficult to push past the guilt and disgust that coursed through me as I helped Jonas pick through clothes and tote bags full of old groceries. I hated having to resort to looting to survive. I hated going through people's belongings. I hated the way it made me feel when I found something good.

This stuff didn't belong to me.

"We have to do this," Jonas mumbled from beside me as he unzipped another duffel.

He could sense the discomfort radiating from me, or maybe it was just blatantly written all over my face. It felt like sometimes he could just read my mind.

"I know," I sighed, "This just feels different than going into houses. Maybe because we're more exposed outside. I just feel like I'm being judged when I'm looking through people's cars."

I glanced up into the rear windshield of the next vehicle ahead and could make out the outlines of the headrests and the pile of bags that sat in the back seat. My eyes hopped past that one and onto the next. My gaze drifted along the lines of traffic with cars that mirrored the same view of belongings left in the stale trapped air. It felt endless. Miles of lives left for the reaping.

Some cars we passed still had people inside—what was left of them. Mummified leather dried down to the bone underneath loose clothing covered in black speckles of mold. The fabric interior speckled with the same rot, but the smell of death no longer lingered.

We searched those cars too. Until our bags were too heavy to carry and our shoulders ached beneath the weight, we searched.

I grew more desensitized the longer we went on. Not just physically numb to the bag and gravity forcing itself down on my spine but to emotions that crept forward with every car we came across. Surprise struck me at each one, then sadness, then grief, then nothing. My body and mind felt the tingling of limbs cut off from blood circulation. I had turned myself off. My consciousness fell asleep, and my mind was on autopilot.

Car after car, bag after bag, I reached into pockets and gloveboxes as a dark pit settled into my chest—void of any feeling. I skimmed over diaper bags and car seats without registering what I was staring at. I pushed aside filth-covered stuffed toys and sippy cups painted with rings of liquid that evaporated long ago without fully absorbing the gravity of the scene before me.

I would sometimes find photo albums and steal pieces of memories like a serial killer taking trophies. I hadn't killed these people—*I was the aftermath.* I was the pent-up grief and anger following behind that faded into a tear-filled morning mist as bloodshot eyes watched the morning sun rise just as they had seen the evening sun fall.

I felt *complicit.* I felt *disgusting.* But I also felt nothing.

The emotions were all too familiar, the pain as well. I had grown tolerant. My mind was censoring itself as if I was going into shock, like a trauma response.

I was growing more uncomfortable with the void the further down the road we ended up. I was uncomfortable with how little I was noticing and how quickly I was brushing past the scenes in front of me. I wasn't taking in any of my surroundings. I was just floating through this space like a dandelion seedling in the wind waiting to plant myself somewhere far away.

How am I supposed to keep living like this?

All it took was one good week, safe and comfortable, to remind myself that this wasn't living. There was more to life than surviving. I think I had heard that quote somewhere before surviving became the priority.

"*Vamos,*" I heard Jonas call out from behind another car, "We should move on. I've got about all I can carry."

There was a small clatter that followed his words, but I continued with no hesitation. I didn't want to be here any longer; I wanted to keep moving. The sun was beginning to bake sweat onto my skin, and I could feel the dust from every vehicle sticking to me like bugs in a glue trap. I already wanted and needed another storm shower. A luxury I could not have.

"I need a break," I called out to him.

I could not see him among the surrounding cars, but I knew he was close enough to hear me. The rustling of his bag bounced off every vehicle around me, yet I could still not place him. I furrowed my brows and slammed the door of the car I was currently investigating before making my way around the front end and scanning the lanes of traffic as I walked through them. I was growing more confused and frustrated with every turn I took and Jonas not being there.

"What the hell?" I muttered to myself as I threw my arms up in frustration and stopped in my tracks.

I began to spin in a circle with narrowed eyes as I scanned every gap and window for his curly-filled head to pop up.

"If you don't come out," I shouted into the air hoping he'd hear, "I'm gonna keep riding and leave you here."

A loud metallic crash answered me and caused me to jump out of my skin. I hunkered down with the anticipation of something jumping out at me, but nothing came. I quickly gathered myself and began to rush back toward where I leaned my bike and bat. I crouched as I ran with light footsteps and my head on a swivel.

"Where are you..." I muttered silently as I approached the vehicle we had left our rides perched against.

When I came upon the rear of the car, I grew more puzzled than before. Our belongings were gone. Vanished. *Poof.*

Both mine and Jonas's bikes were no longer in the place we had rested them, and my bat was among the missing items.

"Fuck," I grumbled.

There was someone here. There had to be. Maybe it wasn't Jonas I had been hearing all along and it was someone else. Lurking and waiting. But if it truly was someone else that I had heard rustling around, only one question popped into my brain:

Where was Jonas?

14

Jonas: After

I winced and gripped the edge of the counter as the needle pulled through my skin one final time, and Melony tied the suture. She took a step back and cocked her head as she examined her work. I glanced down at the stitching across my chest.

"Oh, wow," I mumbled in surprise.

The scene was grotesque and messy. Dried blood stained my chest everywhere except the cut, and the stitches that lined my nasty wound were incredibly uneven in space. The edges around the cut were already blotched in a variety of whites, reds, yellows, and purples. I looked like a toddler's horrible fingerpainting.

"It's not that bad," she defended, "I mean, it'll work. It isn't gonna be pretty."

I nodded. "I can see that."

She rolled her eyes and winced as she twisted to set the needle and scissors onto the blood-smudged counter. She suddenly squeezed her eyes shut as she took a slow deep breath. She reached a shaky hand up and gently clutched her side as the pain quite visibly coursed through her. We stood in silence examining ourselves and the work we had done on each other. It was crude, jagged, and bruised.

It certainly wouldn't heal right and would certainly leave a scar. It wouldn't be Melony's first one, but it would be mine.

I reached out for a clean damp rag to wipe myself off before reaching for the box of bandages and handing some to Melony to cover my stitches. I then cleaned her and placed a bandage over her stitches before I turned and began to walk down the hall toward the bedroom. I could hear Mel's soft footsteps trailing behind me. As I rounded the corner into the bedroom, I felt her cold fingertips graze a spot on the back of my right shoulder. I glanced over my shoulder at her standing in the doorway in just her bra and leggings, blood-stained shirt in hand.

"I always forget you have that," she said as she leaned against the doorframe and grunted before standing back up straight and placing a hand over her bandage.

I pulled open the dresser drawers and picked through the options to find Melony a loose-fitted tee to slip into before I found one for myself.

"Forget I have what?" I questioned as I tossed Melony her new shirt and carefully pulled mine over my head and shoulders.

"Your tattoo," she clarified as she tossed her old shirt onto the dresser and slipped into her new one.

She groaned as she lifted her arms up, and as her head passed through the hole, I could see the pain written across her face. I felt guilty that I couldn't help her.

"Oh," I tried to peek over my shoulder at the tattoo in question, "I forget about it sometimes too."

"Why'd you ever get it? I always saw it but never thought to ask."

I shrugged and felt the sharp burn from my cut shoot through me. "It's a reminder of the best parts of my childhood."

"You should've told me," she replied as she fiddled with the hem of her shirt, "I would've gotten it with you."

"I should've," I mumbled as I watched her pick at the threads of the hem.

Our conversation fell into silence, and I shifted back into moving throughout the room. I picked up Melony's old shirt and threw it into the tiny bin in the corner of the room, wiped away the faint smudges and fingerprints left on the dresser, and began to squeeze past Melony in the doorway to go clean up the kitchen. Before I could completely pass her, she looked up at me with tears in her eyes.

"Jonas," she whimpered.

I stared down at her and glanced at her clenched fists, knuckles white. I couldn't tell where her mind was at. Her emotions had been such a twist and turn from where we were seconds ago. She removed a hand from clenching around her shirt to gently squeeze my wrist. Her hands were cold, and I could feel her trembling.

"What was that *thing*?"

In an instant, I was transported back to the scene we had witnessed in the drive. I saw that creature—its humanlike form crawl and sprint on all fours. The rotting gray skin and the tears that cut wide open to the bone and mangled limbs covered in black and red liquid. I could hear that man screaming, the sound of his flesh ripping as that *thing* flailed about, the screeching, and the terror and blood that gurgled in the man's throat. I pictured the way the creature leaped up and chased after the car like a rabid dog.

I couldn't answer Mel's question. I didn't know what we had seen out there. I didn't know how to answer her. All I knew was that I was afraid, and in the rush of things, I had pushed what I had witnessed aside to save her.

After waiting too long for an answer and getting nothing, Melony's hand slowly released and dropped back down to her side as she turned away and released a trembling breath.

"I think I need to lay down," she whispered as she made her way to the bed.

I watched her from the doorway as she lifted the disheveled covers and slipped underneath them. She rolled and faced the window with her back to me and brought the comforter past her shoulders to nestle into the crevice of her neck. I heard her grumble and lightly moan in pain as her body moved underneath the blanket, and she eventually fell still curled up into a ball. I stared at her for a few more moments. Her hair peaked out of the covers and draped across my pillow. From where I stood, I could see her eyes were still open, and she stared blankly out the window.

I bit the inside of my cheek and took a deep breath as I shifted and walked out of the room. I rounded the corner into the kitchen and was shocked at the true mess we had left behind. The plastic sheet that I had draped over the counter was covered in smeared bloody handprints, and small puddles of red were drying and crusting onto the kitchen floor and counter. The utensils were scattered across the kitchen, and my shirt was wadded up in a blood-soaked ball on the floor. I sighed and headed toward the disastrous clutter. I bent down and swooped up my shirt, the blood still damp and sticky against the palm of my hand. I walked it toward the trash can, tossed it in, and then dragged the bin over toward the counter. I proceeded to wad up the plastic sheet, the rags, the gauze, and the stained bandages and tossed them into the trash. As I looked down at the blood droplets that scattered across the floor, my eyes trailed to my feet.

I was still wearing my blood-soaked sock, now more stained than ever. Not with just a stranger's blood, but mine and Melony's mingling together. I quickly reached down and removed each one, tossing them into the bin as well.

I then grabbed all the utensils we had used and tossed them into the sink before I rushed to the kitchen closet, snatched the mop and Fabuloso out of the darkness, and opened the child-safe cap of the purple bottle.

The more I looked, the more blood I could see staining the tile and countertops. It splattered on the wooden cabinets and the baseboards. I could feel it drying to my skin; my feet stuck to the floor like walking across the stickiness of the convenience store near the soda fountains.

I began to frantically pour the purple liquid over the kitchen floor.

I could feel my heart and lungs pounding in my chest trying to escape the smell of iron and pennies and lavender. I quickly set the bottle on the table and began to scrub the floor with the sponge mop. Out of all the white in the kitchen, all I could see was each speckle of red. It stood out like a grotesque zit.

As I scrubbed, I could feel my chest burning with each push and pull. The burning pain seared through me like a hot iron until I grew numb and caught a glimpse of dark red in my peripheral. I glanced down at myself; deep red soaked into the bandage that covered my stitches.

"*Hijo de puta*," I grumbled to myself.

I rested the mop against the counter and reached for the bandage box with one hand as I began to peel the medical tape off my shoulder with the other. Once the bandage was removed, I stared down at the mess on my chest. It wasn't bleeding as horribly as the bandage had led on, but it was more than I was comfortable with. I pressed several new layers of gauze and bandages against the wound before taping it up and continuing to clean at a slower, less maniacal pace.

Eventually, the floor was clean enough to my liking, and the afternoon sun was pouring in through the windows as it sat almost directly above the house. I turned on the kitchen faucet as hot as it would go and filled the sink with hot soapy water to let the medical utensils soak before I would come back later and wash them. As I reached under the kitchen sink for the small tub of bleach, I could hear Melony's light footsteps approaching from down the hall. I looked at the clock on the stove; it had been an hour since I started cleaning.

"You're up already? *Cómo te sientes?*" I called to her as I poured a splash of bleach into the sink.

She didn't answer, but I could hear her shuffling around in the living room. It sounded as if she was going through her tote bag, a soft rustling as she searched for something. Then the scraping sound of something being scooted across the tile and the light jingle of keys.

I quickly secured the cap on the bleach and sat it next to the sink before I rushed out of the kitchen into the entryway of the living room. Melony stood in front of the door, tiptoeing as she peered out the window at the top of the door. The keys dangled in her hand as her arm dangled at her side. She had slipped on a thin jacket and her sandals. I wondered where she was planning to leave, and why she just stood at the door not moving.

"Where are you going?" I asked softly so as not to startle her.

No answer. She stared out the window at something I could not see from the entryway between the living room and kitchen. I stepped closer, growing uneasy with the way she stood there silently. It was beyond eerie, it was borderline terrifying.

"Melony?" I spoke, "*Estás bien?*"

She began to whisper something to herself. I couldn't make out the words, just that whatever she was saying, she was repeating it over and over and over. I was within arm's reach and placed a gentle hand on her back as I stepped forward and gazed at the side of her face. Her face was pale; the bags under her eyes were dark and stood out like bruises. Terror struck every nerve in her face; her eyes were wide, and her lips quivered as she whispered.

"He should be dead. He should be dead. He should be dead..." I could finally make out her words.

Fear began to course through me as she continued whispering and wouldn't take her eyes away from the window. She was in a trance. Her words stumbled out repeatedly, and I began to grow worried about this being some side effect of her wound possibly being infected.

"Why are you saying that, Mel?" I leaned in closer and reached for the hem of her shirt. "Let me check your stitches. Do you feel hot?"

"That man..." she spoke a little louder, "he's moving."

"What man?" I furrowed my brows, glanced out the window, and spotted the man who had been attacked earlier. I quickly looked away from the gory scene and turned my attention back to Melony. "You shouldn't be staring at that. It's normal; dead people twitch."

I lifted the edge of her shirt, and she quickly swatted my hand away. Her voice was louder this time as she spoke.

"Dead people," she emphasized through gritted teeth, "don't *get up.*"

I stopped in my tracks and gazed up at her through my brows. Her eyes remained locked on the gore beyond the window. She was staring at the corpse and remnants sprawled across my yard.

Dead bodies twitch—that seemed like common knowledge; it was something Melony would've known about. Muscle contractions and gas release that happen as the body shuts down.

Although I was certain she already knew this science, she was locked on as if her wide hazel eyes were the jaws of a K-9 unit waiting to be given the okay to release, metaphorically sinking her teeth in and not letting go of the image she saw in front of her. The way she was unmoving, her hair unbrushed, and her breath so steady and slow she didn't appear to be breathing at all built a heaviness in my chest like watching a horror movie and imagining something in the dark corner of your bedroom. I didn't like it. The way she stood there made me feel like something was watching me, made me feel like something was trying to crawl into my skin. I hesitantly stood up straight and turned to see the "moving man" she was so stricken by.

As I turned and stared through the glass panes, my eyes widened at the scene in front of me. How could she have been staring at this for so long?

Blood streaked my driveway, and chunks of flesh littered the grass and pavement. The body's clothes were torn to shreds along with what skin remained over his abdomen and chest. The blood that pooled around him was black and still slowly seeped out of him as if his heart was still pumping and as if that thick oil-like substance was what coursed through his veins. I assumed it was only because of how much blood there was. A deep enough puddle would appear darker than a single drop against your skin, like the water in a murky lake.

And then, in a tiny sliver of a moment, I saw what Melony had been on about, and I saw it tenfold.

The man's hand and wrist began to twitch and twist in abnormal ways. His leg kicked out straight, and a bulge in his thigh began to form underneath his jeans. His leg bent back again, and I could hear the dull crack of his femur from behind the door as it ripped through the denim.

I could feel vomit rising in my throat as this human corpse began to shapeshift into something monstrous. Dead bodies were supposed to twitch, but this wasn't a dead body, *not anymore.*

The body began to twitch and convulse wildly as the shade from the house receded and the afternoon sun lit up the corpse.

It was a holy spotlight. God was saying, "Look at what I have created for you!"

The sun covered more of the body, and one after another, each limb outstretched, bent in opposite ways than anatomically allowed, and shattered bones pierced through the skin as the black oil burst and trickled from every wound. It felt like watching an exorcism with explicit gore.

Soon after it had begun, the transformation ended. The body flailed over onto itself and pushed itself off the ground until it crawled on all elongated fours. Bones protruded at the joints, black blood poured from every wound, and I could smell the rot and death creeping in through the insulation and cracks in the foundation of the house. The remaining contents and organs that were in this once-human's open chest and abdomen cavity spilled out onto the concrete.

Melony gripped my arm and squeezed harder than I had ever felt as she watched the same scene I laid my eyes on. Her nails dug into my forearm, and her hand vibrated from the amount of pressure she was putting on me. The vomit rose, and I could no longer hold it back. I quickly spun to the side and hacked up all over the entryway tile. Melony's grip loosened, but I could see from my peripheral that she didn't budge one bit as she watched the corpse outside.

A loud shriek echoed through the air like a wild cat screaming in agony. Startled, Melony jerked and finally dropped away from the window. She placed her back against the door and slid down until she sat on the floor next to the vomit with her knees pulled into her chest.

"Its eyes..." she whispered before slapping a hand over her mouth and squeezing her eyes shut.

She released her death grip on my wrist and clamped her second hand over her mouth as well, locking any sound she made inside. Her breathing amplified, and she silently sobbed while I focused on wiping my face free of the acid chunks that spewed from me. I didn't have the energy to ask any of the questions that were racing through my mind. I knew I wouldn't be left with a single answer anyway. All I was left with was another mess of bodily fluids to clean and an image that would scar me until my last day on earth.

I slowly stood and peeked out of the window to see nothing but the remnants of a gory mess. The body was gone.

The following days were drenched in silence. Not the peaceful restorative kind, but the kind that left an eeriness deep in the caves of your chest. It was the feeling of the unknown creeping in on you. Unanswered questions and fearful anticipation. We were waiting for the proverbial bombs to drop if they hadn't already.

"I win," Melony said with no emotion as her Connect4 piece fell into her chosen slot with a light *plink*.

I sighed deeply and pulled the switch that released all the pieces from the cage. She stood up as I began to sort the red and yellow coins into piles. Her back arched, and her arms rose over her head as she yawned and stretched. Once she was relieved, she hovered over the game, her eyes bore into the top of my head. I could feel her gaze from above, and I could hear the soft sounds of her lips parting to speak, but she stopped herself. No words came.

Another round of silence followed.

We hadn't spoken about what happened days ago. I'm not sure we knew how to address it. How would we talk about what we had seen? It left more questions than it could ever answer. It almost felt like a nightmare, but we weren't asleep. Truly, we hadn't slept since. For the most part, we felt safe where we were. I'm sure we both thought that if we talked about it, there would be no going back to normal; we would make it all too real.

Instead of speaking, she sighed, sat back down on the floor across from me, and played the first piece just as we had been doing previously.

Not a single word was spoken.

For hours this would go on. Like routine clockwork, we'd get out of bed, eat from our rationed pile of stolen goods, turn on the static of the emergency radio, and sit on the living room floor playing board games while our eyes took turns flicking toward the small barricades we had placed at both main entrances to the house. We'd do it all in silence, waiting to hear any voice come through the static of the radio. We waited for a warning, a message, a tiny blip in the radar. We'd eat dinner and check our wounds before heading to bed. Most of our sleepless nights consisted of staring at each other. Communicating without words. Reading each other's minds. We talked about it without talking about it. Then, we'd watch the morning sun come, and the bags under our eyes would darken, and the routine would start again. A revolving door that never stopped to let us out.

It was day four—maybe it could've been longer, but I was too trapped in my head to notice. Four days of not knowing what was happening in the outside world. Four days of paranoia and worry. Four days of reimagining that man's corpse transform into a beast in front of my eyes.

I often found myself trapped in daydreams—day-nightmares—of the creature I had seen. My eyes would drift into space as I mindlessly played my turn in board games. I would see its limbs twitch and its body convulse as something else began to take control. I could hear that man screaming before it happened, the sound of his flesh ripping when the first creature attacked him. I was seeing it now.

The terror and blood that curdled in his throat as that... *thing* shrieked. I could still taste the vomit as I watched him come back to life.

Melony touched my hand. Her fingers were soft but cold as they lightly brushed against my skin. As my eyes focused, I could only see her through a blur of tears brimming my waterline. She stared at me and watched as I blinked them away and rubbed my hands over my face with exhaustion.

"I still see it too," she whispered in a quavering voice.

In my eyes, Melony had to have had it worse. She stared at it for so long. She watched it come to life—back to life—and she watched it leave. I could see the exhaustion and horror still riddling her body. Her limbs were weak, and every time she turned towards the window the pace of her breathing would pick up. If I focused hard enough, I swore I could hear her pounding heart racing like a rabbit's.

I brought my hands into my lap as she used the sleeve of her sweater to wipe her eyes. Through the bags under her eyes and the frizzy mess of her unbrushed hair, she was still so beautiful, and seeing her cry physically pained me. We had witnessed something so traumatic and were both bottling it in. I could see her hurting, and she could see me, but we still chose not to speak. It made me sick thinking of anything to say about it. My body didn't want me to talk.

"It's your turn," she sniffled.

I nodded and played my next piece. We entered the revolving door once more.

Plink. Plink. Plink.

Back and forth, we'd take our turns and ignore the white noise of the radio and the silence between us as it filled in around us. I would drift into space as I mindlessly lost the game time and time again. This time my mind traveled elsewhere: the man with a knife to Melony's side.

I thought of the way he had wrapped his arm around her so stiffly to lock her in place—to restrain her as her eyes were wide in fear. I thought about how I felt the moment I saw the knife and how he held it to her. Her wound was not deep, and I suppose I could thank him for saving her life on that front. But if I had another chance, there was no telling what I would've done.

It could've been worse. At least that's what she had told me after I fixed her up. She was right; it could've been worse, and I'd already spent so much time imagining how much worse it could have truly been.

I think so often about my life with her that I always try to avoid what I would do without her. The truth is, I wouldn't be able to do anything. I suppose I got that from my father. My devotion, my love. If the knife had been deeper—if that man had stabbed instead—and Melony would have died, I was certain I would soon follow.

If not from heartbreak, from my own doing.

There were times in our lives when we had taken separate paths. We met other people before we realized the complexity of our relationship. If she didn't choose me, it would be her decision, and I could live with that. But if she *chose* me and I lost her, would I be able to go through what my father did when we lost my mother? A world in which Melony was gone was no world I would want to live in, even if I believed I could survive it.

I'd never thought I'd ever lose her in such a way. We would have a beautiful home with a magical flower garden. We'd grow old together as the flowers bloomed each year, and we'd spend our days sitting outside playing our games. I only ever wished us both peaceful deaths at an old age. Passing in our sleep. But the world is ever-changing. There were more monstrous things out there to consider.

I could hear my mother's voice in my head.

"*You take care of that girl, Jonas,*" her voice a raspy breath as her bony hand squeezed mine. "*She's the one for you. A mother always knows.*"

I always found it so strange how much she insisted Melony was the one. Maybe it was she who planted the thought in my head and wished it to life.

The butterfly that flapped its wings, and the tsunami that came after.

The last coin plinked into a slot once again and Melony sighed at another point added to her total score. She was the only one playing, we both knew that.

"Let's do something else," she said as she pulled the switch and all the pieces fell out of the game.

"What do you want to do?" I asked mindlessly staring at the molecules around her.

"I want to go outside," she quickly stated matter-of-factly like she had been thinking about this request the entirety of the four days we had been locked inside.

I immediately shook my head.

"Whatever that was out there is gone, Jonas."

"Why the hell do you want to go out there? We are safe in here."

"What if we aren't?" Her question lingered in the thick air; I could almost imagine the letters of her words floating above her head.

"Is that what you think?"

She scooted across the floor until her back leaned against the loveseat adjacent to the couch I was leaning against. She was silent, and her eyes darted along the walls and the barricade blocking the front door. She looked everywhere but at me. She said what she needed to say without opening her mouth.

"Where do you think we would go, Melony? Where do *you* think is safe?" I could hear my tone shifting harsher at each word that slipped out.

"There's no need to be like that…" She stared at me with furrowed brows and began to pick at the skin around her thumbnail.

We were both agitated. The irritation and tension in the atmosphere made our moods harsh and tones harsher.

"Well," I replied as I pulled my knees out from under the coffee table and draped my arms over them, "I would like to know. For some strange reason, you think it's a smart idea to go outside when you're complaining about not being safe inside this house. I need to know the logic behind that."

"I just want to see it," she mumbled, "I need to understand what that thing was. I haven't heard from Mom, and I want to go to the house. I need to see if she made it home before—"

She was beginning to choke up and trailed off. After a few seconds of silence, she shook her head and pinched the bridge of her nose. I could tell the type of thoughts she was having; invasive and intrusive thoughts that came as consequences of the unknown. She didn't have answers, and the only way I knew how to help her get them was to let her go.

I stood up from the couch and moved toward the barricade. Slowly and carefully, I began to move each item that blocked the door without making too much noise or mess.

"What are you doing?" she asked from the floor.

"If you're going to go outside and check it out, we must be careful. No noise, and we don't take our time. We go check it out and come right back. I can't say we could go to your mom's, but we can go outside and see if there's anything that might help us get an idea of what's going on. Got it?"

Melony pushed herself off the floor and began to help me remove the barricade piece by piece. With her help, the barricade was down in no time, and the living room was a cluttered maze of misplaced furniture.

Melony placed her hand on the doorknob and hesitated. She stared at the wood grain as her knuckles began to turn white. I could only imagine what she was seeing in her head. I leaned down and picked up the crowbar propped against the wall next to her before placing my hand gently on the small of her back. She gazed up at me before taking a fluttery deep breath.

"We don't have to go. It's your choice," I informed softly.

Then, before I knew it, the doorknob squeaked, the hinges groaned, and the shining afternoon sun and humid air poured into the house.

15

Melony

With no weapon or gear, aside from what I carried on my back, I was surely fucked. Without Jonas, I was surely fucked. Someone had likely stolen our gear, kidnapped my partner, and left me alone in a wasteland of dead cars.

This is bad. This is very bad...

The rattling and shuffling had died down as I crouched through each lane of traffic. It had died down so much I could hear my blood pumping through my body. My heartbeat raced as worry and fear began to rattle me to the bone. I was either growing further away or whoever was out there was leaving. I was alone, and Jonas could have been hurt.

With our belongings vanishing, I tried to recount everything that we had left next to that car.

There were two bikes. The person who robbed us must've known there were two people out here. If it were me, it would be obvious that Jonas wasn't traveling alone. This thought made me assume the person who stole our stuff thought the same and was likely hunting for me.

I stopped and sat on the pavement. The hot plastic bumper of a sedan pressed into my spine as I tilted my head back and squeezed my eyes shut. My heart pounded. I felt like I couldn't breathe. Sweat dripped along my forehead, and I could feel my shirt clinging to me in every spot it shouldn't have. My hands began to tremble.

"Fuck," I muttered to myself as I clutched my chest, "C'mon, not now…"

An anxiety attack started to rumble through me. Tears began to build up in my eyes and burn through my eyelids. The sun beamed onto my face and soaked my vision in red as I squeezed my eyes shut tighter. My breathing quickened, and my chest grew tense. I clenched my jaw as sharp, throbbing pains radiated through my head and chest.

"Get it together, Melony," I grumbled to myself as I slammed my fist against my chest and groaned. "You can't fucking do this right now."

I sucked in the humid air and slowly pushed out deep lungs full until the pressure in my chest finally dissipated. I felt all the tension in my body release and my muscles relax. Soreness flooded through me, and my eyes began to vibrate with a searing pain. I tilted my head down and slowly opened my eyes to a squint. White light and red spots filled my vision. The sunlight caused my head to pound harder and everything around me looked like an over-exposed photograph. The throbbing of my heartbeat pressed against the inside of my skull.

Whomp. Whomp. Whomp.

A shadow slowly overcame me, allowing my vision a moment to recover. The white light faded, and my surroundings became clearer, yet my eyes felt as if they were being stabbed from the inside of my skull. A voice echoed from the shadow that drifted over me and cracked through the throbbing of my brain.

"Don't fucking move," a deep southern drawl commanded.

As I peered up toward the voice through a squint, I was greeted by the barrel of a shotgun aimed right between my eyes. The man behind it wore a ratty cap. The beard that covered the rest of his face was scraggly and peppered with grays. He wore an unbuttoned flannel over a sweat-stained t-shirt. His jeans were covered in stains, and the work boots he wore were lined with a wrinkled layer of silver duct tape. The panic I had just soothed myself from began to rise again, and I started to forget about the searing pain in my eyes and pressure in my head.

"Take the bag off and hand it over," the raspiness of his voice reminded me of Mr. Parker who smoked half a pack a day while he worked on his wood projects.

Although the man spoke his demands, I couldn't move. My gaze darted around him, wildly wide, as I tried to push myself further back into the bumper of the car behind me. I felt like a wild animal trapped in a cage looking around for an exit. I needed to flee. I couldn't push myself away, and I didn't see Jonas anywhere.

My eyes met with the tunnel placed in front of me. I ran my gaze down the barrel until I met the man's eyes. Under the shadow of his hat, I could see the whites of his eyes widen as he stared down the barrel back at me. He looked as if he had just realized something, some key detail I hadn't noticed. Maybe I looked like someone he once knew, or maybe he realized he was aiming a *fucking shotgun* at my head. Unprompted, he began to lower his weapon.

I flinched as he held out his hand and took a step closer. The smell of his musk hit me like bricks. Cedar, sweat, and cigarettes. He inched forward with his hand out as if I were a rabid and that I might bite. I pushed myself back against the bumper trying to escape his touch until it began to hurt my spine. My feet scraped at the loose gravel and concrete and slipped out from under me causing me to lurch to the side and scrape my hand on the pavement as I attempted to catch myself.

The man blinked as he watched me struggle before he took a steady step backward and gave me space. Something in his brain had clicked while he looked at me, and I was trying to decipher what it was when he spoke again.

"Sorry I scared you," he grumbled.

He sounded embarrassed with a twinge of guilt and shame that he had threatened me. I remained silent; my eyes never left his face even as my hand began to feel damp and warm pressed against the hot ground. The tiny pebbles and chunks of pavement began to burn as they pierced into my palm. I was most likely bleeding; I could feel the light prickle of the blood and the stinging of freshly scraped skin, but I didn't dare look away from him.

Instead, I stared.

He backed away. Just a few more steps. He swung the gun over his shoulder with a strap attached to the stock and leaned back against a truck. We eyed each other. I watched each movement and tick of his jaw as he phantom-chewed and the way he picked at the stitching on the front pocket of his jeans. His eyes never left me; I could feel them boring into my skin, violating me. He saw something that I couldn't see, or rather *someone*. You don't stare at someone like that unless they look familiar, or you're deciding your next move.

Finally, after a few minutes of listening to the summer insects trill, he spoke.

"Your buddy is just over there," he jerked his head in the direction behind me, "he might be out for a bit longer, but you can go sit with him if you'd like."

My head snapped back as I gazed behind me and spotted Jonas's feet sticking out from behind a vehicle way down the lane of traffic.

"Oh, God," I gasped to myself as I shot up, lunged forward, and tripped on my size-too-big sneakers as I raced over to his body lying on the hot concrete.

I quickly hit the ground next to Jonas. My bare knees scraped the rough road, and I felt the familiar stinging of sweat and dirt in a wound. I glared back at the man. He stood still, staring and watching with eyes squinted against the sun that peeked around his hat's brim. His jaw ticked, but he didn't shift. I ignored his gaze and turned back to Jonas.

His curls clung to his face with sweat and spread along the pavement in a halo around his head as the sun beat down on him. His caramel cheeks had grown pinker as the sun kissed him. He looked angelic like a painting of a sleeping saint. I grabbed his hand in mine and gently patted his face with my other before pushing the curls away from his eyes and calling for him to wake up. His skin was tacky with sweat and small drops of red began to freckle his face the more I touched him. I flipped my hand over and stared down at the dirt and red that filled the creases and wrinkles of my palm. Pieces of torn white skin were scraped off in jagged lines and small dots and indentations abrased the heel of my palm. As the breeze whisked by and Jonas's sweat mingled with the cuts, my hand began to sting and tremble from the adrenaline coursing through my veins. I turned back to the man. He remained in the same place but gazed off into the distance in the opposite direction.

I wouldn't leave Jonas here, and this man could tell. He would wait.

I sighed and pulled my legs out from underneath me, leaning back against a car as I stared at Jonas. Beads of sweat glistened in the rays of the sun and trailed back into his hairline. His shirt darkened against his chest and lightly rose and fell with each gentle breath he released. I squinted up at the sun as it glared down on us. I had to get Jonas out of this heat, but I wouldn't be able to drag his dead weight into the shade on my own.

I examined the cars around me before standing and taking a closer look at each vehicle I passed. I kept Jonas in my peripheral and didn't hesitate to spare every other glance in the direction of the strange man. I peered at him through windshields and reflections.

He remained leaning against the same pick-up. His head switched from left to right slowly as he observed the world around him. His demeanor came off as if he was keeping guard over something. Over us?

Something about how he looked at me was unsettling. Every look he sent my way made a knot twist in my gut. It had been so long since we had bumped into people that I often forgot that humans were monsters before monsters existed.

Passing each car nearby, I peeked into the backseats and trunks for a sheet, tarp, or something to drape over Jonas. A new thought after another would pop into my mind with each foot I stepped away from the man; I thought about his motives and how sinister they could be. Each intrusive thought was more grotesque and worrying, but it was what the world had come to, and it piqued my anxiety. But somewhere in me, a rational thought sprung forward. If this man truly meant to harm me, he wouldn't wait for Jonas to wake up. He wouldn't stand there so patiently, jaw ticking and fingers picking at the denim stitches.

I observed him from afar as I finally spotted a thin sheet draped over the backseats of an SUV. I quickly reached into the vehicle, and with a slam of the door and shake of the blanket, I was already making my way back over to Jonas.

I could feel the heat from the road seeping in through the soles of my sneakers which quickened my pace. From the time I had left to now, his face had already grown redder. I rounded the front end of one car, stepped over his body, and popped the hood; then, I walked to the car parked directly ahead and popped the trunk. I spread out the sheet between the hood and trunk laying two corners in each before slamming both shut. With the metallic clang, the sheet pulled tight and created a canopy over Jonas—a childlike fort to protect him from the heat. The light underneath softened into a pastel glow just like how the sun would peek through the curtains in his old bedroom.

I glanced over my shoulder at the man. He watched me. He watched with curiosity, and he gave a simple head nod before looking away as if I had impressed him.

I huffed and lowered myself to the ground to crawl under the canopy and sit next to Jonas. The shade created an immediate coolness and protected us from the sun's harmful rays that beat down overhead. It was a relief to feel the breeze without the scorching heat. I wouldn't take it for granted this time. I relaxed and closed my eyes as the wind gently whistled through the tunnel I had created. The sheet overhead rustled lightly, and the temperature in the shade dropped a few more degrees. I could feel the cool dampness of the sweat on my eyelids as I closed my eyes and felt the air around me. The sudden relaxation almost made me forget that I was being watched.

"C'mon, Jonas," I muttered under my breath as I opened my eyes to glaze over his body. "Wake up."

His breathing remained steady, and the sweat on his face had dried for the most part. I scooted closer and placed a light hand on his chest. His shirt was hot and damp against his skin, and I could feel the soft thuds of his heart beating. The smell of his sweat drifted to me from where I sat. I breathed it in as if this were the last time I would be able to.

I could no longer see the man from my position next to Jonas; I had lost my view of him, but I was much happier with my new view. My worry had shifted from the stranger to Jonas lying in front of me. However, the longer I sat next to him, watching the beads of sweat fade away and the shadows of the canopy shift, the thirstier I grew. Jonas would need water as soon as he awoke after losing so much fluid lying out in the sun. I quickly pulled my bag off my back and dug to the bottom for one of the water bottles from the house. After taking a swig, I screwed the cap tightly and placed the bottle next to my feet.

First aid training for my teaching job taught me a few useful skills I fortunately never had to use in the classroom; Heimlich, CPR, treating minor wounds, and the useful tip to never give an unconscious person water. I knew enough about how to assist with seizures and asthma attacks as well as handling allergic reactions, but most of those procedures handled calling emergency services first. We didn't have that luxury now, so it fell into my hands to teach Jonas and retrain myself for such situations.

"If we're going to be here any longer," the man called out with a huff of breath, "we need to find somewhere less exposed."

"I won't leave him," I shouted back.

He sighed before his duct-taped boots shuffled toward me. His clunky footsteps grew closer until his shadow hovered above me, casting deeper darkness over the sheet. I could see his boots at the end beside Jonas's feet before his hand reached down and calloused fingers gripped the edge of the sheet. Suddenly, sunlight washed over us as he yanked on the cover. He tossed the sheet to the ground and stepped over Jonas. With a grunt and grumbly groan, he leaned down, grabbed the back of Jonas's neck with one hand, and began to roughly rub his other hand against Jonas's chest in a circle. He grumbled quietly under his heaving huffs of breath as he tried to force Jonas awake.

"What do you want from us?" I asked as I could sense the frustration and annoyance radiating from him in rippling waves.

"I don't want anything but to get out of here," he huffed.

"So," I glared a hole through the back of his head, "I'm just to believe that you came to a better sense of judgment? That you aren't the same man who knocked Jonas out and stole our shit? Not the same guy who just pointed a *fucking gun* at my head?"

His hand paused over Jonas's chest as he turned to me with wild eyes and a smirk. He appeared almost curious and playful.

"Quite a mouth on you, *little lady*."

"Fuck you," I spat out, "You can leave. I'll stay with him until he wakes up, and then we'll be on our way, far from you."

"Fine by me," he chuckled and sighed in a way that said I was clueless before he turned his attention back to Jonas and continued, "but you're heading into the city. The Grays are more active down that way. I can bet my ass that y'all won't make it to that bridge. That's where you're going, right?"

I hesitated. "Why do you say that? What's wrong with the bridge?"

"Military blockades," he informed, "They tried to shut everyone in, but it got overrun. It's like a feeding ground."

"Feeding ground?"

"Yeah, I see groups of them ugly bastards from time to time. The Grays wander 'round mostly when the sun gets high, and then they hide when it gets too dark. I've learned that they can't see too well in the dark, but they've got good senses. Ain't no way y'all makin' it to the edge of the city before you're dead."

"You study them? The *Grays*?" I asked curiously.

He only shrugged before we both fell silent, and Jonas began to groan and mumble. I lurched forward and gripped his hand in mine as he reached up with his other hand toward the back of his head. His eyes slowly opened to a pained squint as he winced.

"Melony?" he rasped.

"I'm here."

Slowly, his eyes grew wider as he glanced around at his surroundings. When he spotted the man standing above him, his eyes widened, and he jumped forward. Their skulls almost collided with one another.

"Whoa there, Jonas," the man spoke.

The way he had said Jonas's name disturbed me. I had been the only person to say it in so long that hearing it uttered from someone else's lips felt wrong. It felt like something only I could say.

"Hey, hey," I soothed as I gently squeezed his hand, "we need to be leaving, and this man is going to help us."

Jonas gazed up at me in confusion as he returned my squeeze. My hand began to tingle and burn, but I pushed the stinging pain away and kept my eyes locked on him. The confusion written on his face was noticeable, and I could feel his pulse racing through my hands clasped around his. He glanced at the man, then back at me. I could sense his trust in me growing as I stared into his deep dark eyes.

"Okay, well," the man grunted as he stood up straight and took a few paces backward, "Jonas. Melony. I'm Nolan. Shall we get movin'?"

16

Melony

We walked for over an hour. Nolan led the way while Jonas and I fell behind as I tended to him and helped him gather himself. He walked slowly in step with me. It was odd to not be trailing behind him but comforting to walk by his side.

"Are you feeling any better?" I asked.

"Feeling the same as the last three times you asked, Mel," he angrily squinted at the sky and winced before probing his temples with his index fingers, "My head is still throbbing, and the heat isn't helping."

"Is there a knot on your head?"

He reached up and touched the back of his skull, tangling his fingers in his hair.

"It's a small one. It'll probably go down by tomorrow." He fell silent for a moment before lowering his voice to a whisper, "Melony?"

"Yeah?"

"Do you think we can trust this guy?"

"No," I quickly whispered back, "but he gave our supplies back untouched, and he knows more about the city than we do. I'm not asking you to trust him but trust in me that doing this will help us."

"He made us leave the bikes," he paused and glanced at Nolan. "If we need to get out of here quickly, I'm not sure I can do it on foot."

I reached for his hand. "We'll be okay. Within another day or two, when you're recovered and we know a little more about the area and where we're headed, we'll be back on the road. I'll even go the extra mile and come back for the stupid bikes."

He lightly chuckled and gently squeezed my hand.

Together, we trailed behind Nolan as he guided us. As we walked, I observed him. He remained silent our entire course; he never engaged in conversation, but he looked around as if he were waiting for someone. His jaw would tick, and his head would turn. The gun clattered against one of the bags he had offered to carry. Each heavy step was followed by the rattle of the stock and a zipper hitting against one another. He didn't speak to us; he didn't tell us what roads to take or where we were going; he just expected us to follow at every turn. I began to question if he even knew we were following him or if he was so engrossed in his own thoughts to notice.

Every so often he would roll his shoulders and adjust how the straps of the bag sat. He would take a wider step and pick at the top of his jeans. Tufts of his hair poked from beneath the back of his hat and dripped sweat onto his neck.

After moving off the traffic-clogged road, we turned down a few side roads until we ran into a more up-kept outer city town. Neighborhoods were packed together; houses were close and only separated by thin alleyways and fenced in chain-link. The street corners were littered with one-way signs and pedestrian crossings. The stop lights that were posted along the main road had turned into stop signs covered in spray paint. Small convenience stores and boutique shops were sprinkled on either side of the street.

Jonas and I had been through towns like this before, but this one was surprisingly well-maintained. The streets were clean, and the cars that were once on the road had been pushed to the curb as if they were parked there all along. I could only tell they had been moved by the oil patches that stained the pavement where they once had sat. Some cars had even been pushed at the entrances of streets with dumpsters to create some form of blockade. It seemed that every other street was blocked off. Someone had created a new map.

I watched as Nolan bent down and picked up an old Styrofoam cup that had blown into the street.

"Did you do all of this?" I asked him as he tossed the cup into an old barrel-like bin on the sidewalk.

"I tried to keep it as clean as possible," he replied, "It's more sanitary and more like home when it doesn't look abandoned."

"And the blocked off roads?"

"I mapped out everywhere I would ever need to go and blocked the other streets. I don't need to use them, and it keeps unwanted people out."

"That's pretty smart, but seems like a lot of work," Jonas pitched in, "How long have you been here? Do you live in this neighborhood or just visit here for comfort?"

"I've lived here since the first few months after Grays started showin' up. I don't ever plan on leaving."

The ghost town was comforting in a way. It gave insight into what kind of person Nolan was. I felt like I was walking through a past life that wanted to be kept alive. He cared enough to put in the work.

I wandered and drifted away from Jonas and Nolan toward the sidewalk. I heard their footsteps continuing behind me as I approached and peered into the windows of some old shops. Some stores had white lines, or an X, painted on the glass panes. From what I could tell, that was Nolan's sign that these buildings were condemned and beyond repair. However, other stores looked brand new as I peered through the windows. Aside from minor drywall damage and broken windows, it felt like people were still working inside.

I cupped my hands over my face and peeked into another store. The sign above the door had been damaged, but the stickers, decals, and well-placed advertising on the windows told me it was a bookstore. As I gazed into the building through the dirty glass, I saw how much attention this store had gotten compared to others.

Shelves upon shelves were stocked full of books. The floor looked freshly swept, and everything else was neatly dusted. Notebooks, stationery, and other merchandise lined the walls near the register. The inventory was well organized, some books appeared as if they had just come freshly out of a storage box in the back. In a far corner, a small lounge area with four chairs sat in a semi-circle. A small round coffee table sat in the middle of the array stacked high with books; a few had been left open as if the reader had stopped mid-page.

I walked over to the door and cautiously pulled it open. A tiny bell above the door jingled in a high-pitched tone, and I was immediately greeted with the sweet smell of paper and old books. I could also smell a faint perfume as if a candle had been lit within the last few hours. I nearly expected someone to call out from beyond the shelves and welcome me in; instead, the bell lightly jingled again as the door softly closed behind me. As I stepped deeper into the store, I ran my fingers along the front counter and shelves. No dust.

The afternoon sun illuminated the entire room in a calming and heavenly glow. Even if there had been electricity, this store wouldn't need it. The light pouring in gave the place life and energy I didn't think I'd ever see again.

I slowly made my way down the rows of shelves, admiring titles I had once read and ones I had been meaning to get to before the world ended. As I neared the back of the store, I gazed up at a sign that read "Young Readers" in a playful font. In a corner, a tall coat rack filled with hand puppets stood next to a small bookshelf. A chair between the rack and shelf faced the center of a cute, book-shaped rug.

I used to have a similar reading area set up in my classroom. At the beginning of the month, students would vote on a book they'd want to read together. We would spend our free time during classes reading. When we had finished the book together, the kids would be quizzed and graded on how well they paid attention. It wasn't a massive part of their grade but gave me an overall insight into what books or genres each student liked the most. During special events, like spirit weeks, I would sometimes stay after school to do a reading for the students I didn't get the pleasure of teaching directly. I'd even take time off my weekends to volunteer at the public library for book readings. Reading to the children was one of my favorite parts of teaching.

I felt a pit growing in me the longer I stared at the rug. I tried to force it down but couldn't shake the sadness and pain that ached in me. I gazed at the puppets on the rack with pity and sympathy for the lives they once lived and the adventures they once traveled. I mourned with them. I tried to remember the last time I had sat down and read a book. Surely, it was for the children in class, but I couldn't remember.

Quietly, the bell above the door rang. As my head snapped in that direction, the air rushing in chilled over a dampness that streaked my cheeks. I hadn't even noticed I had been crying. I quickly wiped my face with the back of my wrist while Jonas's head bobbed over the shelves as he walked toward me.

"Thought I lost you for a second there," he chuckled, "You didn't say anything, just disappeared on me."

"Yeah, sorry," I sniffled, "I just saw all the books."

He eyed me before spinning around and checking out the shelves. "It smells good in here," he said as he ran his fingers along the spine of a book before plucking it from its spot on the shelf. He smiled at the cover as he turned it over. "I remember this one."

He flipped the book over to show me the cover of *Looking for Alaska* by John Green. A book I had read a very long time ago.

"I remember I read this one in middle school because I saw you reading it one day in class. I don't know if I did it because I wanted you to talk to me about it, or if it was because I saw how emotional and attentive you were to it. I checked out a copy that same day and went home and read it," he chuckled and flipped the book over to read the back. "Cried my eyes out over this thing and ended up being too embarrassed by it to even discuss it with you."

He slipped the book back into the empty slot on the shelf.

"I didn't know you read it," I said softly.

He shrugged. "I rarely ever saw you cry or tear up when we were kids. You could break your leg or split your head open and wouldn't shed a single tear, but a book," he playfully scoffed, "you'd read a book and look like your entire world was caving in around you. I wanted to know what you were feeling."

I opened my mouth to reply, but the bell above the door cut me off. Nolan stood in the doorway and eyed us. He scanned the room before his gaze finally landed on me.

"Take anything you'd like," he said, "Do you read often?"

"It's been a while," I replied as I moved around Jonas and continued to scan the shelves allowing my eyes to flick back up to Nolan. "I used to teach, so reading was a part of the job, but obviously my lifestyle had to change. Do you spend a lot of time here? I saw the table in the back. Looks like you're an avid reader."

He nodded. "I spend most of my days here, even live just a few buildings down to be closer. I'd take my daughter to the library on the weekends when she was just a lil' girl."

"You have a daughter?" Jonas asked.

There was a hesitation that followed the question. Nolan's eyes flicked away for a moment before answering.

"Had," Nolan corrected, matter-of-factly stating as if it did not faze him; but as Jonas looked away in silence, I watched Nolan stare him down, jaw ticking.

The store fell silent once more, and I turned back to the shelves after giving him a sympathetic smile. After a moment, the bell went off again followed by Nolan's clunky footsteps as he walked toward the table in the back of the store. I could hear him closing and restacking books into new piles as he looked for a specific title. I looked up just in time to catch him marching my way. His sincere smile was plastered as he handed me a thick book from his stack.

196

"Here," he kindly held the book in front of me and waited for me to take it. "This was Emily's favorite as a girl. You've probably read it before as a teacher and all."

I gently took the beautiful leatherbound collector's edition, *Alice's Adventures in Wonderland & Other Stories*. I opened the cover and gazed at the pages and illustrations in awe. It was the most used and cared-for book I had ever seen.

"Are you sure?"

He nodded. "Take it. It wasn't this copy specifically, but this is the one I could find when I needed it." He slipped around me and headed for the door. "Take your time in here. When you're done, I'm in the dark brick building at the corner. It's just four buildings down."

"Thank you," I called back as the ball rang and he stepped onto the sidewalk.

Jonas walked up behind me and peered over my shoulder at the pages in my hand.

"Well, that was quite nice of him," he said before he kissed my temple and gave my arm a light squeeze.

"Yes," I replied as I flipped through the pages, hypnotized by the contents. "It was."

The days that followed were filled with peace. Our brief time here had already relaxed me beyond what I thought capable. We spent a lot of your time lounging in silence, growing used to each other's company.

The small two-bed, one-bath apartment Nolan occupied had just enough space for all of us. It was well-furnished and clean. Nolan's muskiness filled every inch of the place combined with the light-perfumed candle he often lit to relax. It wasn't horrible; it was quite homey. After the first few hours inside, I came to enjoy the atmosphere.

Nolan had bookshelves stacked plum full, a soft cushiony couch, and a bed for us to sleep. His apartment was equipped with food stores: MRE's from local abandoned military posts, canned goods from nearby shops, and he even had hooked up his own rainwater system from the roof for hygienic purposes. The man was a survivalist and was inviting us to stay; it was an offer we couldn't refuse.

Most mornings, he would disappear for hours on end and return when the sun set high in the afternoon sky. He wouldn't tell us where he went, and he was usually gone before we woke up.

There was one time when I thought about waking up earlier and asking to join him, but I decided against it. He had been alone since the beginning, and I began to assume that having people in his home may have been overwhelming. He also may have enjoyed solitude and needed space from our company.

I rolled out of bed and slipped into a pair of army pants and a T-shirt Nolan had found for me during one of his early morning outings. As I got dressed, Jonas peacefully slept. I tried not to make a sound or disturb him; seeing him this angelic and well-rested was a rarity I hadn't witnessed in quite some time. Even when we previously had a roof over our head, he still never slept this well. It was simply another reason to be grateful to Nolan.

I quietly left the room and began to walk down the hall when I heard movement inside the living room. I rounded the corner and was surprised to find Nolan standing in front of one of his shelves browsing through titles.

"Good morning," I greeted.

He turned and smiled at me over his shoulder, "Good morning."

"I didn't expect to see you here; you're usually gone by now."

He placed whatever book he was holding back on the shelf before fully facing me. He looked cleaner, wearing a new pair of jeans and a t-shirt with a business logo from a shop I had seen on the strip.

With a smile on his face, he spoke, "I was actually wonderin' if you'd wanna join me today. Just a simple walk, or I could give you a tour. You've been here almost a week now and haven't really had the chance of seeing the town."

"I would love that," I replied with a soft smile, "Let me leave a note for Jonas. I don't want to wake him. This is probably the most he's slept in at least a year."

Nolan furrowed his brows. "You guys haven't settled or stopped? Been on the road this whole time?" he paused but not long enough for a response, "I know you said you're from Brownsburg and that you stopped recently. Did you not stay anywhere nice?"

I thought back to the house—the room with the gaping hole in the ceiling, the corpses, and the black blood that streaked the hall. I remembered how just days ago I wished to go back, to stay there for what was left of our lives. Knowing Nolan's life and community was one way I could be living, all those thoughts seemed childish now. I was dreaming of achieving something lower than what was possible.

"There is nowhere nice," I replied, still lost in thought before correcting myself, "Oh, except here, of course."

Nolan's jaw ticked as he nodded in understanding and walked over to a side table at the end of the couch. He pulled open the drawer and picked up a notepad and pen to hand me. I quickly jotted down a simple note for Jonas—I let him know I would be gone and not to worry—and then quietly rushed to the room and placed the note on my pillow. He didn't shift much as he slept, so it was a convenient place where he would see it when he woke.

Leaving the room, I grabbed my half-empty backpack with only some water, snacks, and my photo album stuffed inside before grabbing my bat that was propped in the corner of the room. I left silently, and the bedroom door clicked shut behind me. Nolan stood near the front door with his backpack that sagged low and heavy on his shoulders. I quickly slipped on my boots and joined him.

The apartment building was small with only three floors and four apartments per floor. The other rooms remained locked, and although clean, a faint smell inked into the hall. A smell of death that had lingered since the beginning I would guess. Nolan had explained to us that he never checked on the occupants. He did not know whether they were still inside, but he knew they were dead. He had told us that one of his next projects was to bury them, but he had too much on his agenda as it was.

We walked down the hall and passed the staircase. Instead, we headed toward the window at the end of the hall. Nolan had also informed us that during his observations of "The Grays," as he called them, he noticed that they seemed to be unable to climb straight up. He had told us a story about how he watched a few of them struggling to get at a raccoon as it climbed up into a tree. After his discovery, he barricaded the staircase and only used the fire escape as his main entrance and exit into the building. Nolan had already taught us so much new information we had no idea about. Jonas and I had spent so much time avoiding the creatures that we didn't realize studying them would've been beneficial.

Nolan forced the window upward and crawled through the opening. He then held his hand through the gap and assisted me out into the fresh air before shutting the window. Quietly, I followed him down the ladder. As soon as my feet hit the pavement of the alleyway, I could feel a knot of worry begin to twist in my stomach. I hesitated and stared up at the window overhead.

"We'll be back before he even wakes up," Nolan spoke from behind me trying to soothe my nerves, "He'll be okay."

"I know," I mumbled as I glanced over my shoulder, "I just haven't been away from him in two years. It feels strange."

Nolan nodded in understanding before he stepped closer, grabbed the ladder's bottom rung, and began to push the ladder upward. I pushed with him to the best of my ability until the ladder was high enough off the ground and locked in place. We headed out of the alley and made it to the sidewalk before Nolan spoke again.

"Is there anywhere you would want to go?" he asked.

"I'm not sure," I replied as I squinted at the morning sun rising, "I think I just needed some fresh air. I know I'm not your prisoner, but I can't help but feel locked away and trapped inside."

He chuckled.

"I think it's because we've been out in the open for so long. Maybe I've grown claustrophobic."

He nodded. "I don't blame you for feeling that way. It's a big change."

"I appreciate you inviting me out."

"Don't worry about it," he brushed me off, "I actually needed some help today so I'm taking advantage of you."

I smiled and gazed around the shops as we walked past them. We were passing the bookstore, and Nolan did not seem interested. I wasn't familiar with the streets or shops past this point and began to wonder what the day had in store for me.

"What do you need help with?" I asked with furrowed brows.

He gestured to his pack. "Part of a ceiling fell in one of the boutiques a few days ago. I didn't notice until yesterday on my walk and didn't have the tools at the time. But I have 'em now, so I'm gonna spend a lot of the day cleaning that mess up, but there's somewhere else I wanna show you first."

"And we'll be back soon?"

"Soon enough," he replied with a nod, "but if at any time you want to head back and check on Jonas, feel free."

I thanked him with a nod and fell silent as I listened to the distant songs of the birds, and the buzzing of insects in the far trees. The breeze was light and whisked through the alleyways and streets. I began to fall a few steps behind Nolan as he rounded a corner and led the way through one of the car blockades into a small section of houses. The sound of insects grew louder as the trees grew closer, and the houses suddenly stopped. The street stopped at a dead end straight into an overgrown field tall with yellow and green grasses. Towards the middle of the field, I could see the faded colored plastic that made up a playground. Nolan stopped at the edge of the road and stared into the grass.

"What do you see?" he asked.

I looked at him, confused, then stared back at the field.

"What do I see?" I repeated to myself, "I see grass."

He chuckled to himself before he began to clarify, "No. For the future. If you were to live here and decide what goes here, what would it be?"

I stared at the grass as it swayed in the morning breeze. The rustling sounded like the faint ripples of a creek, and the sun bounced off the blades creating a wave like the ones that wash the ocean shore. I was staring at the physical form of peace, but the playground that peaked over the tall grass kept drawing my eyes. I could almost hear the faint laughter of children who once spent their days here. I looked at the field and I saw the people of the past.

The past was long over though, and this needed to be a spot for the future. It could be a community hub if Nolan ever intended to find more people out there to fill this town. This park needed to be somewhere where everyone could come together in the future. It was the perfect amount of land to sustain at least a dozen people.

"What about a garden?" I suggested as I looked to him for a reaction. "This could be a community garden. You have the space here to help people."

He tilted his head and stared out into the grass for a minute in silence before giving a small nod.

"It's a good idea," he complimented, "but I'm only one man, and this is a lot of ground to cover."

"You could always start small." I felt the need to fight for this.

Peaceful and away from the hub and clutter of the shops yet a close enough walk to the center of the community made it a perfect space.

"It would need to be mowed, tilled, fenced in. I'd have to find seeds and make sure the birds didn't get at 'em," Nolan began to point out every inconvenience he could think of.

"No," I interrupted, "You have so many shops here and nearby. There must be a hardware store or something to find the right equipment. You have a bookstore where you could learn all the knowledge you need to even start."

He paused and thought about my rebuttal before opening his mouth to counter. "But the seeds?"

I hesitated, but then an idea clicked.

"It was spring when everything stopped. I remember I was prepping my students for the end of the school year. Around mid-spring, hardware stores and outdoor garden centers start selling seed packets. You can start your seeds indoors for the first few weeks until they sprout. In the meantime, you work on this," I informed before I gestured widely to the field, "It could work. I can help."

"You would help?" He cocked a brow.

"I mean," I paused, "only if you invited us to stay. I wouldn't want to overstep, but I have a little experience. Not much with vegetables, but with flowers and herbs. I gardened with my neighbor growing up."

We both fell silent as I waited for him to respond, but he did not speak. He picked at the seam of his pocket, turned, and began to walk back down the way we came. I watched him leave me behind as his jaw ticked and his fingers picked. I turned back to the field for a final look before jogging to catch up.

"I'm sorry," I began to fumble out excuses to save us; I couldn't have Nolan kick us out—we needed this place. "I didn't mean to pressure you into deciding. I know we've already stayed past our welcome, and we will leave if you want us to, but you are living in a paradise. One big enough to share."

He led the way back through the blockade and rounded the corner. He didn't respond, and I began to grow more worried by the second. I felt as if I had talked myself into a hole and ruined Jonas and I's chance at a real life. We would be homeless again, bouncing from place to place and surviving off whatever we could scrounge up.

Nolan steadied his pace down the sidewalk until he reached the bookstore. He reached out for the door and held it open, then gestured for me to walk inside with a sly smile on his face.

"What—What are we doing? You don't want us to leave?" I blurted as I gawked at him.

"We're looking for books about gardening," he spoke with a chuckle, "You don't have to leave. You can't be leaving me to do all this work by myself."

17

Jonas: After

Melony waited patiently as I pried open the front door against the chaotic pile of furniture; we had moved just enough to squeeze out the door, and I slipped into the daylight. Before waving Melony out onto the porch, I scanned the yard and driveway. I noticed the stillness that had once filled the air was long gone, and after being trapped inside for days, I could only notice how loud the world was even without the distant sound of cars on the main road and the faint droning of planes overhead. After a few seconds of waiting, Melony squeezed through the door and closed it behind her.

"The birds and bugs are still singing," she whispered.

"What?"

"They seem to know when those things are nearby. The birds aren't quiet," she informed.

I listened and heard the tranquil sounds of local fauna. They sang loudly against the quiet rustling of the trees blowing in the morning breeze. I hadn't noticed if what she said had been true, but I trusted her. Melony often noticed the minute details I overlooked. She heard sounds I didn't, and she could point out the tiniest differences in the world around us. She was observant and intuitive.

"Then, we should be fine to check things out. If what you say is true, we should have an early warning system if danger is coming." I glanced at her over my shoulder as I thought aloud.

She only shrugged and left more unanswered questions to diminish the comfort I had been building.

I cautiously began to step off the porch and gripped the crowbar tighter in my palm as I watched for any minuscule movement around us. The further I stepped into the yard, the more I began to pay attention to the songs around me. After Melony's observation, I couldn't help but notice how loud the animals were. It was like some strange form of selective listening or super hearing. The sounds echoed around with every footstep I made as if I was disturbing some field of peace. I felt out of place—as if nature was screaming for me to leave—but I pushed forward.

Once we reached the middle of the yard closer to the driveway, I could smell the faint scent of iron and rotted meat as the human remains that painted the property heated up in the beaming sun.

"Oh, God." Melony raised a hand to her nose. "That's horrible. I might be sick."

"Try not to look."

"I don't know how you expect me to do that when it's... *everywhere*," she choked on her words as she held back vomit.

I felt my own stomach begin to churn as the smell grew worse, and I could see the dark red and black of dried blood that had seeped into the ground. I averted my eyes.

"I think we're safe enough to check things out," I said as I gazed around the cars parked in front of the house until I spotted the sedan I searched the other day.

I had left the backpack I had scavenged inside the vehicle. My mind drifted to the maps and articles from the console that remained tucked inside the bag. As Melony stepped away and began to walk up the street in the other direction, I headed directly to the car. I opened the door and quickly tucked the pages deeper into the bag before slinging it over my shoulder and checking for Melony. It felt like I was keeping a secret, but I didn't want to worry her about the conspiracies of mad people, and reading those articles was something I was greatly interested in since finding them. I wanted to know if the pages held any possible answers. I hoped they would give us the answers and relief we'd been seeking. There was so much I didn't know about what was happening, and I feared it would close us off from the rest of the world.

My eyes snapped up as I heard a car door slam.

"It feels wrong searching these cars," Melony shouted to me as if she had no care of what could possibly hear us.

"*Ay, Dios mio,*" I muttered, "keep your voice down."

She rolled her eyes and walked closer to me as she continued, "These people could come back."

"They won't," I said, "and if they do, we'll apologize or tell them it was someone else."

I slammed the car door and huffed out the humid air. The clouds overhead were graying; Melony would say it would be storming soon. If not today, then tomorrow. I had learned a lot from her, and it would surely explain the stickiness in the air. I watched as she placed her hand on her hip and shielded her eyes with the other as she looked into the clouds.

"It's quiet," she muttered, "not like scary quiet, but there's no planes. No cars. It's like the world stopped."

"I would say it did," I replied, and she glanced at me.

"What do you mean by that?"

I gestured to the mess around us. "People don't just abandon their vehicles and go on foot unless they have no other option. These people were desperate to escape. I'm surprised they didn't come knocking on the front door to be let in."

"Maybe they did…" She bit the inside of her lip as she looked over her shoulder at the backed-up traffic behind her.

"Maybe they did," I agreed as I eyed the distance from our front door to the street.

These people likely had sought refuge and pounded on our front door that first night; we just didn't hear them.

"Do you think more people turned into..." she trailed off as she stared at the rotting pile of flesh and blood on the drive.

Yes, I thought, but did not answer her as I looked away. If what we saw had been started by some illness—the "not flu" mentioned in the papers—and the ambulance overturned on the highway was the first sign, then whatever that man turned into had most likely already caused mass infection and spread within the city. Indianapolis was just beyond the highway pictured on the news. I had seen enough movies to know that panic and hysteria in these situations did not bode well for the population. Whoever, or whatever, was in that ambulance had been infected; we saw the gray blur on the television that matched the appearance of the creature we saw attack that man. If one of those *things* had already made it so far out of the city within less than a single day, there was no telling how much disrepair and death had fallen upon the inner workings of Indianapolis.

"I guess we can't really get the car out of this jam to drive to Mom's, could we?" Melony asked as I left her first question unanswered.

"We could walk," I suggested.

"Being out in the open isn't really safe, is it?" she asked as she turned to me.

"I know a shortcut," I said as I pointed to the woods across the road that lined one of my neighbor's properties. "Do you actually think I took the main roads all those times I snuck out to see you?"

"I didn't think you walked," she retorted sarcastically with furrowed brows as if the question shouldn't have needed an answer.

"If I rode my bike, my parents would probably notice I was gone, wouldn't they?" I said with her matched attitude.

She rolled her eyes at my playful tone with a smile before gesturing for me to lead her home. I followed orders and walked across the street toward the trees. Before stepping through the weeds, I glanced over my shoulder at her and saw her clench her fists at her side and release a deep breath to steady herself. Her nerves rattled her, and it wasn't until she opened her mouth to speak that I stepped over the bramble and weeds into the woods.

With each step, I pushed aside branches and thorny bushes with my crowbar allowing us to find our footing. The woods were denser than they had been years ago when I used to walk this shortcut. I could already feel the prickling and itching of tiny leaves and bugs beginning to crawl up my legs.

"Are you sure you want to do this?" Melony asked.

I was sure she was feeling the same irritation of bugs and grass against her sticky skin as I was, causing her to want to turn around. I could tell we both questioned if this discomfort was worth what we'd end up discovering. We both wished to be in the comfort of our home.

"I want you to get your answers," I spoke over my shoulder before mumbling and finishing the thought to myself, "at least some of them."

We walked deeper and deeper into the thicket until I could finally see the backside of a white house peeking through the trees. We were in the homestretch and almost walking directly into Melony's old neighborhood—more specifically her neighbor's backyard. As I pushed my way through the overgrown brush and out onto the other side, I held open the branches for Melony to step through. Upon her exit, she jumped and shook and flailed her body as if she were covered in spiders.

"You're going to have to check me for ticks later," she grumbled as she pinched the neck of her t-shirt and began to wildly shake at the fabric.

"Gladly," I chuckled as I bumped into her shoulder and took the first few steps through the yard.

"You used to sneak through the Fittz' backyard?" she asked with the realization of where we were. "How are you not dead? I'm quite sure Lawrence owns a gun."

"He knew," I chuckled, "Mr. Fittz would be smoking on the back porch most nights when I came poking my head out of the woods. It was like a mutual agreement to keep each other's secrets. Though, that first time I came through here, I did think he was going to shoot me."

"I thought he gave up smoking a long time ago."

"That's what we wanted you to think."

She laughed at my small stupid humor, and we kept moving. As we walked through the Fittz' backyard, the curtains were closed over the glass patio door, and a burnt-out cigarette was perched on the rim of a crystal ashtray. He must have been partaking in his nightly routine sometime recently, but the stillness of the curtains in each window gave me a bad feeling. Not even the air conditioning was wistfully blowing through the home, and I began to think that maybe the cigarette had been sitting outside for longer than I wanted to admit.

We rounded the side of the house and saw a scene like that of my neighborhood. The front doors to many of the houses remained open as if the people living there had been in such a rush they didn't care to properly close them. Garage doors were left half-open, and the cars once housed inside were missing. The scene was just as abandoned as it had been at home; the world just got up and left without telling us.

I began to wonder if we were the last ones left. Melony and I appeared to be the final girls that survived all the movies in the horror franchise. We were Jamie Lee Curtis and Sigourney Weaver. Classic survivors. The last ones to make it out alive.

The worst thing was that I didn't know what was going on. There was nothing that could give me answers or satisfaction. No updates were on the news, and if there had been, we had missed them. Some information had to have gone out for so many people to vanish off the face of the earth; Melony and I had been unlucky on the receiving end. There was no other logical explanation for it.

"How did so many people just disappear?" Melony thought aloud, "Where did they go? It doesn't make sense. This must be some fucked up prank, right?"

"I was just thinking the same thing," I mumbled as I gazed up and down the street.

At the end of the street was the cul-de-sac where Melony's childhood home sat. The brick exterior and white pillars that lined the porch of the single-story home already fronted a much nicer appearance than the home I grew up and lived in. As a kid, I never went inside her house much; she would always come over to mine. Even though they fought about it, her mother eventually gave her more freedom or just began to care less about where she was than my parents had. I suppose her mother grew tired of fighting Melony and stopped trying to control her.

Every time I entered her home, I didn't venture beyond the living room out of respect for her mother's feelings toward me, but from what I could remember, the interior was just as nice as the outside had looked.

Melony had already begun to walk down the street and up the drive before I took a step to race after her. She had climbed the front steps and pushed open the front door before I made it to the mailbox. The town we lived in was small, and Melony's neighborhood was safe enough to leave your doors unlocked; it was a strange custom I had never quite grown to understand.

I skipped up the front steps and quickly followed Melony inside. The house was cool; the thermostat was set to seventy degrees—I could see the illuminated screen at the edge of the living room where the hallway began. Melony wandered into the kitchen and fumbled around with a bunch of bananas well into browning on the counter. Must've been days since her mother had been here.

"She isn't home," Melony murmured as she sighed, walked back into the living room, and flopped onto the couch.

I watched her pick up the remote and begin to slam her thumb into the buttons awaiting any signal or response from the television. Her hand trembled as her arm extended out in front of her. I could see her try to be discreet and gather herself, but whatever she was telling herself in her head wasn't working.

"I've never gotten a tour of this place," I spoke up as a distraction.

She turned to me and dropped the remote in her lap.

"All the years we've been friends," I continued with a sigh and placed my hands onto my hips as if I were disappointed, "and I've barely been inside your childhood home. I don't even think I got to see what your bedroom looked like."

A light smile spread over her lips.

"Which room is it?" I asked while walking toward the hall and peeking down at the doors that lined it.

"Good luck finding it," she scoffed and threw her head back against the couch cushion. "Mom redecorated it as soon as I moved in with you."

She picked the remote back up from her lap. She didn't aim it at the TV but only clenched it in her closed fist. My attempt to lighten her mood had failed. I walked around the side of the couch and joined her on the soft cushions. We both sat and stared at the walls—Melony's stare was directed toward blank space while I eyed the décor.

Quite honestly, it was just as sad and beige as I expected it to be. The colors were bland compared to the character my small home had, and the décor was a very modern farmhouse style in a way that looked as if the woman had purchased every "rustic" labeled item from the hobby and craft store. My eyes scanned over silhouette paintings of farm animals, signs that read about being blessed, distressed wood photo frames, and distressed wood furniture.

The one thing that stood out was the end table closest to the entertainment center. It had the widest view of the room, surely you could see it from anywhere you stood, and on it were two framed photos. I got up from the couch and reached for the frames, bringing them back to my seat. Melony didn't seem fazed at my movement, I wasn't entirely sure she looked at all, but I held the photos in my lap.

"I'm surprised your mom has this on display," I chuckled with a great amount of disbelief.

It was no secret that Melony's mother disliked me ever since I was a child. It was only when Melony and I had made ourselves official that she finally began to accept the fact I was a permanent figure in her daughter's life. So, it was to my surprise that one of the only photos on display in the living room was a photo of Melony and me in our caps and gowns that my father had taken on the night of our graduation. We stood hugged together smiling beaming grins at the camera with our diplomas raised over our heads. Our faces were glowing from the evening sun glistening against sweat as we had just sat in the outdoor ceremony for hours on end. I assumed the only reason this photo was on display was because it was the only good-quality photo she had of Melony that night—I just so happened to be in the shot.

The other photo in my lap was a family portrait, one from an extraordinarily long time ago. A younger, and much happier, version of Melony's mother stood next to her husband, and a child Melony cheesed a toothless grin between them.

I never knew much about Mel's father. I knew all that I was told; he was a good man who had killed himself. That was all my brain could come up with as I stared at his photo. His smile seemed so genuine, and if I was right about Melony's age in the photo, it hadn't been but a few years afterward when he took his life.

He looked kind. Dimples formed in his cheeks underneath his squinted eyes as his white teeth beamed into the camera. His hair was dark, and his upper lip was covered in a mustache. He looked like a cop, which might have been a stereotypical description if I knew what his profession had been—but I didn't, and saying he looked like a cop from a 90's sitcom was as accurate a description my brain could muster.

"What was your dad's name?" I asked.

This question seemed to jar her from her trance.

"Where did you get that?" she asked as she leaned over and placed her hand on the corner of the frame.

"It was on the end table over there."

"Wow," she whispered in awe, "that's an old one."

Her index finger gently traced over her own toothless grin and then moved up to her father's cheeks. She stared longingly at the photo, and I gently pushed it into her hands to let her hold it. She gripped the frame without hesitation.

"Joseph," she finally answered, "but I always heard my grandma and mom call him Joe. Mom never talked about him much after he died. I don't know why. I only ever remember him being kind and funny. My grandma would say that even though he wasn't her son, she loved him like one and that he was probably the best man my mother could've found."

"Did you guys ever figure out why he did what he did?"

She placed her hand over the photo while looking up at me. Her brows softly furrowed as if she were trying to remember.

"Grandma said he served in the military before I was born," she replied, "I'm sure he had demons that even mom didn't know about."

The room fell silent, and I gazed at Melony as she admired the photo of her father. She couldn't take her eyes off his face like she was absorbing every detail so she would never forget. It had been such a long time since he had passed, but I didn't doubt that she still felt a pain in her heart at every thought of him. As the reminiscent feeling in the atmosphere began to warm the home, I began to hear an unfamiliar faint noise in the distance.

"Do you hear that?" I asked as I placed a finger over my lips.

A rhythmic *thwump*. Fast and growing increasingly louder.

"Another helicopter?" Melony suggested.

I jumped to my feet and fumbled straight for the front door as I tripped on the coffee table. I swung open the door and heard Melony's footsteps following. As I stepped out onto the porch, the sound was so loud it vibrated the air. I turned up to the blue sky and watched as three helicopters flew overhead. They grew in distance and the sound faded right before two jets blazed through the clouds in the same direction.

"Where are they going?" Melony asked, "What direction is that?"

We stood on the porch shielding our eyes as we stared into the sky waiting for a second round of helicopters or planes to fly through, but nothing came. The world fell quiet, and a pit began to settle in my intestines.

"We should go inside," I said as I felt Melony's trembling hands touch my lower back, "I'm not hearing the birds anymore, Mel."

I stared at the sky for a second longer before turning and trying to usher her back into the comfort of the house, but just as I turned, Melony pointed up at the sky. I didn't need to turn around to see what caught her attention; the reflection of the glass in the front door showed enough.

Flocks of birds began to swarm overhead, flying in the direction the helicopters and jets came from. They moved in waves, from left to right, and swirled in circles like they couldn't decide which direction to go. The squawking was the only sound that echoed through the air as the ground began to shake.

18

Melony

When I stepped into the store, I noticed the floral perfumed scent I had smelled once before had no longer lingered in the air. I still closed my eyes as I inhaled the air around me; my muscles relaxed, and I began to feel strangely at peace. The bookstore felt like an oasis. Time seemed to stand still as soon as I stepped through the threshold. Back before, I probably would've convinced myself it was some sort of magical realm; I would've made up some fantastical story about a magical bookstore to tell my students about in class the next day. However, I also knew the reason the room had the atmosphere it currently did and was affecting me so much. The harsh truth was the world was much different than before. If I had come across this place before the Grays—when life was normal—it would've felt like an ordinary small-town shop.

The bell above the door jingled, and I felt a chill trickle down my spine as I snapped out of my mind. I heard rustling behind me, and once I turned, Nolan's head peeked up from behind the register as he placed a box of used candles in front of me onto the counter.

"Take your pick," he grunted as he pushed up from the floor and dusted his hands off on his jeans. "There're florals, cake-scented, linens—an assortment for whatever mood you're in."

I felt his eyes on me as I gently lifted each glass jar of wax and read the label.

"You scavenge all of these just for this place?"

He shrugged nonchalantly. "Sometimes you need ambience."

I crinkled my nose as I looked over an apple pie scented label.

"What? You don't fancy a sweet treat?"

"Please, if I smell any of these sweets, I might try to eat the candle. Something floral should be fine," I decided as I pushed the box back towards him.

He silently nodded, plucked a purple tinted container from the box, and reached under the counter for a small lighter. I turned around as he flicked the flame on. I felt a sense of serenity within the room as I gazed over the shelves. It was the peace that came over you when you walked into a quiet library, except this silence was beyond what you could imagine. There was no mechanical whirring of the copy machine and printers, no buzz of the fluorescents overhead. There were no quiet whispers along the aisles between teens and friends. This peace came from the emptiness of it all. A library after hours. No employees, no customers, just me and the books.

Nolan stayed quiet. I could barely notice him shuffling around as I flicked through titles in the nature and survival section of the store. We seemed to forget we were in each other's company. It wasn't until the scent of lavender began to travel through the air that one of us finally spoke.

"You said you used to garden?" Nolan's gruff voice echoed from a few shelves over.

My heart skipped at the sudden noise ricocheting off the walls.

"Yeah," I replied, "An older neighbor of mine had a huge flower garden. She helped babysit me when I was young, so I grew up learning about flowers and herbs. It became a minor hobby as I got older."

"You spent a lot of time with her?"

"I did," I sighed and picked a small book from the shelf to add to the pile Nolan and I had been accumulating.

"I take it your parents worked a lot then."

I paused and glanced up over the shoulder-height shelf at him a few aisles down. He gazed at something behind the shelf I couldn't see, likely another book. His hat covered most if not all his face.

"My mom worked in Indy," I answered, "so my grandmother watched me most of my childhood. She and Mrs. Parker were friends."

Nolan returned a gentle nod, but ultimately fell silent again. I returned to the books only for my gaze to be brought back to him after a few short minutes.

"What about your dad?"

This time my eyes met his shaded face as he squinted, awaiting my answer. I glanced back to the book in my hand.

My dad. I hadn't thought about him in quite some time. I wasn't sure I even remembered what he had looked like. I could hardly picture his face anymore.

"He died when I was nine."

"I'm sorry about that," he spoke with such sincerity, "If you don't mind, how'd he die?"

"He—uh—he killed himself," I stammered and bit the inside of my cheek while closing the book in my hands.

Adding the book to the pile, I squeezed my eyes shut and rested my hands against the shelf. Jonas and I tried our hardest to avoid talking about our families. Of course, in instances when our spirits and moods were high enough, we felt comfortable expressing how much we missed them. It was sometimes difficult to avoid the topic. Jonas acted so much like his mother and shared his father's features that sometimes I would bring it up in conversation. He would sometimes do the same to me. He never knew my family as much as I did his, but he knew I was like my mother as much as I hated to admit it.

Although my father had been gone far longer than my mother, the wound sometimes still felt fresh. I had seen his body; I knew he was gone. I never found my mother; she could've still been out there. It was highly unlikely, but I think not knowing made her death feel less real.

Jonas and I had talked before about the pain of losing our families. Even though he didn't lose his parents to the end of the world, we realized that knowing no one in the world was left made the pain that lingered much stronger.

"I'm sorry for your loss." Nolan stacked another book into his mini pile. "I'm guessin' your mom didn't make it through the beginning of all this?"

"I'm not sure," I sighed and blinked away the searing in my eyes. "I can only assume she was trapped in the city when the bombs fell."

"Well, better that than a Gray."

I nodded in silent agreement and reached to the top of the shelf in front of me for the small pile and walked it toward the front counter. I stood at the register and fidgeted with the pile, aligning each book cover to make the stack as straight and even as possible. Sorrow was creeping into my heart as I stared at the scratched countertop and felt the paperback covers chip and flake beneath my nails.

"Sometimes—" Nolan spoke up and ripped me from my trance, "Sometimes it's hard to keep living in a world like this, knowing I've lost everything. Knowing I've lost my lil' girl. I would do anything to have her back."

He approached the counter with his own stack of books and slid them next to mine. He then leaned forward and rested his elbows down.

"What was she like?" I asked.

He sighed and reached for the brim of his hat. He pulled the cap off his head and squeezed the hat in his hands. The hair he revealed was greasy and stringy. It clung to his head as if the hat was still on and curved slightly outward right around his ears.

"She was a light," he spoke with a smile, "Amanda and I had been together since high school and wanted kids for so long. The problem was she had a hard time getting pregnant, but eventually after years of trying, we had my baby girl. We finally had our baby... but Amanda never left the hospital."

"That must've been hard," I murmured, "losing the love of your life and having to take care of something so fragile on your own all in the same day."

"It was the hardest thing I ever had to do," he replied with a nod, "In one tiny second, I was suddenly a single dad. It didn't seem to matter, though, because Emily became a light in my dark world. It was hell raising her on my own, but I wouldn't go back and change anything about it. She grew up to be just like her mother. Looked like her, somehow got her attitude too. She was a lil' rebel, didn't do anything I said. She dated the wrong kind of guys, talked to the wrong type of friends, did the things most teenagers did. Were you ever like that?"

I playfully scoffed. "Oh, all the time. For the longest time, my mom couldn't stand Jonas. She thought he was the bad influence, but it was really me who made all the bad decisions."

He chuckled and continued, "Eventually, Emily grew out of the phase where she lived to make me mad. She became a fine young woman. She graduated top of her class—not valedictorian, but ya know... up there.

She got accepted into a decent college a few states away, graduated and became a child psychologist. I rarely saw her after she graduated, but she called me at least once a week. She called me whenever she needed anything like asking if she should call a plumber or take the car to a mechanic. I missed her more than anything, and I wished every day that I could be there to do those small things for her."

"Sounds like she missed you too."

His eyes met mine, and he wrung his hat in his hands to the point his knuckles were turning white. His eyes were glazed over, glossy and full as he held back tears. He took a deep trembling breath and began to choke on his words. I could only imagine the strain he was feeling on the back of his throat.

"Then, the world ended," he said as he closed his eyes and dropped his head. "She was states away, and I couldn't get to her. She called me and said the city was goin' crazy. She was panicking and packing; I could hear the f—" he stopped and sniffled, "she was so afraid. Then, this loud banging started to come through the phone, like someone was breaking down her door... that was the last thing I heard before the call disconnected."

He paused, and I watched his jaw tick as he looked at the floor beneath him. I could feel his pain radiating from him, his sorrow and heartache leaked out into the air of the bookstore. Tears began to swell in my own eyes at the thought of losing a child.

I had always wanted kids, had always loved them. Their minds were so curious and full of wonder—that's why I became a teacher. However, I felt I was too young to have any of my own. Jonas and I had only ever talked about it once before Day One, and I had decided we weren't ready at the time. Sometimes I told myself he avoided the topic because he didn't want kids; I believed that maybe he didn't want his children to go through the pain he went through when his parents passed. The topic never really came up again. Then the world ended, and there was no room for children in such a horrible place.

"What happened to her? Did you ever find her?" I asked softly.

He nodded and looked up at me. His eyes were red and watery.

"I immediately went to her. Between driving and walking, it took about a week before I got to her house. When I got there," he exhaled a shaky and angry breath, "the door was busted in and hangin' off the hinges. I take it she had been gone for a couple days, bags still half-packed on the bed, trail of black leading right out the front door."

Oh, no...

I felt a warm droplet trickle down my cheek.

"I'm so sorry," I whispered as I reached over and sympathetically squeezed his hand.

He silently nodded and pulled his hands away. He placed his cap back on his head and pushed away from the counter.

"She's still with me everywhere I go," he said as he reached into his back pocket and pulled out a raggedy wallet.

He flipped open the wallet and reached his fingers in to pinch out two small photos and pass them to me. As I gently plucked them from his fingers, I cupped them in my palms and stared at the woman in the first one. She was young and wearing a cap and gown. Her hair was long and auburn with loose curls. Her skin was glowing and her hazel eyes resembled Nolan's, but not quite. She was beautiful; quite frankly, it was hard to believe she was his daughter. I flipped the well-worn photo over and on the back in smudged blue ink it read:

Graduation is on the 18th! Be careful on the drive!

-Love,
Emily

The second picture in the stack was a family photo of them both. One like the photo my mom had of us at her house. A simple portrait you could book an appointment for at a department store. In the photo, Nolan sat with a small girl in his lap. Her hair was deep brown and her eyes hazel. She smiled wide; her tongue poked through the gap where her front teeth should have been. Nolan looked young, clean, and surprisingly handsome with short hair and a faint smile underneath his even and freshly trimmed stubble.

There was silence around us as I gazed at the photos, but I could feel Nolan growing tense to have them back. I stacked them back together and returned them to him. He gently took the pictures and placed them back in his wallet with the utmost care as if those pictures *were* his daughter.

"I saw you had an album in your bag the other day," he mentioned, "When I ambushed you guys on the road, I saw it in your backpack."

"I do."

"Do you have photos of your family? To remember them by?"

I pulled my bag off my shoulders and placed it on the counter in front of me. I rummaged through the bag and pulled out the album. The green leather cover, cracked and worn, stared back at me. I flipped open the pages toward the middle of the book and scanned through the pictures. Most of the ones in the beginning pages were of Jonas and me. When he gifted me the album, some slots were already filled with our memories—photos of prom, graduation, and just any other occasion his mother or father had photographed—but towards the middle of the album is when things fall apart.

After turning a few pages, I found the photo I was looking for. A family portrait. My father and mother stood shoulder to shoulder as I stood in front of them with a gaping toothless grin. We all looked so happy.

I stuck my thumb into the film and pulled out the photo to hand to Nolan.

"Wow," he chuckled, "look at them teeth."

I bit back a smile.

"What were their names?"

"Joseph and Stephanie Harper," I replied.

He passed the photo back with a smile and glanced down at the album as I tucked the photo away.

"You know all of these people?" he asked as he pointed toward the back pages stuffed full of photographs.

I shook my head. "No, I—uh—if I find pictures while on the road I add them to the book."

"Why?"

"So they can be remembered by someone. Even if I don't know them, they'll still live on."

He nodded and his smile softened as he reached back into his pocket and pulled out his wallet once more. He pinched inside, pulled out the portrait of him and Emily, and handed it to me.

"Well, Ms. Harper, make sure we live on."

I observed him in shock. "Are you sure?"

He nodded. "I have more stashed away at the apartment. I can let one photo slip."

I smiled as I gently took the photo, flipped toward the back of the album, and placed the picture in an empty slot with the softest touch. Once they were comfortably inside, I closed the album and placed it back inside my bag.

After sharing our sentiments, we both turned our attention to our findings and the books we chose to bring back home. Overall, we had accumulated twenty-eight books about foraging and gardening ranging from beginners to expert level advice. We flipped through them and discussed the topics before filtering through and dwindling down our choices.

We had shrunk down our collection from twenty-eight to fourteen before we placed them in a tote bag and began to head to the apartment. The bell over the door rang as Nolan held the door open; the humid outdoor air blew in as I reached over and blew out the candle on the counter. The top half-inch of wax was completely liquid and rippled under my breath.

"Jonas will probably be awake by now," I informed, "so I should probably get back to check on him. I know you said you had something else to work on."

Nolan nodded. "Yeah, some ceiling down the way. I'll see you all later this evening though." He took a few steps off the sidewalk to cross the street before he stopped and turned back around. "Oh, we're running low on supplies, so I was thinking tomorrow we make a run to this school a few blocks away. I haven't been yet because it's more than a one-man job, but we can talk more about the plan later."

"That sounds good," I replied with a small nod.

And as he returned a small wave, he turned and walked to the other side of the street. I flung the tote of books over my shoulder and began to march down the sidewalk, thinking about our time in the shop. It felt so genuine to finally talk to someone new about these past years. I hadn't ever heard anyone else's story, how someone else survived, or talked about who they lost. My conversation with Nolan was the first conversation—outside of Jonas—that I had ever had about the events that came with the end of the world. Although the topics were dark and heartbreaking, I had enjoyed the conversation. I felt as if we weren't alone anymore, and it helped me understand Nolan more.

As I approached the apartment building, I heard scuffling echoing from the alleyway. My heart skipped a few beats, and I could feel the blood chilling in my veins. I slowly and quietly pulled the tote from my shoulder and placed it on the ground against a wall. It was too heavy to run with, and I needed to be ready for anything to lurch out from around the corner. I reached back over my shoulder until I felt the sticky padding of the grip on my bat. I squeezed tightly as I pressed myself against the corner and peaked around the edge of the wall.

My eyes first landed on the trash, debris, and dumpster that swarmed with flies. Other than that, the alleyway was empty. I released the bat and relaxed my shoulders with a deep breath before I heard another shuffling sound. Metallic and rusty like the grating on the fire escape.

"Melony?" I jumped at Jonas calling out to me from the window.

I clutched a hand over my heart as I reached down for the tote bag.

"Sorry," he chuckled and grunted as he sat in the windowsill; one leg in and one leg out. "I didn't mean to scare you. I woke up a bit ago and was just getting some air. Thought I might catch you on your way back."

"Well," I sighed as I adjusted the tote on my shoulder, "now you can help me carry this shit up."

"Got it."

The ladder creaked and groaned as he began to climb down it a few rungs until he could reach for the tote. He took it from my hands and began to climb back up to the platform. I followed behind him.

"What did you find?"

"Books," I grumbled as I pulled myself up onto the grating.

Jonas leaned back against the wall and peaked into the tote with furrowed brows. Confusion drew new lines and wrinkled across his face. He looked cleaner and wore a fresh new set of clothes. His hair was pulled back into a half up half down mini bun that kept it out of his face, and his beard looked combed and less rugged. I could see fresh cuts in it as if he trimmed it with scissors. The bags under his eyes were lighter than usual, and he appeared full of energy. It was a relief to see him this way.

"Why books?" he asked.

"Nolan took me on a tour of the town, and we found a spot where a garden would fit perfectly. Therefore… books," I informed as I gestured to the bag that sat between his legs.

"I don't know if that makes sense to me, but I can assume you had a good time, right?"

I nodded, and he smiled.

"You look good," I commented.

"I feel good," he replied as he pushed himself off the wall and lifted the tote through the window.

He gestured for me to go ahead and waited patiently for me to enter the building. When we both were inside, he slid the window closed and brushed ahead of me, placing a gently hand on my lower back as he passed.

"I think I might've slept too long, but I woke up feeling great. I tried to clean up, hence the trimmed beard," he said as he walked a few paces ahead.

"You look *really* good."

He smirked as he held the apartment door open for me and ushered me in. Once the door was closed behind us, he placed his hands onto my hips and leaned over me.

"I was worried about you," he said softly. His hand gently cupped the side of my face and neck as he craned down and planted a kiss on my lips. He pressed his forehead against mine and closed his eyes. "I'm glad you're back in one piece."

"Are you okay?" I whispered.

His dark eyes opened and met mine.

"I love you more than anything," he murmured, "you know that? If you hadn't had come back…"

I brought my hand up from my side and gripped his wrist near my face. "I'm here; I did come back."

He pulled his head away and gazed into my soul. For once, I couldn't tell what he was thinking, but he stared at every inch of my face. His eyes flicked all over my skin until he reached back in and kissed the top of my head.

"Next time, wake me up," he said as he pulled away.

"Next time, you're coming with me. Nolan mentioned going scavenging tomorrow, the three of us."

He nodded and removed his warm hand from my face. He slowly moved into the living room and sat on the couch.

"Where are we going?"

"A school." I sat down next to him. "He said we can talk about a plan later tonight."

Jonas nodded, deep in thought.

"What did you guys talk about today?" he asked.

I smiled and tugged my bag out from behind me, reached into the pocket, and pulled out my album. I flipped open to the page that held Nolan's photo and pointed to it.

"We talked about Emily."

"Can I see this?" he asked as he leaned in with furrowed brows and carefully pulled the album out of my lap.

He flipped through the pages until he landed on my family portrait. He stared at the photo for a few seconds before removing it from the slot and flipping back to Nolan's picture. Jonas held the two photos side by side and pointed at young me and Emily with a chuckle.

"You two kinda look the same," he finally said.

"No, we don't." I pulled the album back into my lap and stared at the pictures. "It's just because we're both missing our teeth. We don't even have the same color eyes."

"They aren't far from the same color; hers are just a touch greener. You have the same noses and face shape."

Rolling my eyes, I scoffed, and he laughed.

A lot of children look alike. They're young and haven't grown into their facial features yet. Even if I did happen to look like Emily, or vice versa, it was just some strange coincidence, but I couldn't help but think of her graduation photo. I began to flip through the album until

I reached the photos Jonas had taken at my college graduation.

"Did he have another photo? Are you comparing right now?"

I nodded in silence as I gazed down at myself a few years younger. Jonas was right; the resemblance was uncanny. From what I could still picture in my mind of her, Emily and I looked alike. She had appeared a couple years older with different hair, but our facial structure and shape were similar, and our eyes were too close in color to differentiate.

Jonas chuckled again and pulled the album from me, shutting it in the process.

"It's just a strange coincidence. People have doppelgangers. I'm sure there were plenty of people out there who looked kind of like me too," he reassured.

Yet, I couldn't help but feel uneasy as I thought about it. I thought about meeting Nolan on the road and how he had looked at me. I thought about the realization that crossed his face when he saw my eyes peeking around the barrel of his shotgun. Had he seen her in me or was it some coincidence?

19

Melony

We each loaded up half a backpack with things we would need for the trip. The school wasn't far, and Nolan assured us we would be home before dark if we left at dawn. For a short trip, our list of essentials didn't consist of much. Flashlights, batteries, snacks, water, first aid, and weapons. Nolan hadn't run into Grays for quite a while, whereas for Jonas and me, it had only been about two weeks; we had to make sure we were prepared.

When Nolan finally returned home last night, we discussed the route and plan before making a list of everything we would need to bring, and everything we needed to get. It had seemed like a lot.

The thought of the plan overwhelmed me. I didn't want to leave the apartment. It took hours after our discussion for Jonas to talk me down enough so I could eventually fall asleep and not overthink myself into insomnia. Now that the new day was here and we were preparing to leave, my overwhelming anxiety was returning.

I tightened the straps on my bag and took a deep breath before I sat on the edge of our bed and slipped into my shoes. Once the laces were snug, I sat up straight and stared out the window in front of me at the brick wall of another building across the alleyway. I felt Jonas's hand on my shoulder, touching the bare skin exposed from the cut off sleeves on my tee.

"Don't worry," he whispered, "in and out. We'll be okay."

The bed creaked as he got up, and I could hear him shuffling around behind me. When I turned to see what he was doing, he was tucking his hands into his pockets, pressing them flat.

"Let's get going before the sun gets too high," I mumbled as I moved out into the hall and met Nolan in the living room.

He took a deep breath, exhaled a cough, then smiled at me. "Y'all ready?"

Jonas placed his hand on my back beneath my bag. I watched a twitch appear in Nolan's smile.

"Ready to go," Jonas answered.

Nolan nodded and headed for the front door. We followed him out of the apartment, out of the building, and out onto the street. The rising sun was golden in a soft blue light. The light seemed heavenly and tranquil, but I was not at ease.

I was feeling a knot twisting in my gut. Nerves rattled and shook me. My body was trying to send my brain some sort of message that I couldn't understand. A feeling of impending doom. But it was just my nerves.

Jonas and I had been staying with Nolan for a few days, enough to change our habits and make us feel comfortable. We were secure and safe, and today's sudden plans had amped up my anxiety. We were walking into the unknown, so of course my fear was telling me to turn around. But I couldn't push it away.

"You okay?" Jonas asked.

We were falling a bit behind Nolan as he led the way.

"I'm fine."

"You don't have to worry. I know it's going to be hard for you when you see this school in bad shape, but I'm here for you if you need a break."

That's when the twisting in my gut began to churn worse. I hadn't even realized or considered that detail of the trip. I would be seeing a place I had once loved so dearly in decay and ruin. I began to grow overwhelmed with emotion and stopped in my tracks. What would I see inside this school? What grizzly scene awaited me? Children lost? I wasn't ready.

"I don't think I can go," I breathed out.

"Hey," Jonas placed his hands onto my shoulders and soothed, "you're going to be okay. You are so strong. If you don't want to go inside when we get there, that's fine, okay?"

I took a few shaky breaths as I looked into his eyes. So deep like black coffee. I felt sick to my stomach. So uneasy. So afraid. I was beginning to tremble. But that one glance into his dark eyes reassured me. No harm would come my way, and he would be there every step of the journey.

I nodded hesitantly, and he gave my shoulders a gentle squeeze before releasing me and guiding me forward. Nolan had stopped at the upcoming intersection to wait for us. He stood leaning against a brick building watching beneath the tilted brim of his hat. His demeanor felt so odd compared to the Nolan I had shared time with in the bookstore.

"Not much further," he said as he pushed off the wall and took lead again.

Jonas grabbed my hand and led me to assure himself that I was following behind. His hands were mostly soft but tiny callouses roughly poked at my palm. I could feel the sweat forming between our skin as I followed and stumbled along behind him.

The sun slowly rose the further we walked; our shadows shortening with each minute we were in its path. Eventually, we turned onto a back street. The street felt more like an alley than anything, but cars parallel parked on either side, and vines creeped up the surrounding walls and street sign. The street was shaded from the sun and a few degrees cooler. The scene held some sort of magical eeriness. I could see the blue sky and morning clouds overhead, but no light entered the alley. It felt like walking through the woods early in the morning before the sun could ever touch the tree line. The coolness in the air was so refreshing I began to feel the anxiousness in my nerves drifting away.

However, before I could feel too relaxed, we reached the end of the street, and the school came into view.

The parking lot was full of abandoned vehicles and military trucks just as the road had been when we met Nolan. Car doors and trunks were opened and rummaged; debris glided across the ground in the soft breeze. A tall chain-link fence had been erected around the perimeter; tents and small camps were set up inside. In the middle of the lot, a small patch of yard held a flagpole standing tall; the American flag tattered and swayed in the breeze alongside the Indiana state flag. I observed every inch of the fence and perimeter until I saw what I had been dreading.

Corpses.

"They must've been using this place as some sort of regroup center," Jonas whispered.

Nolan nodded. "Having everyone in one spot made it easy dinner."

I began to feel sick. My stomach churned like a ship in stormy waters. I felt the burning sensation clawing at the back of my throat and tears bleeding into my eyes. I swallowed it down, but it refused. I spun around and hunched over behind a car, gagging and dry heaving until the only small breakfast I had eaten forcefully came up onto the sidewalk.

Jonas's hands immediately found me. "Hey, hey," he shushed, "it's okay. Let it out."

I squeezed my eyes shut and groaned as I pushed small pieces of hair out of my face. A pounding force pushed behind my eyes and throbbed at my temples.

"Here." His hand reached out in front of me with a bottle of water.

I hastily took it and swallowed back my queasiness. The water rushed down my throat and eased the burning acid. I could feel it sink and settle into my empty stomach.

"You gonna be okay?" Nolan asked.

"Yeah," I said hoarsely, "just nerves. I'm fine."

Jonas helped me slowly get to my feet and steadied me out before he backed away. His fingertips lingered as his hand trailed off my shoulder. His touch was like being brushed against a cloud. When his hand left, it felt like the remnants of a ghost lingered.

He stepped towards Nolan, and I could hear him whispering indistinct words. When I turned around and faced the two of them, Nolan watched me as Jonas spoke to him. He sent a sympathetic glance, a soft kindness relaxed into his facial muscles. A tension eased off his shoulders. I could see it even through the pulsing in my eyes.

I coughed and took another swig of water before passing the bottle back to Jonas for him to cap and tuck away in his bag. I slowly walked past the two of them and rounded the corner out onto the road; I tried to avoid looking at the fence and what lied beyond it. Instead, my eyes remained locked on the double doors on the front of the building. Jonas and Nolan's footsteps quickened behind me as I grew closer to the chain-link gate.

"Mel," Jonas shouted in a hushed tone, "I think you should wait a second. Anything could be in there."

I can handle it. I am not helpless.

My hands trembled and the throbbing grew fiercer as I reached in front of me for the latch on the gate. I felt beyond sick. I could still smell the death lingering in the air even if I tried to avoid looking at it. The people that were here were long gone. Nothing but fabric and bones picked clean from animals and insects.

This is life. The cycle of life. Natural order of decay.

And although I didn't gaze upon the bodies and brown stained bones, I couldn't help but question how many children laid within the lot. How many families came here seeking refuge? How many were promised safety when it was impossible?

The nausea returned, but I had nothing left to give to it.

The gate creaked open with a sharp metallic whine. I could feel the grinding metal in my teeth and behind my eyes. I might as well have set off an alarm for anything that remained inside.

But nothing followed.

I could hear the birds and the insects trilling in the trees. There was nothing else. No clicking, no shrieking, no pounding on the doors. So far, the place appeared safe. Whatever had killed the last occupants was no longer here—at least for now.

"It sounds clear," I spoke in a normal tone; no longer feeling the need to be utterly silent.

"Doesn't mean it is," Nolan mumbled as he stepped past me into the lot.

I kept my eyes up as I followed him, and Jonas trailed behind me. Nolan held his gun in a defensive position as we stepped heel to toe through the lot. He peeked into tents and swiftly spun around to examine truck beds. When the perimeter of the school, within the fences, had been thoroughly searched, Jonas approached a massive military truck with a canopy over the bed. He used the built-in steps to hoist himself up and climb inside. I stood at the end and tiptoed over the edge to see what he was doing. He walked toward a crate at the back of the truck and pulled open the metal clasps holding it shut. He reached in and pulled out a few small parcels with bold writing. He tossed two down to me.

"Put these in your bag," he commanded.

Chili mac. Shredded beef in barbeque sauce.

"How many of those are in there?" I asked as I looked up to watch him zip his bag back up.

"There were only a few," he informed, "I'm guessing there's more inside. Not getting my hopes up though." His boots thudded against the truck bed as he approached me and jumped down from the tailgate. "You sure you're okay?"

"I am fine."

We locked eyes as he tried to read me. After a few seconds, he opened his mouth to speak, but footsteps approached from behind me, and he kept his words inside.

"Y'all find anything?" Nolan's drawl asked.

"Few MRE's," Jonas responded, "I have a feeling more will be inside. Especially if this place was some sort of outpost or supply depot."

Nolan nodded with a squint beneath his hat. He faced the main entrance. Jaw ticked.

"I don't know what could be waiting for us in there," he huffed, "but from the looks of out here I'm guessing there's weapons. Sights are set up along the fences and some of the classroom windows, casings all over the place. How I see it? Military got overrun. I think it's worth takin' a look. Guns are what we really need in these times."

I scrunched my face.

"Jonas and I have lasted all this time without a gun," I scoffed, "Hell, I didn't even have this bat until about a week ago. Food is a priority."

Nolan nodded. "I agree with you, but we should be looking out for weapons too. If you wanna grow this place like you told me, we're gonna need fire power to protect it."

"I'll keep an eye out," Jonas pitched in, "I'm not sure what exactly to look for, but if I see anything I'll let you know."

Nolan nodded again before backing away and slowly making his way toward the front doors. When he was out of earshot, I turned to Jonas.

"Guns? We don't know how to use them, especially military grade. Sounds like we're doing too much. We came for food," I argued.

"I know," he sighed and glanced to Nolan, "but he has a point. Yeah, we've made it this far without them, but how many times did we get too close? There are too many instances to count where a gun would've helped us tenfold. I know what happened with your dad put you off them, but Nolan seems to know what he's doing, he can show us how to use them safely. They aren't a priority, but I'm not gonna avoid it if I see one. Let me protect you."

His argument was convincing, but I still felt unsettled. I had thought about it once before. A gun could've saved us plenty of times. In the beginning, it was one of the first necessities I felt we needed even after everything, but we didn't own one. My mother removed them from the house after my father died, and I never learned how to use one before then. I thought a gun was something we would come across eventually on our travels like in all the apocalyptic movies and shows I had once seen, but when the time came around, it was never a priority; they were also difficult to find. The longer we survived without one, the more I forgot about it until a gun seemed so minuscule compared to our other means of survival. We survived this far without extra help.

But Nolan and Jonas were right. It was already a struggle fighting for our lives, and if we wanted to create a community for other survivors, we would need guns to keep that community safe.

"Okay."

Jonas patted me on the shoulder before turning away and following Nolan to the front doors. I reached over my shoulder and wrapped my fingers around the grip on my bat, pulling it out of my bag before trailing behind Jonas toward the entrance. The doors were metal framed with large windows. From the outside looking in, I could spot small barricades blocking the entrance. Nolan and Jonas used their strength to push one door open, only allowing someone a thin sliver of space to squeeze through. They both turned to me.

"Seriously," I grumbled as I rolled my eyes and stepped forward.

I slipped my bag off and pushed it through the gap followed by my bat, then sucked in my gut and straightened my back. Holding my breath, I flattened myself against the door and slid into the building. The metal frame and handle dug into my shoulders and lower back.

Once inside, the air felt still around me. It was musty, and I could feel the dust brushing against my skin. I took a second to catch my breath and look around before fully opening the doors and letting the guys in. The windows were tinted allowing shaded light to enter the building, but nothing bright enough to illuminate anything beyond ten feet of me through the second set of doors. I huffed and turned back toward the entrance. Jonas and Nolan stood waiting outside talking to each other. Jonas's lips were moving as Nolan stared and listened, but he must've been whispering; I could not hear his words even through the crack that remained in the door.

In front of me was a small yet sturdy reception desk pressed against the entrance. I placed both of my hands against the side and attempted to shove it away. The wood scraped the floor with a deafening scratching shriek. I gritted my teeth and heaved against the desk. When it would not move any further, I examined how far it had moved.

Inches. Mere inches.

I groaned and turned around, pressing my back against the solid siding. I tried to take advantage of my leg strength; however, even with all my strength, it hardly budged. The corner must've been stuck against something I couldn't see. Annoyance filled me to the brim as I poked my head through the crack—now only an inch wider.

"You guys push the door while I try to scoot the desk," I grumbled, "This thing is fucking heavy."

They both nodded before I retreated inside. I stood on the side of the door and weaseled my hands into a crevice on the back of the desk between it and the door. I planted my feet against the metal frame and baseboards.

"You ready?" I shouted.

Jonas loudly counted to three from outside and on his mark, we all pushed. I pushed off the doorframe hoping that with the help of the door, it would push the desk away in an arching motion. It began to work.

The door creaked and groaned, and the wooden desk slid across the floor with a horrible squeaking—nails on a chalkboard. The sound echoed through the entry room and bounced off the second set of doors. I could feel the high-pitched screech scraping the inside of my skull and scratching the insides of my teeth. After a few seconds of excruciating sound, the desk was far enough, and the door opened wide enough to where I began to slip. My body was almost fully extended from the door frame to the desk, and I stared at the floor waiting for it to violently greet me before Jonas and Nolan stopped pushing and the desk stopped moving. I tried to push myself upward and flat on my feet, but I had no space or leverage. I slowly inched my feet forward until they were beneath me and the risk of landing on my face was no longer imminent. When I got to my feet, I dusted off my hands and gestured to Jonas and Nolan to come inside. Nolan brushed past first and examined the entry; Jonas trailed behind with a smirk.

"*Elegante*," he leaned in and whispered sarcastically at my clumsy slip.

I bumped into his shoulder, releasing a deep chuckle from him as he sauntered off. I rolled my eyes at the back of his head and reached down to where my bag sat on the floor. Once comfortably situated on my back, I grabbed my bat and stood back as Nolan worked on opening the second set of doors. My legs and arms felt weak as I watched him use his strength to get inside the school. A prickly numbness radiated through my limbs, and I wondered how someone old enough to be my father could have the strength to move metaphorical mountains.

The man was determined to get into the building. I watched veins in his arms and hands bolden and protrude from his skin as he pushed and shouldered the door. When Jonas reached in to help, I watched them both struggle. Was this mission worth the effort? The exhaustion they would feel afterward. Did they not know their limits?

After a few minutes, they both backed away, sweaty and out of breath.

"They might've welded these suckers shut!" Nolan exclaimed while catching his breath.

"There's gotta be another way to get in," Jonas huffed as he crossed his arms over his chest.

I sighed and backed against a wall as I glanced around the room for another doorway. When I didn't see one, I slid down the wall until my bottom bumped into the floor and my legs straightened out in front of me. The heat in this section was growing unbearable from the poor air quality and outside heat coming in through the open door.

"Was there not another entrance to check out?" I asked.

No one answered, and I took their silence as a response. We all looked at each other as we thought of a solution, but then Nolan glanced down at his hands, and then his eyes flicked around the floor. It was as if a lightbulb clicked on in his head.

"We could bust one of the windows open," he suggested.

Jonas perked up. Another lightbulb.

"I think I saw a crowbar in the chest outside. I'll be right back," he said before he rushed outside.

I watched him through the dusty tinted windows as he practically vaulted himself into the truck bed with the MRE crate. After several seconds, he reappeared, jumping down onto the ground, and jogging back into the building. I observed from the floor as he passed the crowbar to Nolan and stepped a few paces back. Once at a safe distance, Jonas pulled his bag off his back and reached into it, pulling a flashlight from the depths. I leaned forward and pulled my bag out from behind me to find my light as well.

When I looked back up to watch the upcoming chaos, I watched as Nolan adjusted his grip on the crowbar and cocked it far back behind his head. With a quick and forceful swing and the pivot of his foot and hips, the crowbar connected with the glass, and the window burst.

From his stance, I inferred he must have played golf in the past. I envisioned him in a nice polo shirt and shorts, sporting a clean cap and gloves. It didn't look right in my head, and the more I thought about it the more it felt wrong. *Not a golfer*, I thought. He was difficult to figure out aside from what he told us.

As I stood and dusted off my bottom, Nolan passed the crowbar back to Jonas to which he gratefully accepted and clutched it in his spare hand as a weapon. It reminded me of the beginning. There were details I would never forget—moments scarred in my mind for as long as I lived. Jonas carried that crowbar for the first few months until he lost it at the motel. He had grown so attached to it, and I had grown so used to seeing him carry it that losing it seemed to impact our course and plans moving forward. We had to be more cautious because Jonas had lost his swinging range; due to that, we moved slower and less frequently, trying to remain silent and as still as we could before running into another Gray. I could still picture him walking down the street with blood dripping a trail from the end. I could remember the sound a crowbar made as it struck a skull.

I bit the inside of my cheek as a pang rang through my chest watching him clutch that crowbar at his side. I'm sure to him it felt nostalgic—more in a familiar sense than enjoyable—but I couldn't help but want to yank it from his hands and chuck it out of the building as if it were a bad omen like a ringing in my ears.

Nolan pushed and kicked the remaining glass away from the frame before stepping through the window. He swung his gun to his back and held his light up. Jonas and I clicked on our flashlights and carefully stepped through the opening.

The flashlights did little in the darkness of the lobby. The small beams of light only stretched a few feet ahead of us and illuminated a few feet at a time, but it was better than wandering an abandoned school in the dark.

After a few minutes of waving my light around the room, my eyes began to adjust, and the flashlights didn't seem as useless as before. Straight ahead from the entrance were a few sets of double doors that led into a gymnasium. The doors were solid wood and propped open with attached doorstops leaving a clear view of the tents and sleeping bags that were scattered across the gymnasium floor. From where I stood out in the lobby, I could see signs with arrows that pointed toward different sections of the gym for paperwork and supply aid. As my light swept over the sleeping bags on the floor, I noticed that some were lumpy and full. I didn't step foot into the gym; instead, I turned around and began to scan the other areas of the lobby.

To the right of the entrance was a hall leading to classrooms as well as a glass-paned front office. The main desk where parents would call or sign in to pick up their children was missing, leaving the office looking empty or as if it were getting remodeled. But the dirt pattern on the tile floor made a perfect puzzle piece for the desk blocking the front doors. Directly opposite the office was another hall alongside a small section of counseling rooms about a quarter the size of a normal classroom furnished with a single desk and a few chairs in each.

"Which way do you think the cafeteria is?" Nolan asked.

I flashed my light down both halls. The right seemed to go on forever, doors lining either side of the hall. To the left was nothing but darkness and a single door that looked like it led to a staircase. In the school I worked at, there was a small basement mostly used for maintenance. A lot of the other teachers had told me there used to be a swimming pool down there for the high school swim team to practice back in the day, but I had never gone down to investigate and had only ever seen maintenance and custodians go down. I assumed it was a breakroom or boiler room of sorts.

"Go right," I replied, "the other side of the building is too short."

Nolan led the charge and Jonas held the rear as he ushered me into the middle of them. Our flashlights bounced across the hall. All three beams waved in different directions. Jonas mostly faced behind us, constantly scanning if anything decided to follow. Nolan's focus was straight ahead, quickly moving and searching for our main location. Between the two of them, I had the freedom to explore and point my light into the classrooms.

Most of the doors were closed. The solid wood doors only had one thin window, and the layer of dust prevented me from peering inside. However, from the rooms that remained open, I could see that most classrooms appeared to have been converted into bedrooms or family spaces. The space within the gym must not have been enough to house everyone.

Cots and sleeping bags filled some classrooms, and others were still set up as classrooms with boards and walls filled with posters informing people of the illness and infected. The military most likely had to train children and adults on how to defend themselves as well as make sure they spread information about what happened to infected persons. Propaganda-like posters told children "See something? Say something!" with images of people being cut or scraped. Another poster was sketched out to look like an instructional comic with military personnel defending themselves against a Gray.

Written on a classroom board with chalk was a list of names or terms referring to the creatures: infected, cracklers, rotters, tickers, poppers, grays. They must have had people from all over coming here with new names and sharing them to the point the lingo needed to be taught so there was no confusion.

How long did this place last here to have all this information?

"Up here!" Nolan exclaimed in a whisper.

Jonas and I turned, and our lights crossed into one. On the left side of the hall was a double set of double doors left wide open. As we rounded the corner and entered the large room, the first thing I noticed was the amount of light pouring into the cafeteria. A little less than half of the tables had been folded up and pressed against the far wall lined with windows. But even from behind the large tables, I could tell a couple of windows were shattered. Glass piled onto the floor around the wheels of the makeshift blockade, and the light coming in was too bright to be coming from the remaining tinted windows. The rest of the cafeteria was a chaotic scene.

The remaining tables were askew in no particular pattern—some even flipped onto their sides. Blood splattered across the tile and tabletops; small, dried puddles spilled from the other sides of the tilted tables as if they had been flipped to shield people and the people on the other side were still there.

"I don't like the looks of this," I whispered softly as I stared at the mess left behind.

"You don't think there could still be Grays in here, do you?" Jonas asked us.

I could tell something was bothering him—he looked tense and upset. Nolan looked at us from over his shoulder before gazing around the rest of the room. He hesitated and the ticking of his jaw wasn't comforting.

"Let's just make it quick. There's gotta be some food left behind," he finally replied gruffly, "You two go check the kitchen while I go scope out the rest of the cafeteria. I'll see if I can find any guns."

I took a deep breath as Jonas paused in hesitation. After some thought and Nolan already walking away, he finally nodded before reaching back and grabbing my hand. He gave it a gentle squeeze as he led me into the back kitchen to the right of the dining hall doors. As we entered the kitchen, we had to carefully step over metal lunch trays so as not to make too much ruckus. Dishes and catering trays were scattered all over the counters and floors as if they had just been wildly thrown across the room.

"Do you think someone beat us to the food?" I whispered as Jonas led me around the counter.

He shook his head. "I don't think this is from scavengers."

A pit sank into my stomach as I thought about some gentle lunch ladies trying to defend themselves in any way they could. I glanced back down at the trays on the floors. It would have made sense…

We grew closer to the back of the kitchen, and a horrible stench lingered in the air around us. Jonas let go of my hand and motioned for me to stop. He lifted a finger over his lips as he stared at something ahead. Something in the darkness I couldn't see. I aimed my light at my feet and clicked it off.

The smell in the air was becoming sickening as we stood still and stared into the darkness. My eyes would not adjust any further than the few rows of stocking shelves up ahead to the left of us. I pulled my shirt over my nose and tried to hold my breath as I began to inch toward the shelves, moving around Jonas as he moved in the opposite direction with his eyes still locked on something deep within the kitchen.

Once I made it to the wire shelves, I clicked my flashlight back on and avoided pointing it in the direction Jonas had gone. If there were something in the kitchen with us, I wouldn't want to expose Jonas's location to it.

I scanned my surroundings a few inches at a time with my poor flashlight. The shelves were barely stocked. A few canned goods were scattered here and there, each one I grabbed and placed in my bag. When I neared the end of the shelves, I spotted a pallet of boxes in the corner in my peripheral. I aimed my light at the boxes and read the bold print on the sides.

MREs.

I pulled my shirt down from my nose and held my breath as I bit the end of my tiny flashlight to hold it in my mouth. I rushed to the pallet and pulled a few empty boxes off the top. The second layer of boxes remained unopened. I looked back with excitement for Jonas but could not see him in the darkness. My excitement faded as I squinted and strained my eyes to find him and could not. I turned back to the boxes and ripped one open almost squealing at the sight of stacks of untainted MREs.

I tossed my bag at my feet and held it open with one hand as the other hurriedly shoved the packs inside. I got through a box and a half of meals before my bag was stuffed full and became a struggle to carry. As I swung it back onto my shoulders, I let out a muffled groan as I threw myself off balance. I spun on my heels to catch myself and the flashlight in my mouth spotted Jonas at the end of the shelves. I pulled the light from my mouth and smiled up at him with a wide grin.

"Look what I found," I whispered.

He smiled back. A pure genuine smile. He could hardly hide his dimples under his beard. He then tossed his bag onto the floor, and I helped him stuff it full. Another box and a half. He lifted it with ease and swung it onto his back then held his arm out and motioned towards my bag.

"Let me carry yours," he quietly ordered, "If we need to run out of here, I want you to be ahead of me. That thing is weighing you down."

I glanced at it over my shoulder and flicked my eyes into the area of the kitchen behind him that he had explored. I furrowed my brows as I searched his face for some clue to what he saw.

"Why do you think we'll be needing to run? What did you see?"

He shook his head and reached for my bag.

"I didn't see anything," he argued, "just give me the damn thing."

I didn't argue with him and helped him load it onto his shoulders. The huge lumps of backpacks he now carried made him look like a giant turtle. I chuckled at how goofy his new appearance was, and he playfully chuckled along before he reached for an extra box of meals. I reached out and grabbed the box from him.

"If we need to run," I spoke sassily, "I'll drop it and book it. But right now, you are already carrying too much."

He smiled and nodded silently before turning around and leading me back out of the kitchen.

The rotting smell still lingered, and I couldn't help but get an odd secretive feeling from Jonas. I glanced over my shoulder into the darkness of the kitchen before I was guided around the front counter and back into the light of the cafeteria.

Nolan sat on one of the benches facing away from the table. His head hung down facing the floor as his elbows rested on his knees. The disappointment radiating from his posture hinted that he couldn't find what he was looking for.

I approached the table and set the box next to him.

"Load your bag up," I said with a smile.

He looked up at me and then at the box. The corners of his lips tugged upward into the tiniest, slyest smile as he turned his entire body around and ripped the box open. He began to fill his bag and once the box was empty, he tossed it across the cafeteria toward the double doors. The box slid across the tile and out into the hall. Jonas sat down next to Nolan on the bench, and they recounted what they had seen.

I stood off to the side, waiting for them to wrap up their conversation. I was growing anxious, and the bad feeling in my gut was returning; the adrenaline and excitement from finding the food was quickly wearing off. I stared off into the darkness of the kitchen that loomed over the entire side of the cafeteria. It felt like a void calling out to me, and the longer I stood staring, the more I imagined the smell flowing out into the room.

The pit grew larger as I cautiously stepped toward the lunch counter. I stepped over trays and stayed as silent as I could. Something was wrong, the atmosphere felt different, and I couldn't help but feel skeptical of Jonas's secretive attitude.

My grip on my bat tightened and a layer of sweat began to form a barrier between it and the skin of my palm as I held it down at my side. The closer I grew to the counter, the stronger the smell became. This time I wasn't imagining it.

A rotting stench of decay and old meat wafted around me. I quickly pulled my shirt over my nose and held my breath to hold back the urge to gag. I lifted my light over the counter and aimed it into the kitchen, and then I heard it.

A clicking sound echoed and resonated throughout the cafeteria, but it wasn't coming from the kitchen.

I spun around and peeked down the hall where the box Nolan threw had landed. My angle and view allowed me to see a bit down the length of the hall covering the span of at least three classrooms. There was nothing there.

I began to back away from the counter and the doors. The clicking emanated from the hall again. Louder. Another source echoed in reply. There was more than one coming in our direction.

I spun around and moved into a jog as I approached the table, startling Nolan and Jonas.

"Let's go," I whispered.

They both furrowed their brows in confusion and glanced toward the doors.

"Now!" I gritted my teeth and harshly commanded them to which they both quickly rose to their feet.

I kept glancing over my shoulder as we approached the blocked windows. I reached over and tucked my flashlight into a pocket on one of the bags Jonas carried before I moved along the wall of tables in search of a broken window. When I found one, I motioned for the guys to come, and we all began to push.

The wheels squeaked against the floor, and I froze in my tracks.

A shrill screech reverberated across the walls. Jonas and Nolan stopped pushing and turned toward the cafeteria doors behind us. Within another second, I could hear the shrieking and clatter of multiple creatures clawing their way down the halls. I rushed to the table and began to shove and heave with all my might. My legs and arms began to shake and tremble in fear, and I could feel my eyes burning with tears. Jonas began pulling the opposite end I was pushing while Nolan stood his ground, gun positioned with the stock against his shoulder.

The table moved slowly yet quickly left a gap large enough for the three of us to squeeze through and leap out of the large, shattered window behind it. Jonas practically shoved me ahead of him, and I hopped over the ledge out onto the grass. I paused for half a second as I watched Jonas and Nolan exit the building before my trembling legs took control and I began to run.

"Don't stop, Melony!" Jonas shouted after me.

His voice wasn't faint, which meant he wasn't far behind. My heart pounded in my ears, but I could still hear the shrieking and screaming of the pack of Grays trying to claw their way out of the window. I glanced over my shoulder as I ran into a section of trees. Jonas was only a few feet behind, and Nolan was keeping up with him. Even with two full bags on his back, Jonas tried to stay close and kept up with the route I was making for us. As I continued to look over my shoulder and check on them, I could see the back of the school and the window we had climbed out of. I had never seen so many together; the beasts inside were piled together clawing at the tables and each other like wild animals. They couldn't escape while fighting each other, but it was inevitable that they'd make it out eventually.

We had a good lead on them, but we were going the opposite direction we had come, and I was lost. Eventually the small section of trees ended, and I found myself running onto the side of a wooded road like the one Jonas and I had traveled on to first get into the city. I took a left and kept running. My feet pounded against the pavement. Through the bottom of my boots, my bones felt fragile and broken. I could feel the fire spreading through my thighs and legs like never before.

The shrieking echoed through the woods next to us, but the sound was still so distant. We were far enough ahead we could lose them, but we had nowhere to go except to keep running. A hot trail of tears streamed down my cheeks, but my blurry vision didn't slow me down. I kept running. Waist down I was numb, but I kept running. If I could hear them in the distance, I would be running.

Until a gunshot rang through the air, and I stopped in my tracks.

20

Jonas: Now

Melony slipped through the doorframe into the building while Nolan and I waited outside. I looked around the lot and examined my surroundings.

It was a mess. A massacre.

The chain-link fences were tall and vehicles from the lot had been moved and parked right up against it as a second form of barricade holding the fence in place. Yet, something had still managed to get in. Either that or they did this to themselves. Melony had avoided looking at them the entire walk through the lot; I had seen her straining and struggling, but I was seeing everything.

Black and dried red stained the pavement deep enough to where rain over the past year or two hadn't moved the smudges and outlines. The sun had baked it into the concrete. There was no telling how long ago this had happened. The bodies that had been left out and exposed to the elements were nothing but sun-dried strips of flesh barely coating the bones. The clothes that once covered them were torn and shredded from the wild animals that had somehow weaseled their way in through the fences. The dead were scattered across the lot as if they had been running away from the building.

The feeling I was getting from this place was horrible. I kept glancing back at Melony inside. We had sent her in alone, and I was now regretting it.

"Hey," I whispered to Nolan as we waited, "If anything happens to me in there, you take care of her. Make sure she lives. I'm not liking the vibe of this place."

I turned to face him and watched his jaw click in a chewing motion. He squinted at me with doubt and skepticism—it wasn't hard to miss—but there was something else hiding behind the look. Something lurked deep behind his eyes. Almost as if he had a secret; he knew something we didn't.

After a few seconds of his stare-down, he simply nodded.

"I appreciate that, man," I replied right before Melony popped her head through the ajar door and ordered us to help her.

She quickly disappeared back into the building and positioned herself against the doorframe. With a countdown, we all pushed against the door. The desk screamed inside the building and worry began to strike me deeper. If she wasn't alone inside, something would have surely heard her by now.

Once the desk was moved, we entered the building only to be greeted with another set of doors. Melony took a step aside while Nolan and I struggled to get the door open. No matter how hard we pushed, the door wouldn't budge. Nolan had declared they must have been welded shut from the inside before he suggested we break the glass. From the inside meant there had to have been survivors after whatever happened in the parking lot.

This made me hesitant, but I pushed it away. We needed any supplies that could be trapped inside, so I ran back out to the truck I had climbed into, remembering I had seen a crowbar in the MRE crate.

I quickly made my way into the truck bed. Now that I was outside on my own without the comfort of others, I could really feel the unsettling horror this school held. I didn't want to be here any longer than we needed to, and I couldn't help but feel like Nolan was hiding something from us. Had he been here before? Did he know what happened here? I could tell the energy was throwing Melony off too, and if she had got a bad feeling, I trust what she felt.

I grabbed the crowbar from the chest, and as I stood on the end of the truck bed about to hop off, I saw something in the distance beyond the fence near the trees. I couldn't make out what it could be only that it was a pile of something.

I brushed it away and hopped down from the truck. Trying to compose myself before showing my face to Melony, I rushed inside and handed the crowbar to Nolan so he could do what he needed to. Once the window was shattered, he passed the crowbar back to me to carry. I thanked him as I gazed down at it in my hands.

267

The weight and wieldiness was nothing foreign to me. I could still feel the tension in my arms from the ghostly memories. *Swing, swing, swing.* The blood echoed and pattered onto the pavement like a dripping faucet. I could hear it all. My hands began to tremble, and I tightened my grip on the bar until my knuckles turned white. I couldn't show them I was afraid. Not now. Not as we stepped over the broken glass into the dark lobby of the school. There was no turning back. I was the only one who seemed too freaked out to be here.

The tighter I gripped the crowbar, the more memories flooded back. I could feel the phantom squishy warmth of blood on my socks.

Deep breath, deep breath.

I needed to pull myself together, but this building was holding me back. I was terrified to be inside here. Something horrible happened, and it was more than just an overrun military outpost. I could feel it.

"Go right," Melony instructed.

We formed a line going down the hall. I took up the rear. I felt as if there were eyes on us. Something trailing and following behind. There wasn't a spot my flashlight didn't hit as I kept my eyes open. We walked until Nolan found the cafeteria.

The sight upon entry wasn't comforting. The shattered glass, the tables, the blood.

"You don't think there could still be Grays in here, do you?" I asked aloud.

Melony glanced at me as if she sensed something was wrong. I wasn't hiding my fear well enough, and Nolan's response to the question didn't fix the issue. I squeezed my eyes shut, took a deep breath, and nodded before I reached back and grabbed Melony's hand to guide her into the kitchen. The closer she was to me, the better I began to feel. We were further away from Nolan, and I felt more settled just being the two of us again. I hadn't had a problem with him before, but today something was different.

As we walked toward the lunch counter and rounded into the kitchen, the mess of trays and dishes was an obstacle course.

"Do you think someone beat us to the food?" Melony asked.

"I don't think this if from scavengers," I replied as I shook my head.

The kitchen grew dark fast. The light beaming in from the cafeteria windows didn't extend its reach this far into the depths. The further we walked into the darkness the more I could smell death. The smell lingered around us, not as strong as a Gray or fresh body, but strong enough to make me question what lied deep in the kitchen. I stared off into the dark; maybe I could make out a shape in the void. As I stood still staring, blurs and flashes of shadows moved around ahead of me. A trick of the mind. You see things that aren't there when you are looking into the dark for too long. But something was drawing me toward it.

Melony moved around me and headed to the left of the kitchen toward some shelves. I began to inch and creep to the right, deeper into the darkness. The first few moments of getting into the building and finding the cafeteria had felt so fast but walking into the kitchen felt like time had frozen around me. I kept moving, feeling my way around counters and cabinets. I heard Melony on the other side of the kitchen rummaging through boxes. I was far enough away to where her light didn't reach me, and I didn't want to risk turning mine on.

I neared the end of the kitchen, and the smell was so strong I felt like I couldn't breathe. I could hear a faint buzzing, like insects in the walls. I pulled my shirt over my face to mask the contaminants that filled my lungs, but the thin cloth didn't keep the stench out.

In the corner of the kitchen, I small red light was still glowing faintly on the wall. It must've been on a separate power source. I squinted my eyes, straining to see inches in front of me. The tiny red light highlighted a metallic handle just below it. I approached and the buzzing grew louder. The smell with it. When the handle was inches in front of my face, I could make out the outline of a giant metal door. A walk-in freezer. I placed my ear against the metal and the buzzing echoed and vibrated from inside.

I put my hand on the handle and pulled it out slowly. The door groaned and released from wall with a gaseous hiss. It only made it centimeters ajar before the stench erupted into the room, and I began to gag. I slammed the door shut, ripped my shirt off my face, and hunkered over against the wall. I gagged and dry-heaved until what needed to come up splattered on the floor at my feet. I gasped for air and backed away from the cooler. I stumbled around the kitchen in the dark until I saw Melony's light in the far corner.

I made my way to her, her light perched in her mouth. She swung her bag onto her back and removed her light to smile at me. She had found the jackpot we were searching for.

I tossed my bag onto the floor, shoved my crowbar into a side pocket, and began to fill the main pocket with meals.

For a brief second as I loaded my bag full, I forgot about the cooler only yards away from us; but once my bag was fully loaded, the thought came back. There was death in there. A lot of it, I would wager. The pit in my gut gurgled and churned even on a now empty stomach.

"Let me carry yours," I demanded as I gestured to Melony's bag.

She furrowed her brows at me and argued, but I insisted. What I had just witnessed had been an indication of more than a single massacre. The last occupants of this school must've used the walk-in as some sort of morgue. Maybe it still had power then, but now that it didn't the rot was consuming everything inside.

Whatever had killed the people outside was a separate incident. If I had to guess, I would say something attacked them first while doing their usual routines, and anyone who survived retreated inside and barricaded themselves in. Maybe a few months went by, but they were eventually attacked again and whatever was outside had finally gotten in.

If there were Grays—or survivors—still in this building, I wouldn't want to hang around. If we needed to run Melony needed to be ahead of me. I needed to see her live, so I took her bag. On any normal day, I could outrun her. Today, our bags were heavier, and she looked weaker after throwing up outside. The extra weight on my back was barely an obstacle. Barely weighed me down.

As long as she was ahead.

We took an extra box of meals to Nolan. I could hardly see the look of satisfaction on his face until I sat down next to him. Melony took a few steps back, and I began to tell him what I had found.

"Do you know something about this place?" I accusatorily mumbled, "Something happened here, and you seem like you're holding back information."

"I told y'all I'd never been here before."

But his jaw ticked, and I could feel the tension coming off him like smoke. He hadn't found the guns he wanted, and I'm sure he was upset and angry enough before I started speaking.

"Look," I adjusted myself to face him more, "I just found what I can only assume is a walk-in cooler full of bodies. There're dead people all over this building. *Huele a muerte.* If this is just a get in and get out mission, then we need to leave."

"We'll be getting out of here in just a minute."

"You can risk my life all you'd like, but if you're putting *her* in danger over the possibility of a few guns," I paused and thought of my next words more carefully, "I'd put getting out of here at the top of your list of priorities."

He eyed me with the same harsh squint he had eyed me with earlier outside. It felt as if he was staring into my soul. Trying to read me or curse me. His head snapped away as Melony approached us and told us to leave. We were hesitant as she wildly stared at us, but when she commanded once more, we listened and headed for the large windows.

She slowly pushed at one of the tables until it screeched across the floor, and she froze in fear.

That's when I realized why we were leaving. Melony had heard them before I did. The clicking and shrieking echoed from the hall in multiples. I whipped back around as Nolan steadied his stance and brought his gun up in front of him.

I glanced back at Melony as she struggled to push by herself. Tears seeped out of her eyes and fear was coursing through her. I hopped in to help her push while Nolan stood behind us facing the door to the cafeteria. As soon as there was a gap to fit through, I pushed Melony ahead and watched her jump onto the grass. She waited there until I made it out before she began to run.

Don't stop.

Don't stop.

Don't stop, Melony!

She kept looking over her shoulder, and her ponytail whipped behind her with every turn of her head.

I'm right behind you.

She ran into a small, wooded area, weaving between the trees. I trailed behind—almost keeping up with her. I was beginning to feel the burn in my legs and the pain from the bouncing bags in my shoulders. Twigs and thorny bushes brushed against my calves and knees. My sweat mingled with the fresh cuts and scrapes and my legs began to sting until I couldn't feel them anymore.

I kept following her.

Neither one of us knew what direction to take, but I had once seen Melony run for miles before she even stopped to take a breath. It had taken me almost ten minutes to find her curled up behind a tree, and that was her running from living people. Running from Grays? She wouldn't stop until she couldn't hear them anymore. We had a good head start, and as I looked back through the trees, they were still inside the building struggling to squeeze through the same gap we had. Yet the noise was still so loud. So many in one place.

After a couple of minutes of running through the trees, she finally brought us out to the side of a road. An unfamiliar one. She barely paused before she took a left and kept running on the pavement. The ground was no longer soft and with each step I took I could feel the pavement echoing through my bones. Up my ankles, calves, and thighs all the way into my head. The pain was spreading, but she kept running, and I kept following. Unfortunately, I was slowing down.

Nolan began to catch up to me with a worried yet fiery look in his eyes. He held his shotgun in front of him, not in his aiming stance, but off to the side, pointing at me. I slowed significantly as I watched him face me, bring it up, and shoot.

The gun went off in a faded boom as if I couldn't hear it. Maybe it hadn't had gone off.

I felt a hard punch to the gut. Warmth.

A light fire in my stomach and chest.

Toes cold.

The pavement scratched my knees. Then the back of my head bounced off the mountain of bags on my back.

The sky was so blue and bright. I was in the trees. The leaves were so close to my face, I saw them in a blur, but they were there. Just right above. Between me and the sky.

"Jonas!" Melony yelled, "Oh, God. Oh, no!"

She was right beside me, her freckled face hovered over mine. She was like an angel. I tried to reach my hand up to touch her, but I couldn't tell if I was moving. Instead, I felt her familiar skin and fingers wrap around my hand and pull it up to her face. She pressed my hand against her cheek.

It was covered in red.

My stomach was burning. I couldn't feel my legs.

"It's okay," she whispered to me as she reached down and cupped my face in her hand.

Something screamed in the woods, but she didn't move.

"Mel," I choked and coughed out.

Another punch to the gut. The pain seared and a wave of cold numbness washed over me. I let out a shaky breath and felt my fingers twitch against her face. I could feel her tears under my fingertips.

"Melony," I strained again, "you need to go."

They are coming for you.

"No, no," she shushed, "it's okay. Don't try to talk, it's okay."

I tried to push myself off the ground, but another punch and more fire began to spread.

"Stop, stop." She shoved me back down.

"Melony, please."

I reached and clawed into my pocket and pulled out my folding knife. I couldn't turn. They couldn't be the ones to kill me. I needed to die before they got here. I slowly pulled the knife out and flicked it open. I reached over myself and pushed it into her hand.

She furrowed her brows; the confusion bled through her tears as she glanced at the knife and back at me. I wrapped her fingers around the hilt and guided the blade over my chest.

"Melony, I don't want to turn," I mumbled.

I could feel the cold spreading up my legs. The warmth poured out of me even as the fire in my gut grew wilder. I felt tears fall back into my hair. I knew what was coming…

"I won't," she argued while trying to pull away, but I used the rest of my strength to hold her hand steady over my heart.

The tip of the knife poked into my skin, and for the meantime, it was taking my mind from the darkness and cold that was creeping in.

"I need you to," I pleaded, "please, I can't turn. I can't be one of them."

"Jonas…"

"This isn't your fault. This is what I want," I comforted.

The tears streamed down her face and mixed with the blood on my hands. She looked so painterly against the blue sky. Her hazel eyes gazed down on me, glossy and full. Her freckles scattered like stars. A map of the heavens. Her skin was so soft as it touched me. *Siempre mi angel.* I smiled softly at her and wheezed in a deep breath as I began to push against her hand. She squeezed her eyes shut.

"I love you more than anything, Melony Harper," I whispered to her as I felt the sting of the blade puncturing my skin. "*Gracias, mi flor.*"

I winced as I pushed the blade deeper, faster. I could hear her sobbing, and the screams that spilled from the woods sounded closer.

"Please, go…" I commanded as I did the final push and felt the world stop around me.

Melony yanked her hand away from the knife shouting and sobbing. I could still see her against the blue light of day climb to her feet and make a run to the tree line. The trees above me grew blurry and the darkness crept in. I felt so cold.

But she had got away.

She made it.

21

Melony

Blood coated my hands.

"Please, go…" He guided the knife deep.

NO. NO. NO.

"Oh, my God," I shouted and screamed, "Fuck!"

I pulled myself away and stared at him. His arms fell limp to his sides as he closed his eyes; his chest stopped rising and falling, and a faint smile remained on his lips. Red ran all over the road. Red stained every inch of his stomach and chest. It coated his arms and hands. Splattered on his face as he had coughed it up. I felt the warmth on my legs; it dripped from my knees and down my shins. I looked down at myself covered in him.

Blood on my hands.

I couldn't breathe. My lungs felt full of water. Thick and red. I didn't want to move, didn't want to leave him. He was just lying there.

Please, get up.

He was lying there. Not moving. Not breathing. The knife was still in his chest. I couldn't leave him like that. Not my Jonas. My hand reached up to my neck and I pressed my shaking thumb into my pendant. Why wasn't he moving? Why wasn't he holding me? He needed to breathe. I pushed the pendant deeper against my thumb until the metal petals stabbing into my skin pulled me out.

He was gone. I couldn't bring him back. Dead. His knife still in his heart. I helped push it in. His blood ran across the pavement. Seeped into the cracks.

An eerie shriek came from the trees. I needed to move. I had to leave him. I turned with blurry vision and headed for the opposite side of the road into the trees that lined it. I ran a few yards deep and glanced back at the road. Jonas's body remained still. He was so still.

The terrible shrieking was closer. I was beginning to smell them now. Overpowering the metallic scent that lingered in my lungs. I had to get away. Jonas wanted me to live. He wanted me to go.

I looked up at the sky. The leaves of the trees shook in the breeze. I trembled with them as I began to climb. Branch by branch I pulled myself upward. Climbing until I was high enough off the ground the Grays could not reach, and I could see the road from the branch where I sat.

The branches were full of green, but when the breeze blew right, I could still see Jonas from a small opening. Wave after another I caught glimpses. He lay there alone. Then a Gray approached. It sniffed around him but did not touch. It raised its head toward the sky and bellowed its call from deep within. Its skin looked as if it were melting off its bones. Bones popped through the skin in places it shouldn't have. The discoloration was sickly and the scent of death that engulfed it was thick enough to swallow.

Another second, another Gray. They came a few at a time, sniffed Jonas's body and then the ground like wild animals on the hunt. They were no longer interested in him. His heart no longer beat. His lungs were no longer full of air.

I observed them from my branch. The breeze dried the tears against my face and crust the blood against my skin. My wrists and fingers felt tight, and my knees felt sticky. I was beginning to itch, and the dark void of emotion was settling in nicely. I felt numb. Even as I stared at Jonas's body on the road, I felt empty. It was as if he held my every emotion and memory, and they died with him. But I knew it wasn't emptiness I was feeling. I was feeling everything at once. The sorrow was running so deep that I was numb. Tears still streamed down my face. I was still quietly sobbing, but the numbness made it feel like I was going into shock. I was reacting but not feeling. I was staring at him lying lifeless but not screaming for him to wake up or move.

I was his flower stripped free of my petals in the wind. Stomped out by someone walking past without a second thought. There was nothing I could do.

He was dead. Gone. Killed.

He was killed.

Nolan.

I was beginning to feel hot. Burning with rage and anger. The tears that streamed down my face were no longer sorrowful, but full of rage. I was shaking and on fire. My blood boiled inside me. I could feel it bubbling under my skin. I wanted to scratch it out. The stickiness and itching were killing me. The red began to flake as I dug my nails into my arms.

Why? Why had Nolan shot him? What was the purpose?

The thought of that man was sending me over the edge. I wanted to jump down from the very branch where I sat and ran until I found him. The adrenaline was pumping in my veins. I think I could've done it or would've if I hadn't heard Jonas's soft voice in the back of my mind.

Stay still, they'll hear you.

I stopped moving and watched the beasts on the road as they scoured the area with their poor eyesight and horrible stench. They wouldn't find me, and if they did, they couldn't reach me.

I brushed them away and thought back to Nolan; I'd rather be filled with rage than be numb from despair.

What had happened?

The gun had gone off. I heard the boom echo through the trees and the birds that lingered in the sky screeched and called out in fear. Silence followed the shot. When I turned, Jonas was falling to his knees. Nolan turned away and kept running. He grabbed my arm as he passed me.

What had he said?

I couldn't hear what he was yelling at me. I could only hear my own heart.

What did he yell?

It echoed around me like a drum, but through the rhythm I heard his words so faint.

"Emily, we have to go!"

Who was Emily? The name was familiar.

But I stared in horror as deep crimson soaked the front of Jonas's shirt and he hit the ground. My bat fell out of my hand and hit the pavement. I thought Jonas had died right then. I ran to him. I was terrified he was already dead, but he wasn't. He was staring at the sky like he had never seen it before. His face was full of awe as if he was looking into heaven staring at an angel.

Nolan hesitated. I heard his footsteps behind me as I comforted Jonas, told him not to move. Nolan had been there watching me. He was deciding whether to drag me away or leave me there. He chose the latter when I heard his footfall quickly stomping off.

Nolan had shot Jonas and left me to fend for myself.

That prick!

The rage was filling me again, but I didn't move. I watched and waited as the Grays gathered. They bellowed and croaked and clicked like a conversation. Their misshapen human forms pained me to stare at, but it was intriguing how they acted. I had never actually sat and watched them like zoo animals before. I was always running from death; but today, death had finally caught up, and I wanted to watch. It was distracting how much they looked like decaying humans but acted like animals. They were creatures like no other.

Monsters. Beasts. Death.

A living plague that roamed to destroy us all. The Reaper coming for everyone's last breath. The disease had crawled out of hell. It spread among animals and then to humans. We turned to this.

Death crawling on all fours, sniffing out the next meal, attacking unprovoked with primal urges and violence.

Jonas and I had avoided them for so long, yet here we were almost face to face. Killing ourselves to not turn into one and observing from the trees. So close. The air hung, thick like the black smoke of a fire. The rot in the air choked me and curdled my stomach. Yet, they stood around unfazed, having a hidden conversation told in code.

After a few minutes of their warbling, they took off. They leaped and ran on all fours. Their fingers and hands clawed against the road as they ran in the direction Nolan had gone. They were tracking down his scent and luckily not mine.

I would wait in the tree until I could no longer hear them calling through the woods. Their screams were so shrill you could hear them for miles, so when the woods fell silent, and the birds began chirping again the sun was already past the mid-point in the sky. Late afternoon.

I had sat on the branch for hours staring at Jonas. His skin had grown so pale. His life faded from him. I carefully climbed down one branch at a time. I scraped my legs, stomach, and palms against the bark with each move and slide I made down the tree. Finally, I reached the ground and hopped down with a thud against the dirt. The brush and twigs snapped at my ankles as I climbed out of the woods and onto the street. I slowly made my way over to Jonas and knelt at his side.

His skin was cold and clammy as I reached out and touched his cheek. Feeling him beneath my skin broke the dam I had just built. The rage faded and the sadness poured out. I began to cry, uncontrollably. I sobbed and could barely breathe. He was right in front of me, yet he wasn't. I still felt like the knife was in my hand. I could still feel the warmth of his hand against my cheek and how his fingers twitched and tapped against my skin.

Now, he was so *still*.

I could barely see him right in front of me through the burning tears in my eyes. It felt like fire pouring from my eyes and the strain on my throat felt like something was trying to claw its way up. I couldn't take it seeing him like this, but I couldn't move away. He needed me. He was so close yet so far.

"Jonas," I mumbled through strained breath.

I called out to him but couldn't form a sentence to say. I wanted to apologize. I wanted to beg him to come back. I wanted to tell him I loved him too. I couldn't do any of it. Instead, I grabbed at my throat and fell onto my back beside him. I tried to take deep breaths, but only let out quick wheezes. It felt like the world was closing in on me as I stared up at the sky covered in his blood.

I felt like I was floating upward. I was being pulled into the blue, floating somewhere between the ground and the canopy above. Is this what he saw? Is this what he felt? I was running out of tears to cry. I could feel my tears drying up, and the sun and heat beamed down on me until it felt like I was melting into the pavement with him. I didn't want to leave him here. I would lay here with him until he was nothing but sun-bleached brittle bones.

But I couldn't do that to him.

I stared up at the bright blue sky and the trembling green leaves until I could finally catch my breath. I couldn't cry anymore, and my chest was too sore to properly breathe or move. I ached from head to toe, and my brain throbbed inside my skull. Slowly, I began to release shaky breaths.

The sky above was so calming. Jonas had left staring at the sky like we had when we were younger. We would lay in the clearing on The Zinnia Path when the grass was tall, and the clouds were blowing through the sky. I would look over to him and see the smile on his face as he squinted at the harsh bright blue above.

He was at peace; he was at home.

I sat up and gazed at his face. His smile had fallen flat, but he had died with one. I smiled softly as I stared at him; the last of my tears ran over my cheeks as I bit the inside of my lip and glanced at the woods.

"I'll be right back," I whispered to him and kissed his cold forehead before I stood up, heavy with blood-soaked clothes, and walked over to my bat lying on the road.

After retrieving it, I walked into the woods. The birds sang and whistled and led me away from the road. As I walked, I whacked and pushed bramble and weeds away to create a path with my bat. I followed the birds and the bugs, weaved in and out of a winding path of trees until I found what I was searching for.

The sun was an hour lower in the sky when I stumbled across a small clearing shaded by the canopy. It was tiny, but the gaps between the trees were the widest I had seen since walking into the woods. I stood in the center—the widest part of the area—and gazed up at the now colorful evening sky. It peeked through the few branches overhead. The view was beautiful.

I cleared the path even wider as I walked back toward the road in half the time it had taken me to get to the clearing. I leaned over Jonas's body and pulled his arms from the straps of the bag that laid beneath him. I tugged the bags out from underneath him and slipped them onto my back. They were heavy, but bearable. I wouldn't be running, and the journey wasn't long. I then squatted down, grabbed Jonas under the arms, and began to drag him.

I dragged him along the path as gently as I could. I tried to avoid any major thorns and branches that could harm him. The trek was slow, and I was growing more exhausted by the second. By the time I had pulled him into the clearing, the sun was in the early stages of setting.

I set him down in the moss and dirt as gently as I could before I pulled the bags off my shoulders and rested them on the ground against the trunk of a tree. I spotted the crowbar poking from the side of Jonas's bag and pulled it free from the pocket. Then, I returned to Jonas, reached down, and removed the knife from his chest as gently and carefully as I could. I didn't feel anything as the knife gently glided out through bone and muscle. I should've felt something and that's what was hurting the most: the numbness. My pain was locked behind a barrier in my mind. My body and brain were in so much shock that clarity had faded, and the world in front of me seemed unreal.

Once I had prepped Jonas, I found the center of the clearing I had stood in before by gazing up at the sky and finding the same view. Once the gaps in the trees and sky looked the way I had remembered, I fell to my knees and began to scrape at the dirt with my hands. When my hands grew tired, or I began to struggle, I used the crowbar to wedge up some dirt, and the knife to help carve around roots. I dug until I couldn't feel my fingers, and then I dug some more. The night came quickly, and the moonlight overhead was enough to guide me through it.

Hour after hour passed in the darkness under the moonlight. With each hour, the hole grew a little deeper. The crickets and frogs chirped and croaked and kept me company as I scraped through the dirt layer by layer. It caked beneath my nails and into the creases of my palms. The blood on my hands no longer looked like blood. It was mixed with dirt and dew. By morning, the hole was long enough, wide enough, and barely hit hip deep.

The birds chirped before the sun rose, and the frogs and bugs subsided. The coolness and dampness of the air shifted, and I could tell the sun was coming. The moon had vanished, yet the sky felt bright. I looked down at my hands as they trembled in my lap.

Blood and mud.

My fingers burned and stung and the small wounds that grazed the surface sparkled like rubies in the morning light.

I climbed to my feet and pulled myself out of the hole. My hands were aching and sore, and I almost crumpled under my own weight as my fingers and nails dug into the dirt and pulled me to the ledge of the grave. Jonas still lay next to me on the moss, gazing up at the sky. I sat beside him and dangled my feet into the space below. I was exhausted; I hadn't slept nor eaten. I couldn't even remember the last drink of water I had. I didn't have time for breaks. Jonas needed to rest, and I wouldn't until he could.

I reached into his pockets and pulled out the wallet he still carried. I set it to the side before I slowly dragged him into the hole. I put his feet in first, making sure his head was propped up and held so as not to hurt him before I slowly lowered his top half in.

Finally, he lay at the bottom, facing up toward the sky like we had done throughout our childhood. Like how he had died.

With a trembling, weak breath, I climbed out of the hole and sat on the ledge with him. I grabbed his wallet from where I had sat it and opened it. The first thing my eyes landed on was his old driver's license. It expired last year. He had no use for it, expired or not, but he kept it anyway. A man and his wallet. Behind his license was his ID card and behind that was a photo. I pinched it out and looked down at the smiling faces.

Junior prom. The same photo in my locket.

I looked up at the sky to keep the tears that were welling in my eyes from streaming down my face. I sniffled and wiped my eyes on the collar of my shirt as I stepped into the grave, reached down, placed Jonas's hands over his chest, and tucked the picture beneath them. He should hold it forever.

I climbed back to the edge and continued going through the wallet. He still had his credit and debit cards tucked into the slots, and when I opened the large pocket, I found two one-dollar bills. I chuckled at the thought of him saving it in case the world came back together. I flicked through them and found a piece of paper folded between the bills. I furrowed my brows as I pulled it from the pocket. It felt heavier than a piece of paper should have, so I set the wallet in the dirt next to me and opened it.

Something fell out into my lap, and when I spotted it, I froze. A thin gold ring.

It sat in my lap, and I stared at it as if it might bite me. It couldn't be what I thought it was. Why was it in this paper? Why did he have it? How long had he had it? I didn't move and kept my eyes on the ring. Frozen as thoughts raced through my mind.

I love you more than anything, Melony.

It was for me.

"No…" I whispered to myself as I stared at the ring in my lap.

Where did Jonas get it? Why did I have to find it now?

I reached into my lap and pulled out the ring. I held it in my palm as I began to unfold the paper and tears flooded me. My hands shook; my whole body shook. A contagious trembling that spread throughout me like wildfire. I could hardly see the words on the page scrawled in such familiar writing. Pencil and eraser marks were scribbled all over the page.

Mel,

We have known each other for far too long. Our childhoods were spent together, followed by our teenage years, and then we grew up. It took too long for me to realize that we were meant for each other. From ten years old to seventeen was too much time wasted not calling you mine. *Siempre has sido mi flor.* And now that we can never tell how much time we have left, I'm afraid I'm too late.

Since the beginning of this hell, there's been this nagging at the back of my mind. It's a tiny voice that tells me to watch over you. Sometimes I think it's my mom haunting me. She tells me that you're the one for me and to take care of you. Sometimes I think she'd be ashamed of the situations I've gotten us in. But being here, at the apartment with you, makes me feel normal.

I found this ring at the yellow house. It was sitting in the jewelry box on the dresser. I grabbed it without thinking a second thought, and I'm staring at it as I write this. Luckily for me, I think I found a perfect fit. (I may or may have not tested it on you while you slept.) I should've married you when I had the chance. I should've made you Melony Carrera before we even moved in together. I don't know why I didn't then, but I'm doing it now.

I had to write this speech to prep myself. I probably won't use any of it or read from it like a teleprompter, but I want you to have this letter as a token. As my vows. I will always be here. Always be with you. Through the end of the world and past that. I will be with you as we rot into the Earth. I hope you say yes.

Te amo, mi flor,

Jonas

I stared at the page. Unable to move. The sun peeked through the trees in a bright orange glow, and I couldn't take my eyes away from the page grasped between my fingers. My hands had stopped trembling, and the ring felt hot in my palm. I must've reread the letter seven times before I laid the paper on my thighs and opened my palm.

The gold band was thin and sparkled against the morning sun as if it had been recently polished. In the center of the ring was a small stone. A tiny diamond nestled into a spot on the band.

I gently slipped the ring onto the proper finger. Left hand. Ring finger. It slid on perfectly past the dirt and mud. The ring was mostly snug but wiggled a bit. Only a touch too loose. Barely noticeable, and not loose enough to fall off.

"I'd always say yes," I whispered to him as I stood up from the edge of the grave.

I grabbed his wallet from the dirt and tucked the note back inside before moving the wallet beside the backpacks. I returned to Jonas and gazed down at him lying pale and motionless in the cold Earth. My head was beginning to throb as I fought the urge to cry again.

He was at peace; he was home, I had to remind myself as I took a deep breath and dropped to my knees against the moss and dirt before starting to push the pile in.

The clumps of mud and dirt fell with a clatter on top of him. With each armful I pushed in, the further away he became. Halfway through the pile, the tears began to fall on their own. No noise or sound came with them. They spilled over the edge of the dam as waves rippled against the barrier. It didn't feel real. I pushed the last bit of dirt over his body and evened the ground. I patted and slapped the mud to pack it in before I rose to my feet and walked a few feet into the trees in search of a makeshift marker. I found a large branch that had recently fallen and brought it back to the grave. I used the crowbar to dig a small hole and planted the stick inside. Once his plot was noticeably marked, I backed toward the tree and rested against the trunk staring at the work I had just finished.

My entire body ached and cried for me to relax. The tension in my muscles was throbbing, and I could hardly keep my eyes open as my eyelids felt the weight of the world dragging them down. I lazily pushed one of the bags to lie flat on the ground and fell over onto it. My eyes closed, and the world felt as if it were spinning around me until I faded into darkness. I did not dream.

When I woke, the sun was still high in the sky. Midday. I looked around, lost to my surroundings, confused about where I was until I saw the thick stick protruding from the ground in front of me. I looked down at myself to the blood stained into my clothes and the mud caked into the cuts and cracks of my hands and gold ring still on my finger. A wave of numbness swept over me. I cried all I could and was so full of sorrow and grief I did not want to move.

However, deep down, there was this blazing, roaring, molten pit leaking into my bloodstream. Anger was replacing the sadness that kept me still. I needed answers, and I was going to get them.

I stretched, tucked the wallet into my pocket, and cleaned up the area. I picked up the crowbar and tucked it into the same side pocket of the bag I had found it in along with Jonas's knife. I propped my bat against the tree trunk as I swung the bags onto my back. Before leaving, I kissed my mud-covered hands and patted them against the ground Jonas lied under. I then grabbed my bat and marched my way out of the clearing.

I'll be back.

On my way out, I found a few medium sized rocks and carried them with me to the edge of the tree line where Jonas's blood painted the pavement. I piled them together on the side of the road as an indication of the clearing entrance.

Now that I was back to where this all started, I did not know which way led back to the apartment. Yesterday, I had seen Nolan keep running in the direction we were originally headed, but there were no tracks left behind on the road to follow. If I kept on as he did, I would surely get lost.

I grumbled to myself as I looked all around me for any tracks or idea in which direction to turn. I stopped and stared at the trees across the road. The trees we had run through to get to this point.

I was certain I knew my way back to the apartment from the school. I remembered what turns and the route we had taken to get there. If I could find the school on the other side of these woods, I could find my way back. It would not be a warm welcome. I was likely not welcome back at all. I would bet Nolan thought I had died alongside Jonas. He probably thought I refused to let go and turned. Though I was not dead, by the time I found him he would wish that I were.

22

Melony

I followed a rough path as well as I could until I could spot the building in the distance. The edge of the trees was a few feet away, but I didn't step out. I remained among the trees and listened as I eyed the building closely. I watched the darkness beyond the shattered cafeteria windows for any movement, and I listened for any small sound. Any shriek or click or croak.

There was nothing. Nothing but the singing birds and the screaming summer cicadas and the buzzing of wasps and grasshoppers.

I hunkered low and kept my eyes on the windows as I carefully and quietly crept out of the brush out into the open. I hugged the trees, creeping along as close as possible in case I needed to retreat into them. One foot in front of the other, moving heel to toe in the grass until I eventually was out of direct sight of the windows. I was on the side of the building facing the brick and chain-link.

From outside the fences, I looked upon the bodies I had avoided that lay face down within. The bodies were sprawled and scattered across the lot, and there were more than I had remembered. People died hiding behind trucks and cars, cowering against the bumpers. What was left of them was left to be lost to the ages and decay that followed.

I scanned the surrounding area before I moved an inch. When my eyes reached the tree line, I spotted a charred pile of black ash. Misshapen figures and bones sprawled across the burned remains. The pile was several feet high, and flakes of black and white fluttered away in the slightest breeze. If only we had noticed this disaster sooner, maybe we would've turned around. Maybe we wouldn't have gone into the building.

I moved along the fence and kept my eyes on the front door that still sat open. My only glimpse into the building was from that opening; beyond the tinted windows, there was nothing I could see. I hurriedly made my way around the fences and across the street into the alleyway we had come from. The same alleyway I had vomited in from seeing such a sight as the corpses that littered the school parking lot. I felt empty looking at them now. I was blinded by fury and resentment, and it blocked any other emotion I could possibly feel. It blocked the sadness and the nausea; it blocked the pain that ached in my chest. But I couldn't stop it. The fire deep in me wanted a reason. I needed to hear his excuse. I needed to hear Nolan say why he shot Jonas. I needed to be the one to bring judgment and justice to him.

There was no one else who would.

I stealthily made my way through the narrow street along the cars that lined the curb until I hit the open and familiar road. It would lead me straight to the apartment. Straight to what I wanted.

I rounded the corner and straightened myself out. I needed him to see me standing tall, unfazed, strong. I wanted him to see the anger and vengeance headed his way. I wanted him to beg and plead. I needed it.

I tightened my grip on my bat and adjusted the straps that dug into the flesh of my shoulders. Dried mud and scabs flaked off my wrists and fingers. The tips of my fingers and palms ached and burned. My hands were starting to shake, and my legs felt weak. The pain I had ignored since yesterday was swinging back like a wrecking ball. I had overdone it last night and something in me wanted to stop, but I couldn't let it take control. I couldn't stop, not now—but it tickled at the back of my mind. A voice shouted at me, muffled and indistinguishable. I could almost hear it in Jonas's voice.

Turn back. Go to the yellow house. Get out of here. There's nothing that will change what happened.

Maybe that voice was right, but there is something that would make me feel better.

I continued down the sidewalk until I reached the apartment building. I turned down the alley and climbed the fire escape. My feet thudded and clanged against the rusty metal grating. I wedged my fingers into the crevice of the window and lifted until it groaned for me to stop. Swinging one leg in, I sat on the windowsill, balanced between outside and in. I stuck my head in next and listened. The complex was quiet. There was no shuffling,

No movement. I crawled into the building and closed the window behind me. The carpeted hall creaked beneath my feet with each step toward the end. When I reached the front door, I rapped a gentle knock, and when no one answered, I walked inside.

The apartment was more silent than the rest of the building had been. The living room was just how we had left it yesterday morning. The same disheveled books and unfolded blankets and ransacked supplies. Nothing had changed except for the pile of MREs that was stacked on the kitchen counter.

Nolan had made it back.

I dropped my bags and bat on the floor in front of the door with a clatter. I heard tiny flakes of mud crumble to the floor beneath me as I marched down the hall and pushed open the bedroom doors, avoiding the first door on the right. After searching, I had concluded that Nolan wasn't home. It was just me alone in the apartment.

I was walking back toward the front door when I stopped, standing still right in front of the door I was avoiding. Involuntarily, something took control of me and reached out for the doorknob. I bit the insides of my lips, pursing them in a line in fear, and squeezed my eyes shut as the door creaked open. Through my eyelids, I could tell the light around me grew brighter and I decided to open my eyes.

Against the middle of the wall was the bed. The comforters and sheets were ruffled and unmade with the indentations of someone recently sitting on the mattress. The leftover imprints of Jonas and I from the morning before. He had been getting ready for the end of his life without ever knowing.

I hesitantly stepped into the room; my fingers lingered on the doorknob as my shoes creaked against the floor. Against the wall adjacent to the door was a small vanity. I avoided my reflection, but from the corner of my eye, I could see the amount of red that covered me. I paced myself toward Jonas's side of the bed we had last slept in and gently grabbed his pillow. I brought it into my chest and buried my face in it. I could still smell him. It was like he was right in front of me.

I pictured him wrapping his arms around me as I inhaled him. I breathed him in as he held me tightly. He was right in front of me; I could almost feel him. My legs buckled, and I dropped to my knees, face still buried into the pillow. I took another deep breath and felt his arms fade. His last touch slid away until it was just me kneeling alone in our room.

I screamed into the pillow until no sound would escape my lips. I sobbed into it until the tears soaked the case and the fabric no longer smelled of him. It smelled like salt, iron, and earth. I pulled my face away. Strings of snot and saliva pooled into the shape of a weeping face. Red and brown blurred into one another and stained the wet cloth. I was more exhausted than before.

I rested the pillow on the bed and struggled to get to my feet. My legs were numb and tingly, and I could barely keep my eyes open. The tears burned the raw skin and bags beneath my eyes; they felt swollen and sore. My entire face felt puffy and hot. The warmth spread to my neck and chest. My cheeks were sticky and felt unbearably grimy. I stumbled to the vanity and looked at myself in the mirror.

"Oh, my god..." I slurred in a hushed voice.

I couldn't recognize the girl staring back at me— not even compared to the last time I had seen her. Her cheeks were red and rubbed raw. Her freckles were hardly noticeable under the caked-up dirt and oily smudges that painted her skin. On the side of her face was a dark red handprint like she had been slapped with a handful of paint. But I knew what it really was. It flaked away and stained the skin beneath a gross shade of pink. The girl was covered in blood and cakey dirt. I coated her arms, fingers to elbows, and her legs, knees to ankles. Her clothes were tattered, crusted, and stained. She looked like she had risen from the dead. A walking corpse that breathed and cried.

I felt like I was going to collapse staring at myself in the mirror. I couldn't tell if I was awake or even alive. I turned back toward the bed and took one long look at the messy sheets and now dirty pillow. I was beginning to itch, and the grime all over my body felt eight inches thick. I went to the duffel bag of clothes stashed in the corner and rummaged through for an old, oversized shirt of Jonas's, a pair of military cargo pants, and some boxers. I went to the bathroom and locked the door behind me. Nolan's water system saved me from the trouble of scrubbing myself over the sink. I stripped down to nothing but bare skin and stepped into the shower. The stream was small, weak, and cool, but enough to make the scrubbing easier.

As I scratched at the dirt and dried blood, I felt as if my fingers were rubbing away with the grime. Right down to the bone they ached and trembled with each motion I made against my skin. The water ran red and thick down my body from my shoulders to between my toes. The last of Jonas's life trickled and trailed all over me like rain cascading down a mountainside. I placed my face beneath the stream and held my breath as the water gushed over my forehead and cheeks. Droplets of water trickled into my hairline and zigzagged across my scalp.

I was washing him from me. He would go down the drain to swirl the pipes with dirt and disgusting gunk for as long as the water continued to run. With each layer that came off, I felt lighter. I felt as if the mental block was lifting, and the pain was coming back.

When I stepped out of the shower, I stared at the water as it swirled the drain while I patted myself dry. The wetness that ran down my cheeks wouldn't leave; every time I wiped it away it returned, and through my blurry vision, I saw the last of the water run down the drain, finally disappearing into the depths and darkness.

My stomach grumbled and gurgled as I slipped into my new set of clothes. A sharp pain followed the sound. With my wet hair dripping onto my back and shoulders, I made my way into the kitchen. My movements were slow and lethargic as exhaustion twisted around every limb. When I rounded the corner of the hall and stopped, I could feel my legs trembling weak beneath my weight. I hadn't eaten in over twenty-four hours, and I couldn't bring myself to. My appetite was long gone even as my stomach knotted in pain. I knew I wouldn't be able to keep anything down.

I stared at an MRE pouch sitting on the edge of the counter and only grew sicker at the sight of it. I couldn't help but think of Jonas…

A few months after Day One, Jonas and I were still living at his place, barricaded in, and living off whatever the cars parked around us had packed. We rationed and struggled, but it worked for us until we needed to scavenge next. Walking through our small town provided us well enough for months before Jonas decided we needed to move south. I was never sure why or when he decided it was best, but it seemed to just happen overnight. I agreed and followed him; I would've followed him to the ends of the earth.

As we left home, we had set an objective to check out Indianapolis—it wasn't far from where we were, and it was likely the military was there. We assumed Indy would be our refuge and safest option after the bombs fell, but when we got there, no one was left aside from abandoned outposts and transport vehicles. We stayed right outside city limits for almost a month living off MREs and whatever we could find.

I stared at the package, remembering Jonas and me laughing together as we read the instructions for the first time. It was the first moment of relief we had had since we made it to Indy. It was hell being so close yet so far away from home. I was scared when I was awake and had nightmares while I slept. Nothing could comfort me the way he did.

I sighed and picked the package up from the counter and held the weight of it in my hand. I could feel anger rising again as I began to clench my jaw. My fingers tightened around the MRE as I spun around and launched it at the wall. I screamed as I grabbed one after another, throwing them across the room with all the strength I had left in me. There was a flashflood of memories sloshing around in my head.

But with every thought and moment that replayed in my head, another overpowered it. The same one played over each second like someone re-recorded over old tapes. A double exposure layer. A piece of seaweed that kept washing ashore.

The gunshot and Jonas falling to his knees. I couldn't unsee it and couldn't shake the feeling that it was my responsibility to do something about it.

I took a deep ragged breath as my arms dropped to my sides and I stared at the mess I had created. I had thrown more than MREs. I had tossed books and small pieces of furniture across the room. I had destroyed almost everything within range of me without even noticing like a tornado blasting through a small farm town.

I gazed over my destruction before I spotted my gear in the corner by the front door. I bit the inside of my cheek as I pictured the blood that had streaked my hands and the blood that had been pouring from Jonas's stomach and chest.

I grabbed my bat and headed out the front door. I rushed down the hall and out the window onto the fire escape. I hurried down the ladder, catching myself when

I missed a rung, and jumped down onto the grass-cracked concrete. I didn't know where to go, but I knew one place to start looking.

I turned around the corner and followed the sidewalk four buildings down until I stood in front of the bookstore. The bell jingled above me as I pushed the door open and stepped inside. I peeked over the counter and between the shelves. Nolan wasn't anywhere to be seen.

Time felt as if it were flying past. The world was spinning faster around me, ticking like the hands on a clock. I felt dizzy and sick.

I groaned as I tilted my head back in frustration. I took a few deep breaths as I paced the aisles. There was nowhere else I could think to look for him. I continued pacing and ran my fingers along the shelves, trailing along the titles and empty spaces on the shelves until it clicked.

The empty spaces. Our search for gardening had led to plenty of books being misplaced. I glanced at the stack still neatly piled onto the counter. I pulled the door open and stepped back out onto the sidewalk to continue down the street.

The walk was quiet. Peaceful even. The silence brought some form of meditation with it, some type of regret or pause. I was growing agitated at the thoughts that were arising and the doubt that was starting to stomp out my fury.

What would I do to Nolan when I saw him? What would I say?

Jonas wouldn't want this.

And that's the voice that was pissing me off.

I squeezed my eyes shut and tried to push away the thoughts. Bring back some of the peace. The silence. I passed through the makeshift barricade and could see a figure sitting on the sidewalk in front of the field. The thoughts began to drift as I approached. My nails dug into my palms as I tightened my fingers around the bat handle. The birds and bugs echoed down the alley until I stepped out into the open behind Nolan sitting on the ground. My shadow lurked beside him, and he looked at me over his shoulder. There was a smile on his face.

"Emily," he chuckled and grinned at my appearance, "You're back!"

Emily? Where had I heard that before?

He turned back to the book that sat in his lap. A shovel rested at his feet. He looked different than when I had last seen him. His clothes were clean, and he was no longer wearing his hat. He looked free and happy instead of his grumbly exterior.

"Why don't you sit down and enjoy the day with me, sweetheart?" he said as he patted the ground next to him.

He thinks I'm his daughter.

I wanted to yell. I wanted to grab him by the shoulders and yell in his face, but I couldn't. He was so different now. Something had shifted in him. I didn't know what to say so I sat. I stared at the tall grass as it swayed in the breeze. A yellow and green ocean of waves.

"Oh," Nolan glanced at my hand, "Where'd you find that? It looks good on you."

I looked down at my hand and stared at the ring as it sparkled in the sun. The light bounced off the gold and reflected the incoming evening sky.

"You don't remember who I am, do you?" I asked as I gazed at his face for some flicker of a reaction.

He looked up from his book, confused. He searched my face as if he thought my question was a joke. I could see the gears slowly grinding behind his eyes as he asked himself why I would ask such a thing. His green eyes met mine and held contact for a few seconds before they widened. He was remembering. His lips parted but nothing came out.

"Why'd you do it?" I asked.

He shook his head and scurried to his feet. I shot up with him and followed as he began to rush away.

"Nolan," I spoke, and he stopped in his tracks at the crack in my voice. "Why did you do it?"

I could feel the tears swooping in. I was never the confrontational type, but Jonas wasn't here to save me anymore. He wasn't here because of the confused man in front of me. The pressure in my chest tightened, and the pain began to spread. A ringing began to engulf my ears, and my nails dug deeper into my palm.

"Please," I cried, "just give me a reason."

His face softened from fear and anger to simple fatherly frustration.

"He wasn't good for you, Emily."

"I'm not Emily!" I screamed back.

He flinched as I jerked my bat forward and pointed it at him.

"I'm not your fucking daughter! I just want an answer. Jonas didn't deserve to die!" I shouted through waves of tears.

He stepped closer with his arm out trying to comfort me. "Emily, calm down. Don't say those things."

"I'M NOT EMILY!" I screamed as I shoved him to the ground and brought the bat over my head.

Without thinking, I brought it down. And back up. And down again.

A dull crack echoed from his skull, and I jumped back, releasing my grip. The world that was spinning so fast seconds before seemed to come to a halt around me as the bat clattered to the concrete with a reverberating echo. I stared at him lying on the pavement.

The hair on top of his head quickly became wet with blood as it seeped from the open wound on his head and out onto the ground.

"Oh, my god..." I quietly gasped as I stumbled back away from him, "I'm so sorry. I'm sorry."

I mumbled and cried as I fell to my knees a few feet away from him. I pulled my knees to my chest and rested my head against them as I sobbed and waited for Nolan to wake up though I knew he wouldn't. He didn't move. It had been over twenty minutes, and he hadn't moved. He never opened his eyes.

I killed him.

"I'm so sorry," I cried to nothing, "I didn't mean to."

I am a murderer.

Something had come over me, and I couldn't handle him not taking accountability. He wouldn't admit what he had done, and the anger that had been fueling me overpowered whatever sympathy I had left for him. I had killed him for what he did to Jonas, but I couldn't call it justice. I couldn't justify what I had done.

There was only one thought left on my mind: I was alone now.

As the sun began to set, I released a shaky, regretful breath full of tears before I pushed myself off the ground. I took one last look at Nolan before I turned to the sidewalk where we had sat only moments before. I glanced at the shovel that had sat next to his feet then up at the woods behind the field. I wiped my face, huffed out a sigh, and grabbed the shovel before heading into the woods.

Two bodies in two days. I dug two graves in two days.

Night had fallen by the time I had finished. The shovel was much quicker than by hand, but left blisters in my palms. It was less of a punishment than what I deserved. I tossed the shovel out of the grave and went back out into the field for Nolan. I dragged him by his feet to his grave and rolled him in. Numbness overcame me as I shoveled the dirt back over him.

The night was still dark, and the moon barely reached halfway through the sky when Nolan was fully buried. I stumbled through the bramble and weeds and waded through the tall grass until I made it to the sidewalk. The shovel clanged against the concrete as I dropped it and walked away.

I walked through the barricade and down the sidewalk four buildings past the bookstore until I reached the fire escape. The ladder squeaked and groaned as I climbed it, and the window screeched as I pulled it open. The floor of the hall creaked beneath my every footstep until I made it to the apartment door.

Everything after felt like a blur.

Days passed, and then weeks, and the summer heat began to die down as the crisp autumn air was right around the corner.

I spent my time in the apartment curled up beneath the covers, suffocating in the stuffiness of the bedroom.

I would wake up to the sun beaming through the window. It coated the bedroom in a beautiful golden glow. I would smile and roll over only for that smile to fade when the bed beside me was empty and everything that had happened flooded back in. The light seemed to shine directly on Jonas's side of the bed every morning like a punishment and reminder from a god I didn't believe in. It felt surreal.

Today, I flung the covers off my body and sat up on the edge of the mattress. I dropped my head into my hands and harshly rubbed my face. I was drained and empty. I could feel everything inside of me being swallowed up by a deep dark pit. A black hole had settled within me.

The floor groaned as I stood and stretched, and dust sparkled in the sunlight as I tossed the comforter in the air by the corners and watched it float down evenly over the bed. I walked to the corner and slipped on some partially clean clothes. The metal button on the cargo pants knocked against my finger with a tiny clink.

I stared down at my hand after buttoning my pants. A thin gold band lit up my ring finger. I twisted it with my thumb until the tiny stone sat on top before I dropped my hand at my side and walked out into the living room.

The first few days that followed so much death I couldn't even climb out of bed. Moving within the apartment and eating was a big step in the right direction.

For the past few days, it was the same routine: Once a day, I would muster up the strength to leave the room and venture throughout the dimly lit apartment. Most days, I couldn't stomach a meal, but I tried to eat anyway. The crushing anxiety and realization of my loneliness would slither in and force my meal to end early or be brought up entirely.

I was alone, and it was the hardest fact to grow accustomed to other than Jonas being gone. For as long as I could remember, I had never felt lonely; I always had him.

But now, I had nothing.

However, today I had a plan. Today would be different. Today was the day my routine changed.

I grabbed an empty bag and packed it. Two MREs, a few bottles of water, an introduction to gardening book I had already read over two times, a pair of thick gloves, and a long-handled hoe from Nolan's entryway closet. Then, I was out the door.

The air in the hall was crisper than the musty smell that lingered in the apartment, and when I opened the window to the street, the air felt even better. The breeze was wonderful compared to the straight stuffy heat inside the apartment. The wispy hairs that framed my face fluttered and tickled my skin as I stepped out onto the platform. I inhaled the morning air until my lungs couldn't take any more and slowly descended the ladder. The streets and sidewalk were debris free as I made my way down to the barricade before the field.

I squeezed past the cars and through the street until it ended, and the open field stared at me head-on. I glanced at the ground where my bat still lay next to a deep red stain waiting for the rain to wash it clean. I dropped my backpack on the sidewalk next to the shovel and entered the grass with the hoe.

Hours upon hours, I raked and cut away the grass until a large section of the field was short and choppy. I took a break and sat on the sidewalk to eat a meal before I got back into it. I tilled the ground and pulled up roots and piles of dirt until the sun went down. I went home, slept, and woke up the following day to till the field. The gloves didn't keep me from getting blisters as I worked, but the ground was getting soft.

Each day, I brought the same book and reread the pages while I ate my lunch. When I was finished, I would continue working until I was covered in sweat and dirt, and the sun began to set. Another day had passed, and I had used my time to find a creek not far in the woods where I had buried Nolan. That day I read about irrigation, and how I could use the creek to water the future garden.

Eighteen days had come and gone before the ground was ready to plant, and after eighteen days, I needed a break. The sun rose as it had each day in the weeks before—shining on the empty place next to me in bed. I sat up and stared at the nightstand beside me. The green leatherbound photo album sat atop staring back at me. I reached out and picked it up. The weight of it fell heavily in my lap. I stared down at the well-worn cracks in the cover and traced them with my fingers before taking a deep breath and opening the album.

I smiled down at the photos that welcomed me. Jonas's handsome smile peered up at me from the pages, faces I could only cherish in my memories.

Every morning, I woke up and had to remind myself that Jonas wasn't here. I could still feel him all around me like he would be back in a few hours. He seemed like he was just out on a supply run, but I knew that wasn't the truth. He wouldn't be coming back. He was gone. I would never wake up to him by my side again or hear his heavy sleepy breath. I wouldn't see that stupid smirk on his face or hear his laugh. I could only see him here. In the past.

As I flipped, page after page, photo after photo, I began to realize that Jonas was in everything I did. I had lived over half of my life with Jonas by my side; everything I ever did we did together. Riding bikes, playing games, prom, graduation, the end of the world. He was there for everything, and he always would be. I flipped again and stared down at the letter I had nestled into the pages then glanced at the ring on my finger. I smiled with tear-streaked cheeks and closed the book. Setting it on the nightstand, I got out of bed and walked to the corner of the room where I kept Jonas's bag. Blood still soaked the exterior.

I stared at it and took a deep breath. "I can do this," I muttered to myself with a quavering voice before I grabbed the strap and carried it to the bed. I unzipped all the zippers and pockets before I flipped the bag upside down. Everything inside clattered onto the mattress in a mess.

With each item I plucked from the pile, I found a permanent spot for it around the bedroom. His metal tumbler that matched mine would sit on the nightstand; his wallet was placed next to it. Pairs of socks went into a dresser drawer, his first aid kit was taken to the bathroom, and any snack went into the nightstand drawer.

It was like he never left. He had never packed his bag and never ventured out beyond the apartment with us.

I reached for the last thing on the mattress: a folded stack of papers that I had never seen before. They were crumpled and torn. Blood soaked and stained the edges as it had seeped through the bottom of his bag. I unfolded the stack expecting to be hit by more grief and handwritten notes but was only met with utter confusion as I gawked at the pages in my hands.

"What is this…" I mumbled and trailed off into thought as I stared at the red ink that annotated printed articles and maps.

I plopped down onto the bed and began to lay the pages out before me.

How long had these been there?

I left them sitting sprawled out across the bed as I absorbed the information. After a few minutes of trying to read the nonsensical notes of a madman, I hesitantly got out of bed and packed a small bag.

So many questions were running through my mind, but there was no one to answer them. The only person that could was gone.

I made my way out of the apartment and out of the building onto the fire escape. Once I hit the ground, I walked a different route. Away from the bookstore and the garden. Away from the town.

The sun was heavily shaded as I tiptoed around the school and toward the woods. I made my way through the overgrown weeds and brush as it clawed at my legs. Eventually, I reached the end of the trees and the edge of the road. I turned left and walked as the birds sang and chattered and the breeze rustled through the leaves above.

Up ahead, a small formation of rocks sat on the road near a shadowy red stain on the pavement; when I reached it, I turned into the woods. The path was slightly overgrown; the weeds I had once pushed away were shifting back stronger, but eventually I made it to where the trees began to separate, and a large stick poked out of the mossy ground. I sat beside it and reached up to my neck, pressing my fingers against the zinnia pendant.

"I found the papers in your bag," I said aloud, "I don't understand what they mean. Why did you keep them? Were you hiding them from me?"

The leaves whispered in response, and I looked down at the moss that was beginning to spread over the edges of the grave and the grass that was starting to poke through the dirt.

"I killed Nolan," I blatantly stated as I stared at the ants and pill bugs crawling in and out of the dirt. "I thought I did it for you," I paused, "then I thought I did it to make me feel better for what he did. I thought it was what he deserved, but I struggle to sleep. When I do sleep, I have nightmares of the bat coming down over..."

My thought trailed off as I squeezed my eyes shut and tried to push away the image. I pushed my thumb deeper against my pendant and took a ragged breath before opening my eyes back to the bugs wriggling over the ground.

"I can't help but think that you'd be so ashamed of me."

The wind whispered again, and as the leaves rustled above, I could almost hear his voice.

I will be with you as we rot into the earth.

I sighed a breath of relief as a tear fell down my cheek. "I'm holding out hope for it," I mumbled back with a smile.

AUTHOR'S NOTE & ACKNOWLEDGEMENTS

As We Rot has been a project of mine for years. Between the struggles after COVID-19, part time jobs, and just life itself, there were points where giving up was a tempting option. Over the years, the idea for this book shifted and morphed into completely new concepts due to my overactive imagination and possibly multiple undiagnosed mental illnesses. However, with each new idea and turn of the page, there was always someone to pull me back; so, I would like to take this tiny section to thank the anchors that kept the floating cloud I call a brain still.

Growing up, my parents never pushed me towards becoming a doctor or a lawyer or one of the big professions; instead, I was pushed to do something I enjoyed whether that be art or writing. Although my family hardly knows anything about me writing a book, my first thanks go out to them for giving me the freedom to choose my own life. We aren't as close as the picture-perfect families in film, literature, and media, but I know they always love and support me no matter how far I am willing to go. That's all I could ever truly ask for.

To Brooke, Mari, JJ, and friends for not cringing or giving me odd looks when I said I was going to write a book.

That helped a lot! Friends are just the family you choose, and it's clear that I've finally made some of the right choices. The feedback and clarity you all provide help spark my motivation.

I edit and write and create on my own, for the most part. It's a struggle being a broke aspiring writer trying to publish just one simple dream. However, there has been one person who has stood by my side through every second of this journey.

Tony, a dedication page just isn't enough to say how much you have helped and pushed me through each new day. Distraction after distraction you were always on the other side to guide me back. You've always understood how much this project meant to me, and I can't finish it without giving you your credit for talking me through my blocks and sharing your own ideas when problems needed solving. Along the way, there were issues with the story of Jonas and Melony, and every time I was able to work through them was because of you. I hope you'll be by my side for every future project that comes. I would hate to have to write another book without your help.

Lastly, thank you, to everyone who has read and bought this book! Without you, my first novel would probably be my last. Thank you so much for your support!

www.ingramcontent.com/pod-product-compliance
Lightning Source LLC
Chambersburg PA
CBHW010531100726
47903CB00011B/2973